Hot for the

PRINCIPAL

ALEXANDRIA GONCALVES

You are enough. A thousand times enough.
— ATTICUS

BLURB

Victoria had always had her life planned out... until that one moment when everything was ripped away leaving her feeling empty, scared, and insecure. Now, the only two pieces holding her together are her best friends.

Enter Auston Scott. A handsome stranger with green eyes, a bearded jawline, and sexy as hell three-piece suit. This new Principal—and her boss—looks as if he has just walked out of a GQ magazine.

Can Victoria let go of her past so she can fall for the man of her dreams and ignite a passion that she didn't know could exist outside of the novels she teaches her English students?

She knows she shouldn't go there, but what she doesn't realize is that the new Principal holds a dark secret, one that could tear Victoria apart.

DEDICATION

I want to dedicate this novel to a few people.

The first being my fiancé, Denis. Throughout the last five years, you've been the one person to support me through all my highs and lows. Thank you for always being there, and for being my hero.

The second is to anyone who battles anxiety, grief, or insecurities. There are so many pressures we deal with in life that cause us to feel pressure to give up. However, I don't want you to give up. I want you to thrive because you deserve a happy ending to your story too.

CHAPTER ONE

G atsby was a loner who didn't deserve Daisy, so his death was kind of deserving.

That's it?

How can a student end their essay for their grade twelve academic English paper like that? How do students think they are going to survive in university ending an essay like that? I remind myself that the question was to state if *The Great Gatsby* was an outdated novel, or if it was still relevant today. Overall confusion dawns on me, as I try to make sense of this student's conclusion.

I put the paper down on my desk and rub my temples. How did I end up here? In my hick hometown? As a high school English teacher? I lean back in my chair and thank God that lunch is about to start.

The bell rings signaling to everyone that it's lunchtime. I don't have class during the period before lunch, so I usually spend that time marking students' work... or on Netflix watching *Friends*.

I stand up to disinfect the students' desks, as I do every morning, but I've made it a habit to do so during lunch as well because everyone is getting sick. With the beautiful winter in Ontario, students are sicker than usual, especially since exam season starts next week. I go around the thirty desks to make sure they're somewhat clean and put the spray back in the brown cupboards that usually stay locked.

I look around the room and sigh. The walls are all off-white bricks with a blackboard taking up a full side, well almost—there is an active board that sits in the middle. What was once just a simple chalkboard has now become a large screen that projects my computer screen to students. It also allows me to write on it, like a chalkboard. Instead of chalk I use a pen that connects to the special surface of the smart board. On the opposite side of the smart board there are windows. Some classrooms at Angel's Catholic High School don't have them, but thankfully mine does. I open up the bland grey covers and allow a small amount of sunshine to come through. My desk sits near the door and shows a little glimpse of who I'm to my students. I have a pencil holder that looks like a typewriter and a framed photo of me with my two best friends; Hannah and Emma. I walk back over to my desk while straightening a few of the desks along the way.

"Hey babe!" My best friend Hannah walks in with a spring in her step and plants herself on the desk in front of mine. Hannah and I have been friends since grade nine. We have been stuck together since our first day of high school and that was eons ago. Appearance-wise Hannah is my polar opposite, but we're utterly compatible on the emotional front. I'm five-foot-five, with long brown hair that hits the middle of my back, hazel eyes, and a bronze skin tone. With caramel blonde hair, blue eyes and white skin, she's practically a model, standing over me at a stunning six feet. She could definitely be a model if her dream wasn't to be an artist.

"Hey, how was Art class?" I reach under my large, square

brown desk and grab my bag. Pulling out my Greek salad, I lean back in my chair and put my feet up.

"You know what, I think these students are finally starting to get it. It's grade nine, so I don't expect them to be fantastic but this one girl, Joana? I can see her becoming an artist. She does beautiful work."

"Well, I'm glad you're hopeful for your students. I had a student end their grade twelve paper like this." I shuffle through the mass of papers on my desk and hand her over the essay. I watch her eyes scan the conclusion, and she spits out her coffee, laughing. Luckily, the spray of liquid missed the papers on my desk. I open the top drawer of my desk and grab wipes to clean off the coffee that was sprayed everywhere.

"Oh my God Vic, I actually feel bad for you. Teaching English is definitely not easy…" She looks at me, sympathetically, and I roll my eyes.

"How did I end up becoming a teacher? In my country-ass hometown?" I ask, throwing my body back and feeling my chair almost tip. I always wanted to be a writer, and I know I still can be. I have all summer to try writing a novel, but as soon as I'm in front of a computer or have my writing book in hand; I freeze. My anxiety gets the best of me, and I end up just putting everything aside and telling myself I'll write my book the next summer.

Four years later, that notebook still sits in my bag. Blank. Every. Single. Day.

"Oh babe, we live in a competitive world…I always assumed I would be an artist with my work hanging in some beautiful art gallery, but apparently life had different plans." Hannah crosses her legs and shrugs. I continue eating my salad when I hear squeaky running shoes coming down the hallway.

Here comes Emma, the last of our trio. Emma is naturally beautiful with short black hair, brown eyes, and an olive skin tone. I love Emma because we're both short, which makes us feel better when we're standing next to Hannah. The three of us became inseparable in tenth grade when Emma moved to Simcoe from Edmonton. Although Hannah and I had already been friends, Emma's magnetism drew us to her on the first day of tenth grade. It was a dramatic change, but she made friends with the perfect girls.

"Oh, my God! Sorry for being late, some boy thought he could lift more than he could handle and ended up with the barbell coming down on his forehead. It was a disaster, I just took him to the office to head home." She takes a pause and sits down beside Hannah. "Why do boys think showing off is a good idea? Especially in Gym class? As if you're not six feet tall, sexy, and all man… you're fifteen, five-foot-five, and your balls haven't even dropped!" I laugh, I can't help it. This is why I love Emma. She doesn't hold back, but she's a ray of sunshine on a shitty day. We continue to talk about our day, and then suddenly, Emma slams her hands down on her desk.

"I forgot to tell you guys, Principal Hiffin put in her notice for retirement. She won't be back for next semester!" Hiffin is an elderly woman who has been a principal for over twenty-five years. She could be mean, but if you got on her good side, then you were all good. Even at twenty-nine years old, I'm still afraid of principals… especially since she was mine.

"What? But we're just getting to exams for the first semester. How are they supposed to find a principal in the middle of the year?" I ask Emma. She always has all the answers. She's the one you go to when you want a good laugh and the inside scoop on everything going on in these brick walls. Last year she caught two teachers going at it in the boys' locker room - after school hours, of course. It was still no less of a shock. Emma didn't tell anyone except us, but eventually, the fuck buddies got caught…and lost their positions. You would think teachers would know not to mess around with one another.

"Well, allegedly they already found one. He will be coming in from the city and apparently, he's a hard ass. Doesn't really like to socialize and keeps to himself." Lucky him, I think, wondering if he will be able to talk his way out of going to the bar on Friday night. Every Friday after school, all the teachers go to Kline's, a local bar, for drinks. The girls and I always try to get out of it.

Emphasis on *try*.

"Is he another old person? I swear it's so difficult to keep the older staff up to date on all the latest technology we use." Hannah groans; she's not just good at Art, she's also a tech wiz. Which is why she's always called in to help the older teachers when they can't get their computers to turn on. I laugh to myself, remembering the time that one of our colleagues unplugged his computer with his foot. He would have thrown the damn thing on the ground if it wasn't for Hannah coming in and plugging it back in.

"Apparently not…" Emma takes a bite of her ham sandwich and continues on with her mouth full, "From what I know he's only thirty-three, a total hard ass for rules, but sexy as hell. I haven't seen him, but that's what I've heard…" She shrugs. I'm curious as to where Emma gets all her information from. She loves participating in extracurriculars; nothing that has changed from when we were students. She frequently attends conventions and meets with various teachers around Ontario. It came to benefit us as she would get all the scoop from one side of the province to the other.

"Now I'm intrigued, I can't wait until after exams to find out for ourselves!" Emma smirks and pretends to swoon. I roll my eyes at her. All three of us are almost thirty and single. We would go out and meet men, but in a town of four-teen-thousand people, most already have families or are elderly; the pond is limited. I close my glass container and put it back in my bag. Emma throws hand sanitizer my way, and I put a small circle in my hands. The strong smell of alcohol and flowers filling the air. Emma tries her best to mask the smell of sweaty teenagers with the highly fumigated hand sanitizer.

"Do you have your exams ready, Vic? They start tomorrow, right?" Emma asks me, and I nod.

"Yes, they do, thank God." I take my legs off my desk and stand up to stretch. I feel the pull between my shoulders, giving me release from sitting for over three hours. I should consider moving around more during my lessons. "Then I will be marking until Friday, and then long weekend!" I do a little shake of my hips. This is one of my favorite times of the year, usually on long weekends teachers have to stay up marking. This year, however, the exams will be over before the long weekend which means we can actually spend our time relaxing before the new semester.

The bell rings and our girl time is over. Emma grimaces, knowing her next period is grade twelve Fitness. Which means it's a mixture of people who may not want to be there but need a Gym credit; the perks of a high school curriculum.

I wave the girls goodbye and go to the front of the classroom to erase the notes from my earlier class. I hate having to use this pen to erase things. I have to click the little eraser icon on the screen and drag it along the plastic material. The scratching sound of the pen dragging is worse than nails on a chalkboard. My shoulders slump due to my last period being grade ten English. These students don't have a care in the world for school. I prefer teaching grade eleven and twelve because at least they make an effort with their studies. After all, post-secondary is only a couple years away.

The classroom becomes louder as students filter into their seats. Every student has a phone now, and it makes teaching so tricky. If you take away a student's phone, you become a "bitch," but if you don't take it away, they're distracted the entire time.

"Good afternoon guys, if you could put your phones away that would be appreciated. I don't want to have to take it away, but if I notice it becoming a problem; it's gone." I pause to watch some nod their heads, and some roll their eyes. "We're almost done with the semester, just a few more things to go over. I will be giving you guys the rest of the class to study for your final exam that's coming up." I walk over to the computer and start the final review slide of the term.

"Oh my God, finally!" I say aloud to myself. It's finally three o'clock, and school is over. I thought I dreaded this more when I was a teenager, but it's so much worse as a teacher. I want to get out of here and have an evening to myself before I have to be here again tomorrow morning. I grab my bag from underneath my desk and throw it over my shoulder.

Locking my door, I head towards the front doors to the parking lot. These hallways always leave me anxious. I try to walk as fast as my heels will take me to get out of here. People always liked to say, "You're going to miss high school and university, they're some of the best days of your life" and I still disagree with that statement. School was my worst nightmare come to life; there is nothing that could make me go back.

At all.

I step outside into the bright sun which is shining at the end of January, I cannot believe it. Anyone who lives in Canada knows that it's almost always snowing in January. There is snow on the ground, but not enough that I have to wear a full snowsuit and boots to work. I make my way to my black Mini Cooper parked in the staff lot. Trying not to wipe out on the ice as I walk around my car to the driver's side as I try to keep my heels from gliding against the thawing. I unlock my car, open my door, and slide down into the faux leather seats. I throw my beautiful black leather shoulder bag onto the passenger seat and turn the car on. Maluma's *Mala Mía* starts blasting through the stereo, nearly giving me a heart attack. Music is part of what keeps me alive, so I tend to have it blaring at any time of the day.

I put the car in reverse and pull out of my spot to head home. I can't believe another term has gone by, a time of the year that always leaves me feeling anxious and excited. A new semester means new students, fresh minds at work, and more assignments to work on. I roll to a halt at the stop sign near my house and feel my phone vibrate beside me in my bag. I look in my rear view mirror and see nobody behind me, so I grab my phone.

Hannah: So once exams are over, drinks at DP on Saturday?

Me: Absolutely! Emma coming too?

Hannah: Duh!

I'm about to answer back when a sleek black BMW pulls up behind me. I can't see the person behind the wheel to gauge if they're irritated or not.

I take my foot off the break and throw my phone back on the seat. I turn left towards my house and drive for another eight minutes before pulling up my driveway. I live on the outskirts of Simcoe, just far enough to be away from people, but close enough that I don't dread running errands or my drive to work.

I pull up to my house. It's a beautiful, simple rustic country bungalow with large glass windows framed by wood pieces that make them pop. Most country homes have a wrap around porch, but mine has a multi-stone square porch in front of the French doors. My porch would be much larger if I didn't have a swing bed installed, but I wanted to be able to sit in my front yard comfortably because it's where the sun sets. I saw the idea for the bed swing on Pinterest and had our local contracting company come in and install it. It's the perfect place to sit on a beautiful day.

I park my car in the separate garage and grab my bag on the way out. One thing I hate about this house is the independent garage. The snow and I aren't friends, so the trek isn't ideal especially since I wear heels ninety percent of the time. I walk carefully, dodging the ice on the driveway while closing the garage. I reach the French doors and unlock one. Throwing the door open, I kick off my heels as I walk in and throw my bag on the lavender ottoman sitting against the wall in the foyer.

This house used to be so different. Save for the swing, the exterior of my house has always been the same. Once it became mine, I had some walls knocked down, the walls repainted, and I revamped the master bedroom, kitchen, and laundry room. Emma and Hannah love coming over because of how big and rustic everything looks.

I put my containers in the dishwasher and grab a bottle of wine out of the fridge. The next two days are full of exams, so I will be marking for what is going to feel like a year. I take a big gulp from my glass of wine and get ready for the upcoming exam season.

CHAPTER TWO

After a long week full of exams, the weekend is finally here.

"Cheers to another semester being done in this hell hole," Hannah shouts. People look over at us and make annoyed faces. One thing with small towns is that everyone is judgmental, it doesn't matter if they don't know who you are, they don't hold anything back. I notice a group of girls sitting in a booth chomping down on some delicious-looking nachos and drinking fish bowls.

Literal fishbowls.

Full of alcohol.

Usually when you see fishbowls on the menu it's like thirty percent alcohol and sixty percent slush and juice. Well, at Dallas Pub the bartenders don't hold back. They don't pay for the alcohol, the business does, so why should they care? That's why the group of girls are loud and rowdy. They have enough alcohol in them for the entire weekend. Are they of age? Who knows. In small towns it's easy to get away with under-age drinking.

"Can we get on their level? Let's order some fish bowls

next!" Emma raises her hand to attract our waitress' attention. I look at the menu and see they have a peach Bellini bowl.

Yeah that's *definitely* what I'm getting.

The waitress comes over and we each tell her which flavour bowl we want. Hannah winks over at the bartender as the waitress tells her our order. Out of the three of us, Hannah is definitely the one who has fully accepted her sexuality. Man or woman, she doesn't care. As long as there is a connection, she is happy. Emma and I wish we were as sexually confident as Hannah. However, once Emma gets to know a man though, her confidence soars. She has the physique of a goddess and a personality of gold; any guy would be lucky to be with her. Me on the other hand? I have no idea how I would describe myself. I'm not an introvert, but I'm not exactly an extrovert. I'm just a woman who loves taking photos of my life, writing, and hanging out with my best friends.

The waitress disturbs my train of thought as she brings over these monstrously large fishbowls. Her arms are straining as she carries three fishbowls in a small circular tray. She sets them down quickly, the glass clinking together. I glance over at the group of girls and our drinks are larger than theirs. I look up at Hannah and then look at the bartender and she sends a wink our way.

Oh.

Well, thank you, Ms. Bartender.

Twenty minutes later, the three of us have downed half our bowls and ordered burgers. We figured it's better to get some food in us or we are going to be pulling a Coyote Ugly on the bar really soon.

"You see that brooding man over there?" Emma points over to a man sitting in a suit at the bar. I grab her hand and bring it down.

"Emma, you can't just point at people! It's rude." I hold her hand down and slide my bowl over with my other hand to take a sip through the straw.

Jesus, there is a lot of alcohol in here.

I do a little shake of my shoulder, you know, when you drink an entire sip of just alcohol. I swish around my straw in my bowl so that the alcohol mixes with the ice and juice. I take a second sip and the delicious peach flavor assaults my tongue. This drink tastes like a liquified version of fuzzy peaches, my favorite.

"Oh, he's definitely not from here. He doesn't look as if he's here for a long time…" Hannah stares at the mysterious man.

"He also doesn't look like he's here for a good time." Emma snorts into her drink, which causes Hannah and I to join in.

"Okay, we are such losers, but that was hilarious." I turn and study the man. He's in a small-town bar, wearing a fitted grey suit and tie? He definitely isn't from here. I can't help but stare at him.

He turns his head, looking behind him towards the door. I almost choke on my drink. From behind he was gorgeous, from the front?

Holy.

Shit.

He has green eyes the shape of almonds, which adds to his mischievous look. He has a neatly trimmed beard and full lips that compliment his jaw. I'm gawking at him, but I don't have a care in me. I can't help but have the urge to run my hands through his thick, dark brown hair. He has it styled in the perfect quiff. I wouldn't mind wrestling with it a bit.

"Earth to Vic!" Hannah throws a wadded-up napkin at me.

"You know staring is rude!" Emma mocks my former words back at me. I jump and turn my attention back towards them and notice there's now a burger in front of me.

"Oh yum!" I grab some fries and stuff them in my mouth.

"What were you just thinking?" Hannah smirks and Emma nods, agreeing with Hannah's question.

"Uh, I was just thinking about how he's definitely not from here." My face flushes as I lie. They have been my friends for over ten years…they know when I'm lying.

"Yeah, okay, that is definitely not what you were thinking!" Emma pushes. I roll my eyes at them and pick up my burger, taking a huge bite. Some juices from the burger slide down my fingers and I moan. The perfect ratio of meat, cheese, and vegetables to make my eyes roll to the back of my head in delight.

"You know, if you don't answer I'll smack that burger right out of your hand." Hannah threatens, and I put my burger down at lightning speed.

"Okay, jeez, don't take it out on my food!" I finish swallowing. "You know what I was thinking, that man is gorgeous. Like drop dead, not from around here, gorgeous!" I laugh at my play on words. I look back towards him and notice he is looking back at me. My eyes widen instinctively and I start to panic, thinking I may have said that a little too loud. When I turn and look at the girls with a look of panic, my worries are confirmed. Their eyes are wide, not with surprise, but laughter.

Fuck me.

"I said that really loud, didn't I?" I groan and throw my head back. This is why we usually drink at my place; there is no way I can embarrass myself in my own home. I peek slowly back towards the man and notice that he's gone.

"Vic, you totally said that out loud. It was priceless.

Everyone knew who you were talking about, too." I groan even louder. I pick up my burger and take a huge bite.

"I'm going to need more alcohol to deal with whatever I just did." I say to the girls with a mouth full of burger. They laugh, nod their heads and Hannah raises her hand to get our waitress' attention...again.

God, where is that light coming from? I lift my head up, pain radiating through it from the sudden movement, and look over to find my curtains ajar.

Ugh, I forgot to close them yesterday when I got home. Which, with this hangover, doesn't surprise me. I look over at the little rose-gold clock on my mirrored nightstand and read the time: twelve thirty-four. I groan and throw the covers over my head, trying to remember how the hell I got home. I remember us drinking one, or maybe two more fishbowls? Okay, maybe I don't. I start to recall the girls and I drinking more, then dancing around the bar, before the bartender offered to drive each of us home.

Oh yeah, that's how I got home.

"Fuck, my head is killing me."

"Holy fuck," I shout and shoot upright from the bed.

Oh God, I shouldn't have moved that abruptly. My head swirls and my mouth feels as if it's full of cotton balls as I try to speak. I notice Emma and Hannah are both laying down on my floor with towels and pillows. "You guys scared the shit out of me. I didn't realize you stayed here last night." I crawl to the edge of my bed and stare at them. Why the hell are they on the floor, and not in my bed with me? This king mattress is more than enough for the three of us, and we've done it plenty of times before...

"Oh yeah, just look at us peasants down here while you lay in your throne of a bed." Hannah growls and sits up while holding her head.

"Both of you shut up." Emma peeks out from under a towel, "How much did we drink last night? I just remember passing out on the floor, unable to even make it to the bed, apparently." Emma tries to sit up but decides against it. I giggle watching her struggle like a newborn calf trying to walk.

"Get your asses up here." I throw open my covers and watch them struggle to get into my king size bed. There is obviously enough room, but I think moving makes them feel as if they're going to hurl.

"What the hell were we thinking last night?" I stare up at the ceiling. I knew we were going to celebrate another semester being done, but I didn't expect us to go that hard... in public. I groan and shove my head into my pillow.

"I don't know, but I don't think this headache was worth it." Emma turns so she's facing us. Sudden emotion hits me. I don't know how I got so lucky getting to grow up with my best friends, have them go through the shittiest time of my life with me, and still be here fourteen years later.

"Vic, are you okay? You look like you're about to cry." Hannah and Emma both look at me with concern.

"Yes, yes I'm okay. I just realized I really love you guys." I laugh. They both "aww" in unison and hug me.

"Okay, enough of this. Why don't I get the coffee going and we can make some breakfast?" They start nodding as soon as I mention coffee, so it looks like I need to get my hungover ass to work.

"Vic, I swear if you weren't a teacher you would be a chef. The bacon and eggs are absolutely delicious!" Hannah moans and grabs another piece of bacon from the plate sitting on the island. This is a typical Sunday that happens at least once a month. The girls will come over on Saturday night and we watch movies, either horror or romcom; no in-between. Then we order pizza, drink wine, and enjoy ourselves.

Yeah, maybe that's why we're single. I rinse off my plate and put it in the dishwasher, pouring myself another round.

Because you can never have too much coffee.

"Okay, my loves, I'm going to call a cab so I can go pick up my car." Emma rinses off her plate as well and throws it in the dishwasher. Hannah shoves another piece of bacon in her mouth and nods her head to Emma.

"I'll split it with you because I need to grab my car too." She finishes chewing and follows suit with the dishes. I finish setting our mugs on the top rack and close the dishwasher. I turn around and the girls are standing at the door, waiting for me to come say goodbye. Luckily, I had Emma pick me up on the way to Dallas Pub, so I don't need to pick up my car.

"I swear, you say you're hungover, yet you never stop cleaning." Emma smirks at me and I stick my tongue out at her.

"Well, I'm somewhat used to this, we do it quite a bit." I wink.

"She's not wrong. We do this quite a bit, so we should be used to it." Hannah shrugs and throws her black purse over her shoulder.

"I will never be used to drinking three fishbowls. Never!" Emma exclaims dramatically, while I cringe at the sudden loudness. Emma should have chosen a career in Theatre, not Fitness. We hear a car honk from outside and look to see a taxi in the driveway.

"Well, this is where we part." Emma throws her arms around my shoulders. I hug her back only to have Hannah throw herself into the hug as well.

"You guys are too much. We are going to see each other on Tuesday for the new semester!" Emma pouts and I can't help but laugh. We could spend every hour together and it would never be enough. I push them out the door with pouts on their faces and blow kisses to them as they walk towards the taxi. I shut my door, smiling.

My friends are seriously the best.

I grab my phone from on top of the ottoman and bring it to the kitchen to charge. As I wait for it to turn on I walk to the dishwasher, put a pod in it, and close it to start its cycle. I hear a ping from my phone, letting me know that it has finally turned on. Walking over, I immediately open my camera roll.

I love taking photos, it's one of my favorite things to do. I have a wall in my hallway dedicated to showcasing the photos I've taken throughout my life, placed in an assortment of black, white, and mint colored frames to add a little character to the house. The pictures provide constant reminders of the amazing things that have happened in my life. Despite those good memories, a pang of sorrow tightens around my heart, and I try not to let my sadness overtake me. Shaking it off as best as I can, I start scrolling through last night's photos and realize that when we're drinking, we shouldn't take photos.

Oh my God.

I find a photo of the three of us on the bar. Well, we definitely pulled a Coyote Ugly, but at least we looked good doing it. I send the photo to my printer and grab one of my extra frames from the closet in the hallway, ready to put it up on the memory wall.

After putting up the picture, I laugh and send a photo of it to the girls. They didn't remember last night as much as I did. Even so, all of us remembered the gorgeous, suited man from the bar.

Yum.

I have today and tomorrow off until we are back to school on Tuesday and decide I'm going to do a self-made spa day. I walk to the bathroom attached to my bedroom, put some Epsom salts and bubble bath into the tub, and start the hot water. My bathroom is my own personal sanctuary. The bathtub sits beside the window, with a stack of metal baskets on a ladder holding toilet paper, towels, soaps, and of course, books. Hung above my bathtub are cut up pieces of burlap, on which I've written the word "relax." I have a crazy obsession with the beautiful rustic look; that's why my entire house looks like it's from Pinterest. Quickly grabbing my coffee from the kitchen, I get ready to settle into the bath, with my laptop perched on the chair to watch some Netflix.

A couple hours later, after draining and filling up the tub a handful of times, my body is completely relaxed. I pull on the plug and stand up, wrapping myself in a big, white, fluffy towel as the lukewarm water spirals down the drain. I leave my hair in its messy bun on top of my head and put every-thing back in its place. I move the mouse on my laptop to check what time it is, and find that it's already six o'clock.

Well, I guess I should make dinner for one. I walk to my bedroom and grab my grey sweats and a t-shirt that reads, "Boys in books are better." This shirt is over ten years old, but I will never throw it away because it was gifted to me from my mom when I was nineteen. My mom loved customizing anything and everything, so she made me this cute shirt using fabric markers and I wear it when I'm staying in. I walk to the kitchen, set my mug in the sink and open the fridge. I realize I need to go grocery shopping at some point this week because my choices are very limited with an almost-empty fridge. I grab the pack of ravioli I bought at Costco and decide it should be enough for dinner tonight.

As I start to boil the pasta, I picture the guy from last night again. I don't know what it was about him, but he was captivating. He was one of those men who are so well put together that you can't help but think about them days later. He looked so brooding, but man, it suited him. Just like the suit he was wearing. I shiver and look down to see that the water is boiling over, the water jumping over the top of the pot and onto the hot stovetop.

Oops.

I grab the pack of ravioli and put it into the water. Waiting for that to cook, I grab some sauce and cheese to bake with the ravioli afterwards. I put some eighties tunes on my phone and decide a party for one while cooking is exactly how my night is going to go. My dad was always a fan of eighties rock, a trait I must've inherited since I'm air drumming *Cum on Feel the Noize* by Quiet Riot. I jump around while singing along, quickly stirring the pasta while the song plays its guitar solo. The lyrics pick back up again and I jam all the way to the fridge to grab some wine. I remember the days when I would come home from university on the weekends and sit in the garage with my dad, listening to anything from the seventies and eighties. They're some of my favorite memories, us sitting there singing with beers in our hands, and my mom coming out and laughing at us. She would never really take part in our tipsy singing shenanigans, but she loved to sit and take photos of us.

Those were some of the best days of my life.

I drain the ravioli from the pot and spread it in the pan with the sauce, topping it with cheese. It's definitely a lazy girl dinner, but it suits my night. I throw the glass dish in the oven and put the dirty dishes into the sink. I hate throwing pots into the dishwasher. They take up so much space.

Any Way You Want It by Journey comes on and I grab the nearest spoon to start using as a microphone. I jump as cold pasta sauce splashes across my face. I look down and notice I grabbed the spoon I used to spread sauce over the ravioli. I shrug my shoulders and use a cloth to clean off my face. I continue singing, but realize that clean utensils make for the best microphones.

I'm sweating by the time the beeper on the oven goes off; I just spent the last ten minutes dancing around the kitchen. I can't be the only person who does this when they're alone at home. I wipe my forehead with the back of my hand and pull my perfectly done ravioli from the oven and get ready to dig in.

CHAPTER THREE

I pull into the school parking lot at precisely seven in the morning. Our staff meeting is supposed to start any minute now, so I grab my bag and haul ass out of my car. I look down at my outfit and feel confident to meet the new principle. I'm wearing a black turtleneck, a tweed skirt, and thigh-high boots. Yes, I'm one of those teachers who dress to impress. The sleek black BMW I saw the other day is parked in our teacher's lot.

Well, someone is getting paid well for a small-town occupant. I speed walk up the stairs, headed for the teacher's lounge to the left of the chapel.

I hope I'm not sweating that bad. Moisture collects under my arms, but thankfully, I wore black to hide any stains. I slow my pace and check to see that it's just after seven; they're only five minutes into the meeting. I walk in casually, but immediately stop when I see the man from Dallas Pub on Saturday standing in front of my colleagues. My eyes widen as I look at Hannah and Emma, who are smirking.

They didn't think to text me? I ignore the mysterious man's eye contact and take a seat next to Emma. I grab my phone and hold it in my lap and see that the girls did text me...

Hannah: Oh my God Vic, where are you? We're in the meeting waiting to meet the new principal.

Emma: VIC, YOU NEED TO SEE THE NEW PRINCIPAL! YOU ARE SERIOUSLY GOING TO DIE.

Emma's text messages are followed by a bunch of laughing emojis. Why is the guy from the pub here?

"As I was saying," he looks directly at me because I interrupted him, "I'm excited to start a new semester here and look forward to getting to know all of you. I'm sure there have been rumours that have already commenced, but if you have any concerns, feel free to stop by my office." He nods his head at everyone and my colleagues start to filter out of the room.

What the fuck? This is our new principal? You have got to be kidding me, my embarrassment from Saturday comes full force. I can imagine what he thinks about me already. I look over at the girls and they are already looking at me, giggling.

"Oh my God, just when I thought teaching couldn't get any worse." I groan into my hands, keeping my head down. The girls stop giggling beside me and I open my eyes to notice two beautifully expensive black Salvatore Ferragamo shoes right in front of me.

Fuck me.

I raise my head slowly and take all of him in. He's wearing a grey three-piece suit with an accented red tie. I keep moving my gaze upward and can't believe how gorgeous this man is, not to mention young. I finally make eye contact with my mystery man—now known to be the new principal, and my new boss. I straighten my back, trying to look put together, and plaster a smile onto my face.

"Hello sir, I'm sorry for interrupting you earlier. I had a mishap at home which made me late. I'm Victoria Mateus."

"Hello Ms. Mateus. Let's ensure that this does not happen again, I'm not a fan of interruptions." He nods his head at the three of us and walks out.

"Uh, nice to meet you too?" I look at the girls confused. What the hell is his name? I grab my bag and throw it over my shoulder. That was a pointless meeting. Albeit I was a tad late, but it didn't seem like a valid reason to come in forty minutes before we usually start.

"Well, he seems pleasant…" Emma notes. I scoff, and the three of us walk towards my classroom. We have thirty minutes before we need to disperse.

"What the hell is his name? He didn't even introduce himself to me." I grab my classroom keys from my bag and shove them into the lock. I didn't expect this guy to be this rude, but I guess if he's coming from the city it makes sense.

"His name is Auston Scott and I think his reason for being such an asshole to you is because of Saturday night. He recognized us right away and treated us the same…" Emma grimaces and sits on the student's desk in front of mine.

"Well, great. We just finished dealing with one crotchety woman, now we have to deal with a cranky man? Why don't principals ever seem happy? They literally sit at their desks all day." Hannah pipes in, slightly angry. She's right, though. We've spent our entire career with an old angry woman, and now we have to deal with a young, sexy as hell, and brooding man. Life isn't fair sometimes.

"Actually, I don't sit at my desk all day, but I will take it into account to walk around more." My eyes widen and we all turn our heads to find grumpy, mysterious Mr. Scott standing in the doorway. "I just came by to give you three these." He hands us all a piece of paper. "I will be coming in within the next few weeks at odd times to observe your teachings. I hope your lectures are a lot better than your gossip circle." He turns and walks out. My mouth is left hanging open.

Who is this guy and what's his problem?

"Well, cheers to the new semester, guys." I throw Hannah's words back at her from the other night. I say goodbye to the girls as we hear students filtering into the hallways and decide to print out the syllabus for my new students.

This semester I have academic grade twelve in first period, an online Creative Writing course that I monitor during second, third period break followed by lunch, and finally applied grade ten. This semester is jam packed, and I don't know if that's a good or bad thing yet. Depending on the group of students I'll have in my class, will help determine that decision.

That was the longest day in teacher history. As if this morning didn't already suck, *Mr. Scott* surely knew how to make it worse. He assigned Hannah, Emma, and I to lunch duty. We absolutely hate lunch duty. Who wants to miss their lunch break to listen to a bunch of kids screaming, and talking about things I'll never be able to erase from my mind. On top of that, I have another grade ten English class at the end of the day and these students might actually be worse than last semester's. I finish erasing the board and lay my head against the chalkboard.

Give me strength, please.

I finish my little prayer and move to organize all the desks back into straight lines, then gather my stuff. I actually feel bad for the way I treated my teachers in high school. Had I known how tiring it is, I would have been a lot nicer to deal with. Not that I was that bad; I tried my best to stay quiet and do my work. But if I had a class with either Emma or Hannah, we became slightly disruptive.

I grab my bag, throw it on my shoulder, and walk out of my class before locking the door. I look down the hallway to see Mr. Scott standing there, watching students filter out of the hallways.

Okay, at this moment I really wish that he would sit in his office more. Our words from earlier are coming back to bite us in the ass. I straighten my back, feigning confidence, and walk towards him to exit the school.

I quickly make my way down the hall towards Mr. Scott. As soon as he hears my heels clicking, he looks my way. I inwardly scoff.

"Ms. Mateus, I was just curious if you think the clothing you're wearing is appropriate for a school environment?" I look at him as if he's ludicrous. I think my eyes might just pop out of their sockets. My outfit is absolutely gorgeous. My curvy figure may fill it out a little bit more than if I were thinner, but I love looking good; I don't dress for anyone but myself. He can tell I'm a little taken back by his question.

"I'm sorry Mr. Scott, but I have been working at this school for almost five years and have never had any complaints." My eyes narrow into slits as I look at him. I understand he's in an authoritative position, but I don't think he has any right to question my attire. The man dresses as if he is ready to walk down a goddamn Dolce and Gabbana runway show.

"Very well then." He looks me up and down one last time, something darkening in his gaze. He nods and turns, walking away from me. I roll my eyes. He's probably not used to seeing a curvy girl have confidence with fashion, why else would he make such an ignorant comment? A few minutes later, I continue my walk towards the front doors. My fingernails are biting into my palm as I make my way out of the school. I despise when men think they have the right to judge a woman's outfit choice.

Hannah and Emma are talking outside the front doors when they notice my storming face. Emma looks confused while Hannah seems concerned.

"Babe, why do you look as if you want to punch someone?" Hannah puts her left arm through mine and Emma links hers through Hannah's right.

"You will not believe what that arrogant fucking guy just questioned me about! He questioned me about my fashion choice. *Me.*" I may be a little bit dramatic right now, but I have never had problems with my choice of outfit at work. In fact, Hiffin usually complimented my outfits, because she knows what I went through as a teenager between these walls.

"No way." Hannah's eyes widen in surprise as Emma's nose scrunches in anger. They are both as appalled as I'm. We carefully walk over to our cars and stop behind them.

"I know. You can imagine the look on my face when he said that to me. My fashion has been the one thing that has kept me grounded since my life hit the fan." I look up to the sky and groan. I glance at my best friends to find Hannah looking genuinely upset, while Emma has a devilish look on her face.

"Emma, what the hell are you thinking?" Hannah asks, intrigued by her mischievous look.

"Well, if Mr. Scott is so uncomfortable with your outfits, I think we should really give him something to feel uncomfortable about." Emma's eyes sparkle at the thought of getting back at him.

"Guys, I don't want to start problems. I'm not going to change how I dress because of him. My fashion choice is what brings me confidence and peace every day, and I won't let anyone take that away. Everyone has something that brings them confidence and for me, it's fashion." I shrug and try to believe the words I just spoke. When I was a little girl I would always go into my mom's closet to try on her many dresses and heels. My mom always said that my choice of clothing and love for books would forever keep me happy, even as a little girl. I know that now, that statement is truer than ever. I tell the girls not to worry and that I'll see them tomorrow, before heading to the grocery store. I have absolutely nothing in my fridge right now, so off to Fresh Growth I go.

It's about a five-minute drive from the high school to Fresh Growth. It's one of my favorite grocery stores since it's all organic and fresh, hence the name. It's not as packed today as it usually is, which makes me happy. I grab the reusable bags from my trunk and get ready to spend a few hundred dollars on groceries.

Two hours and a bill of two-hundred and fifty dollars later, I have purchased enough groceries for a family of four.

You know what they say: never go grocery shopping while hungry. Since I had to skip my lunch today, I was starving. I would have taken my lunch on my spare, but Mr. Scott decided to inform us of our lunch duty only ten minutes before it began. As I'm walking out of the store, someone bumps into my cart. I'm about to tell the person to watch where they're going, but the words die on my tongue. Mr. Scott looks up, noticing he was so occupied by his phone that he didn't see me coming out of the store. I roll my eyes, which he obviously notices.

"Rolling your eyes is rude, Ms. Mateus." I smile sweetly, *and fakely*, at him.

"Being on your phone and not paying attention to your surroundings is also rude Mr. Scott." I continue smiling at him as I wait to hear his reply.

"You're right, I'm sorry. Have a good night." He walks past me, and I grunt. Can the universe leave me alone for five minutes? Who was once my delicious mystery man, is now my annoyingly gorgeous boss.

I walk to my car in a huff, pack everything in the trunk, and start the car to get home.

Is it horrible to stop at Wendy's on the way home when I just picked up groceries? I guess this is what they mean by adulting. Even when you can do whatever you want without anyone judging you, you still guilt yourself into making the better, albeit less exciting, choices. At the last second, I turn my car left rather than right towards home, making my way to Wendy's to deal with my emotions. Nobody ever said there was a correct way to adult.

Half an hour later, after putting all my groceries away, I sit on the couch and turn on the T.V. I load up the Passionflix app and get ready to watch a delicious romance.

Who wouldn't love romance books coming to life in a way that actually does them justice? I decide between a few movies and go for Gabriel's Inferno. Now, why can't I deal with an alpha man like Gabriel Emerson? He's gloomy, brooding, and somewhat of an asshole, but when you get to know him he's protective, intelligent, and loving as hell. Why can't I find a man like that?

I roll my eyes thinking of damn Mr. Scott. He's the

complete opposite of the amazing men we read about in romance novels.

I open up my delicious Baconator and put the fries alongside it, finally getting ready to enjoy my delicious dinner with Julia Mitchell and Gabriel Emerson.

CHAPTER FOUR

I s it bad to masturbate to the thought of your devil-like boss? I sit at my desk at the end of the day and think about last night. After my date with Gabriel Emerson, I needed a little me time with my vibrator... with no other than Mr. Scott in mind. When I saw him this morning with his black slacks that were tight in all the right places, a black button up, and an emerald tie, I may have had to squeeze my legs together.

I put my head on my desk and groan. It's only Wednesday —how the hell am I supposed to deal with this for another five months?

I plead to the time Gods; summer, please come quick.

I'm startled by a knock at my door and I look up to see Mr. Scott arching an eyebrow at me. God dammit, do I not get a rest from this man? I barely ever saw Mrs. Hiffin when she was here, why can't he follow suit?

"Hello Mr. Scott, what can I do for you?" I straighten my back and smile tightly at him. My memories from last night come to mind and I cower. I try to keep my face neutral as well as my posture. He catches everything, so I don't want to give him any further suspicions. He comes into my classroom and looks at all the items on my desk. It's not cluttered, but it does give him an insight into my life.

"You must be close with Ms. Brock and Ms. Ribeiro?" he nods at the photo on my desk and I look at him puzzled. As much as I don't want to talk to him, his voice is guttural, husky, and modulated. Squeezing my legs together, I look back up at him. So much for a neutral posture.

"Uhh… yeah, we have been friends since grade ten. Is there something I can help you with Mr. Scott?" I question him with an eyebrow raised.

"Yes, I have two things to follow up with you. On Friday, I will be coming into your last period class to watch you teach."

Fuck, that's my worst class. It's like trying to tame damn monkeys. I'm going to warn them tomorrow that he will be in, and to be on their best behaviour.

"Also, we will be having a staff meeting after school on Friday at four o'clock. I have a few things to go over with everyone." He looks at me and I notice he takes in my attire. Today I'm wearing a long-sleeved, pink knit sweater tucked into the front of my jeans, paired with my brown leather boots.

"Is this more work appropriate for you, Mr. Scott?" I can tell he senses my sarcasm by the way his jaw clenches. I inwardly fist pump. This semester may actually be fun, if I continue with this sarcastic attitude… or I may end up jobless.

I don't know if that's a game I really should be playing…

"Yes," he nods his head in approval and I roll my eyes again. This guy has a lot of nerve.

"Will that be all Mr. Scott? I have lessons to plan." I raise an eyebrow and I can tell I'm really pissing him off. His eyes become slits and his jaw tightens. He nods his head towards me and walks out.

I let out a deep breath once I hear his footsteps farther down the hallway. I look down at the lesson I have planned for tomorrow and shudder. It's a lesson on Hamlet, and I'm not a huge fan of Shakespeare. As an English Major and teacher most would assume that I think he's the God of English Literature, but no. I despise that our curriculum is still focusing on his work. We have so many new and upcoming writers that I believe are better choices, but every time I bring it up to the board, they laugh and dismiss me.

I think for my grade twelve academic English class I'm going to switch things around and let the students decide what book they want to use for their culminating assignment, worth thirty percent of their overall grade. It allows me to see their own unique perspectives, and which aspects they enjoy in a novel. As a bonus, it'll give me some summer reads to look forward to. I make some quick notes about what I will want to see from them in their assignments before closing my binder.

I pull out my phone and notice that it's three forty-five. Hannah had to head out right after school today for a hair appointment, but Emma should be out on the field running the girl's rugby try-outs. I decide to go outside and see how everything is going with her, so I lock my classroom and head down the stairs.

The sun has been out all week, and the plus temperatures has caused the snow to start melting. Most likely not for long though - the weather app is forecasting a storm this weekend. I step out into the sun and already I can hear Emma's voice screaming.

Damn, she has some good vocal cords. I tend to forget

that since I don't spend much time with her in coaching mode.

I walk slowly through the dead yellow grass toward Emma. Our school is lucky enough to have a beautiful field, where all our sports take place. To the left of the entrance is the football field, which is surrounded by a track. It's a two for one, making everything a lot easier when it comes time for track and field. There is a long jump pit behind the bleachers, which are next to the track. Some strategically-planted trees line the way to a large field, about the size of six Olympic sized pools with some soccer nets placed in between. This field is usually where try-outs take place, since it's spacious and allows for more than one activity at a time. I notice that the boy's hockey team is also training outside today. They usually go to the local arena, but I guess Coach Riley wants them outside today. Hockey is the major sport at Angel's High School; we offer every sport, but we take pride in our successful hockey team. I glance away from the hockey team and make my way towards Emma, who is wearing grey Lululemon sweats and a black Angel's High School rugby sweater.

Emma looks away from where the guys are practicing and waves at me.

"Hey babe, how was your day?" She looks over at the try-outs and shakes her head. "C'mon girls, that's how you tackle? Get lower or you will get wrecked during a game!" She shouts at them, and I grimace.

"Hey, my day was all right. Those tenth graders are spawns of Satan. I've never had a class so careless and mean; I need to think of some ways to tame them." I wrap my arms around my body. The sun is out, but the chill is definitely still here.

"I'm sure you will think of something. It's only the first

week, and you care about all your students so much. They will notice that, and become angels instead of demons." She winks at me and I laugh.

Emma and I both turn our heads at the sound of a bunch of boys hooting and hollering. My eyes widen at the activities that are taking place before me.

Mr. Scott is dressed in gym shorts and a tight, black short-sleeved shirt, and he is flipping over a tire. Not just any tire though - a tractor trailer tire. A tractor tire can weigh anywhere from two hundred to six hundred pounds.

"Holy Fuck…"

"Thank you, Jesus!" Emma yells up to the Gods above. We stare as Mr. Scott's arms bulging as his shirt tightens around his large muscles. He squats to lift the tire and grunts while pushing it over. He does this a couple of times until he reaches the middle of the field. The team starts hollering at him as they run to give him high-fives.

Myself on the other hand? I feel like a heated mess… on my face and in between my thighs. I notice the girls on the rugby team are also staring and giggling. I feel as if all of our hormones may be a little erratic after that presentation.

"I feel so bad that Hannah has to miss this." Emma laughs.

I nod but I can't take my eyes away from Mr. Scott. A principal should not be allowed to be this physically attractive. No wonder the board kept an old woman in charge for twenty five plus years. I use my hand to fan my face as I try to cool myself off.

"Emma, what the fuck is he doing out here with the boy's hockey team?" I peel my eyes away from Mr. Scott being praised and I look at her.

"Mr. Riley's wife finally went into labor. Mr. Scott has been put on coach duty because nobody else wanted—nor knew how—to do it." Mr. Riley's wife's due date was three weeks ago; it's about time that baby wants to get out.

"Well, good for Mrs. Riley… and for us, apparently." I smirk. Emma nods her head in rapid motion. She looks like one of those teeth toys you would wind up as a kid, to watch it open and close quickly. I laugh at her and give her a nudge. Even though he irritates me, his looks make up for his poor attitude.

"I think I'm going to head home now. Did Mr. Scott tell you about the meeting on Friday?" Emma groans without answering my question, which means she knows. I start to walk away and tell her that I will call her tonight.

Forty minutes later I've gathered all of my stuff from my classroom into my bag, cleaned off some desks, and placed Hamlet on everyone's desk for tomorrow morning's class. I grab my bag from my chair, my phone that's on my desk, and lock the door.

As I'm making my way down the hallway, I pause.

Mr. Scott is drinking from the fountain. He is glistening with sweat and taking in water as if he hasn't had a drink in years. As if everything is going in slow motion, he turns away from the fountain and grabs the bottom of his shirt to wipe his face.

You know when people say washboard abs and you think of some Sports Illustrated magazine with a shirtless man on the cover? That's exactly what I'm witnessing right now, right before my eyes. My mouth sits agape as Mr. Scott's abs ripple as he wipes his face free of sweat.

I'm just gaping at him when a cough sounds, and takes me away from my fantasy of Mr. Scott. I shake my head and realize that Mr. Scott is now in front of me, glaring.

"You know Mr. Scott, you probably shouldn't be lifting your shirt up in the middle of the hallway. You are a principal in a *Catholic* School." I say quick and turn on my heel.

Jesus Christ. My face is burning up; I have never been so careless in front of a colleague, not to mention a boss. I think back to the night at Dallas Pub when I made those comments about him, and I sag my shoulders. He probably wants to fire my ass.

I speed up my pace to get out of the school, into my car, and get home. I've had enough imagery today that could last me a lifetime of dark fantasies for masturbation about Mr. Scott.

Once in my car, I lock the doors and lean my head on the head rest. I turn on my car and turn the air-conditioning on blast.

In the middle of winter.

I take a deep breath in an attempt to calm my nerves. I should have just kept my mouth shut and walked away from Mr. Scott, but after the comments he made about my fashion choices the last few days, I felt the need to snap at him.

Laughter fills my room as Hannah and Emma sit on Face-Time with me. I just told them about the incident in the hallway with Mr. Scott.

"Okay, you guys can stop laughing now! It's not that funny. I'm worried I may have just dug myself into a hole!" I practically scream into my phone. I got home and made myself dinner to try to calm my nerves, but even four hours later I'm still anxious.

"Oh Vic, why are you overanalyzing it? I'm sure he knew you were just being sarcastic towards him. He made a comment about your fashion sense, so it only made sense that you would make a comment back about him." Hannah states as Emma nods along. I lay back onto my bed with a thump, and groan.

"He can't fire me for this, right?" I question the girls. There aren't many options for teaching in Simcoe; I would have to move. That thought alone makes my eyes rim with unshed tears.

I could never sell my home.

"Girl, please calm down. No, you can't be fired. If so, you could get him fired as well for his comments." True. He made the comments about my attire first, which would just make us even.

"Okay, okay." I take a deep breath for the millionth time today, "I'm feeling a little better. I think I'm going to head to bed and turn my brain off. It has been on overdrive today." I laugh lightly into the phone.

"You should have a session with your trusty rabbit. I'm sure after what you saw today it would help release some stress!" Emma yells into the phone.

"Oh my God! You're hopeless, I'm hanging up now! Goodnight, I love you guys."

"Love you!" I hear them both yell back as I hang up.

Maybe Emma is right, another night with my vibrator doesn't sound so bad. I look over to the drawer where it sits, and smirk to myself. Nothing comes from a fantasy; it's just a fantasy, after all.

CHAPTER FIVE

T*hank God it's Friday.*

The lunch bell just rang, indicating that lunch has just finished. I'm nervous all over again because Mr. Scott will be joining my class today. I warned the students yesterday about it, and I pray that they won't be shitheads.

They start to filter in from the hallway and I stay standing at the front of the room. I have the attendance sheet in hand and decide that instead of passing it around, I will be asking each of them individually to raise their hand in attendance. It will take up more class time, which is a plus because I feel sick. My nerves are frayed and my stomach feels as if it is ready to empty its contents.

I have never enjoyed being criticized; maybe that's why I never started writing my novel.

And people can be extremely mean when they don't like your work.

I shake my head at those thoughts because that's not what's important right now. I glance down at my outfit and make sure everything is in its place. I decided to wear a square-neck long sleeve bodycon dress in black, with my cheetah print booties. Nothing extremely fancy that Mr. Scott can complain about, but enough to make me feel like myself and give me that extra boost of confidence I need for the day.

Every student is currently sitting at their assigned desk and Mr. Scott isn't here yet. I look around and notice some of them are on their phones.

"Guys, if you could please put your phones away. The bell has rung which means class has officially started. I don't have a problem with making you put your phone on my desk, so please get them out of sight." I state the last part in a hurry because Mr. Scott just walked through the door. Can this man try and be casual for even just one day? He looks like a GQ model, not a principal in a small town. He is wearing maroon slacks with a black dress shirt tucked in. It's actually pretty simple for him, but man if I don't feel myself drooling.

I clear my throat to get everyone's attention while Mr. Scott sits on the desk at the back. He has a folder in hand with a pen hanging off the top. I look at all the students and smile.

"Okay guys, to start off class we are going to be taking attendance." I hold my binder up with the sheet sitting on top of it and grab the pencil I have tucked behind my ear.

"Uhh, but Ms. Mateus, you usually just give it to us and we mark ourselves?" A student says aloud which results in my cheeks heating up. She has a smirk on her face, the cockiness evident in calling me, a teacher, out.

For fuck sakes, I know what I usually do... I just want to take up extra time.

"Well, today is different. When I say your name, I would like you to raise your hand, or say 'here.'" I smile and hear a student mumble "this is gay."

My nostrils flare—I absolutely despise when students, or anyone for that matter, uses the word gay.

"Brad, that's language I will not tolerate *at all*. Either you be quiet, or I have no problem sending you to the office for the rest of the day." I raise my eyebrow at him and he rolls his eyes but nods in agreement.

Fuck, if my parents had heard that I had said something like that in class, I would've been grounded for at least two weeks. My mom didn't tolerate any hateful slang. I remember as a kid I had said the word gay, and my mom put hot sauce in my mouth.

Portuguese parents really know how to discipline.

I look at everyone and start calling their names one by one. Whoever is here and listening has been marked with a check, whoever is not here, or not listening is getting an x and a call home for absence.

"Maria, would you mind taking the attendance sheet down to the office?" I handed it to her.

"Maria got to do it yesterday. That's totally unfair!" One of the students says aloud. I try to keep my snarky response to myself, but I look over to Mr. Scott who gives me a look that says *what are you going to reply back?*

I take a deep breath and try to keep myself from being sarcastic in front of my boss.

"Well, Maria participates in class and doesn't talk during lessons, so for now, she will be taking the attendance down." The kid rolls her eyes and continues doodling on her notebook.

If these kids keep rolling their eyes, they're going to get them stuck in the back of their head. I snicker to myself and realize my mom used to say the same thing to me as a kid.

My lesson went off without a hitch, thankfully, and the students are doing their assigned classwork. Mr. Scott still sits in the back, analyzing each student and myself. I have caught him multiple times staring at me, despite me not doing anything.

I stare at him as he speaks with one of my better students and notice how his lips move while he talks. Is that weird? I bite my lip and shake my head.

I notice a student holding his phone on his lap and watching videos rather than doing the work I assigned.

"Connor, phone on my desk. I shouldn't have to tell you guys twice about having your phones out." I point to my desk and see Mr. Scott looking at me from the corner of my eye.

"No, my dad told me that I don't have to give you my phone. It's my property." He smirks at me and continues to mess around on his phone, probably texting his dad.

"Connor, I won't tell you again-" I'm cut off before I can finish my sentence.

"Mr. Stewart, as a grade ten student you should know that the school doesn't tolerate any technology in class that isn't issued by the school. Give me your phone, and your parents can pick it up from the office after school." Mr. Scott puts his hand out. My face reddens with anger as Connor gets up and gives his phone to Mr. Scott.

I can manage to take care of my own class, I don't need him to help me control my students. My chest vibrates with anger, and I turn away from Mr. Scott to plan out next week's lessons. I need a couple minutes to keep me from losing it on him in front of my students.

Him jumping in just portrays me as weak in front of my students, which means they could take advantage of me if this happens again, especially if he is present in the classroom.

"That will be all for the meeting. Thank you for taking the time out of your schedule to stay for the staff meeting today." Mr. Scott nods and everyone starts to filter out of the room. I let the girls know that I will be out in a couple minutes; first I need to give this man a piece of my mind. He has his back turned to me when I clear my throat. He slowly turns around and leans back on the desk with his legs crossed at the ankles.

"Yes, Ms. Mateus?"

I clench my jaw. Does this man ever smile? What does he have to be so angry about? Anger fills my chest, but there may also be a slight underlying of sexual frustration there too.

"Why did you have to speak up in my class? You embarrassed me in front of my students and made it seem like I can't handle them." By the time I hit the end of my sentence my voice was almost a shout.

"Lower your voice," he grinds out.

"Excuse me?" I throw my head back and let out a fake laugh. He's worried about me embarrassing him now? Well, he should have thought about that before he interrupted my class.

"Ms. Mateus, I was only trying to help. Mr. Stewart didn't seem to be listening and more times than not, when a principal gives them an instruction, they listen." He sounds so calm that it only irks me more. My irritation causes goosebumps to rise on my skin. I don't know if this man is on a power trip, but I can't stand it. After dealing with Mrs. Hiffin for so many years, I'm not used to having some man come in and try to help.

"Mr. Scott, I understand you were trying to help, but these are my students. Many of them I have taught in the past. If I needed help, I would have asked for it." I cross my arms in front of me and look at him.

"Are you always this stubborn? Or do I just bring it out of you?" He raises an eyebrow and I groan. Men are impossible, maybe that's why the girls and I haven't actually tried to rectify our relationship statuses.

"You bring it out in me. You come here looking like a goddamn GQ model, trying to change things around, and being strict as hell while doing so without consulting those of us who have been here for years!" My face reddens when I realize that I called him a GQ model. I see something shift in his eyes - desire, maybe? He raises his thumb to his lip and tries to contain his smirk.

Is he doing something other than scowling? I'm in trouble.

"Well Ms. Mateus," he states as he starts to walk towards me. I take some steps back when I realize he's getting close, and my panties can't help but start to dampen. He comes so close that there is just less than a foot between us. "You better get used to having a principal who looks like a GQ model and wants to change things. It's inevitable, and you are just going to have to accept it." I don't know if he or I have started to lean towards one another, but all I know is I have to get out of here fast. His voice is like a rumble I feel all the way to my toes. I bite my lip and notice that we are mere inches away from one another.

I go to squeeze myself out from between him and the desk before I do something I'm going to regret, but before doing so Mr. Scott puts his hands down on the wall beside my head and I notice he is trying to restrain himself from doing something he may regret as well.

I bite my lip and notice how his eyes are staring at my lips. Without thinking I lean forward and touch my lips to his.

I pause.

Fuck, what do I do now? Why did I do that? Before my

thought process can continue, Mr. Scott groans, wrapping his arm around my waist, and kisses me back with so much force my legs wobble. He holds onto me tightly so I don't collapse from the intensity of our kiss. I bite his lip lightly and wrap my hands into his hair, pulling at the strands.

Next thing I know we're in a frenzy. Our lips don't stop, and neither does the passion coming from both of our bodies. I pull his body against mine and feel the *large* bump under his zipper. I moan out loud with the pleasure of our bodies against one another. Once again, goosebumps rise on my skin, but this time it's because of the electricity buzzing throughout my body.

"Fuck," whispers Mr. Scott, after abruptly stepping back. An expression of pain passes through his eyes and before I know it, he has grabbed his bag and stormed out; slamming the door in the process, startling me.

What the fuck just happened?

My skin tingles as if I just stepped out of a sauna and my body is begging for release. I lean my head back on the wall and take a few deep breaths, waiting for my hormones to go back into the shell they have been in for the past few years. This isn't what I expected to happen. I assumed that I would lose my shit, he would reply back rudely, and walk out. *Clearly* that didn't happen.

I bring myself off the wall and go to grab my bag with shaky legs. I check my phone and notice the girls have sent me multiple messages asking me what's going on. I text them back SOS, which indicates they need to come over immediately. Ever since we were in high school that has been our emergency code and we know that when one of us texts it, we go, no questions asked.

Twenty minutes later I have switched into my comfy

clothes, and am sitting on my couch. The door is unlocked for Hannah and Emma, so they can just walk in when they get here. We have done this enough to know how it works. Remembering the most devastating SOS we ever had to deal with brings pain to my chest and water to my eyes. I look over at my memory wall and shudder a breath.

The door opens a couple minutes later,

"I got the wine," Emma shouts while kicking off her boots. Hannah shuffles in behind her and is carrying another bottle…and a box of pizza.

Once they are settled down beside me, I fill them in on everything that happened after the meeting from my shouting to my body being captured between his. I look up at them after releasing everything and notice both of them have their eyes wide and their jaws open.

"Okay, I didn't expect that to happen…" Hannah states, the look of confusion still fresh. I look over at Emma to see what she has to say, but all she does is chug her entire glass of wine. I grimace and follow suit. I mean, there is no way we won't get at least five bottles done tonight with the shit that just happened.

"Well, okay…" Emma pauses. "This will be fine. There may be some serious awkwardness, but you guys are going to have to push past this. I mean, he's your boss and you guys kissed and… Hannah, help me out." Emma looks over at Hannah, who looks as if she's ready to burst into a fit of giggles now.

"I swear to God, Hannah, if you start laughing, I will push you off this couch." I grumble. I get up to grab myself another glass of wine from the kitchen. Resting my hands against the counter I think about what happened less than two hours ago. My hands rise to my mouth as I remember the way his plush lips felt against mine; he has the perfect lips for kissing.

Fuck, this isn't going to be good. I walk back over to the couch and tell the girls that I can't talk about this anymore and that we are going to binge watch some Netflix, because what cures a girl better than a gruesome horror movie?

CHAPTER SIX

I pull up to school and stare at it in horror. I have no idea how this is going to go. Should I go talk to him? Should I just leave it?

Give me strength, I pray.

I grab my bag from the seat beside me, lock my car, and begin my walk to the safety of my classroom. I look down at my outfit; I look pretty put together for someone who spent the first twenty minutes after their shower panicking. My grey t-shirt is tucked into my suede wine-red skirt with a simple thigh-high boot. It's not ideal for the end of January, but a girl needs a pick me up after Friday night.

As soon as I walk into the school I see Mr. Scott leaning against the doorway, staring me down.

Holy fuck. Of course today is the day he decides to wear simple black trousers, a black button up, and suspenders. To top off the entire look? He has his sleeves rolled up, showing off his extremely toned arms.

Every woman's weakness. My steps falter as I walk into the school and just as I'm about to pass him and enter the safety of the hall, I hear his voice,

"Ms. Mateus, in my office." He nods his head for me to follow him to his office. I clench my jaw and follow behind him. I smile at Michelle, the school's secretary. She waggles her eyebrows at me and I squint my eyes back at her. She has tried to set me up with both her sons, but that is never happening. Michelle is great, but her sons? Not exactly my type. They never really spoke to me in high school, but they knew what was going on and never cared. That spoke volumes to their characters.

We walk towards his office and I'm a few steps behind him, wanting to keep some sort of distance. His office is hidden in the back corner of the administrative office, which is nice because it sits in a corner with full floor-to-ceiling windows. It's probably the nicest room in the building, but that's beside the point.

We walk into Mr. Scott's office and he motions for me to take a seat while he closes the door. I look around, impressed with what he has done with the space since becoming in charge. He has a beautiful wall of books behind his desk, both old and new books lining the wall. Ms. Hiffin had been here so many years yet she never cared what her office looked like, because it was only used for scolding students... and teachers. I sit in the plush seats in front of his desk, and my cheeks heat. I bite the inside of my cheek and look up at him after hearing him take a seat in his large leather green chair.

"I want to apologize for Friday. That was completely unprofessional, and I will ensure it won't happen again." He stares at me, awaiting my acceptance. I bite my lip.

Is it bad I want it to happen again? Being on the curvier side I have always hated a man picking me up, but I want Mr. Scott to pick me up and slam me against the wall of his office and make my lips raw.

I press my thighs together, and my clit throbs, my gaze

still cast downward. His groan shakes my thoughts and I look up at him to see a dark expression has crossed his face.

"I…" I what?

Suddenly Mr. Scott gets up and rounds his desk so quickly I don't have a chance to react. He cages me in, *again*, by putting his arms on the rests of the chair and his body radiates heat, and I don't mean body temperature. I look up at him, my eyes slowly making their way up his body. This man is built like a Greek God. Those men with perfectly chiseled bodies made of stone? Yeah, that's definitely what's hidden beneath his clothes.

"Ms. Mateus, I need you to be of a level mind. You don't think I feel the way you do? Feel that fucking chemistry that goes straight to my fucking dick?" He growls in my face. I'm at a loss for words. My anxiety decides to take flight because I have never been in this situation before with a man. Most of my encounters with men have been extremely tame. What do I do when my boss states he has the same attraction as I do?

Fuck.

"Auston," I cough awkwardly, "I mean Mr. Scott… I don't know what you want me to do. You come in here looking like this," I motion my hands down his body, "You can't expect me not to react. I mean, you remember what happened that night at the pub," I admit, a bit embarrassed. He smirks, remembering when I - very obviously - gawked at him.

"Oh, I remember. I went to my car and jerked off into my fucking hands like a teenager because of this sexy and confident woman who openly gawked at me." He bites his lip and I see the struggle in his eyes. I lose my own mind and grab his face, smashing our lips together. He moans loudly, maybe too loudly, and lifts me up out of the chair.

He picks me up and sets me on his desk as he steps

between my legs and continues his attack on my lips. He slowly moves down my neck, and my nipples pebble against my bra, causing me to release a light gasp.

"Fuck, Victoria. You are so sexy with the sounds you make," he moves his way to the soft spot behind my ear and I moan as I palm his dick through his slacks.

Oh my God. His fingers start to climb underneath my skirt and just as he's about to reach my panties, there's a soft knock on the door and a voice asking Auston if he can meet someone in the main office. I don't really listen to who it is because my mind is turning with what just happened.

"Fuck." He groans quietly, "One moment, please." He rearranges himself and smirks down at me and I can't help but blush. Did I just make out with my boss? Again?

"I'm so sorry Mr. Scott. That got way out of hand..." I stand straight and pull my skirt down to make sure I look as normal as ever, despite having just been teased by a God.

"Please, call me Auston." He pauses, "It's not your fault... I just can't control myself around you." He shrugs. I bite my bottom lip while smiling, and grab my bag. My face must be the color of a tomato right now, and I'm struggling to understand what's happening. My life is usually a series of misfortunate events, but this? This is way outside of what I'm used to. Anxiety? Sadness? Insecurities? Yeah, those are the terms I would unfortunately use to summarize my life.

"Well, looks as if we will have to save this chat for another time." I smile slightly towards him and make my way to the door to open it. I thank him for the meeting and say my goodbyes as I walk back by Michelle. A knowing look passes in her eyes and she zips her lips shut. I roll my eyes, trying to play off that nothing happened.

I shake my shoulders out and walk quickly to my classroom. I unlock the door and put my bag underneath my desk, then lean back in my chair while looking up at the ceiling.

What the heck just happened? I shake my head in disbelief as a cough sounds behind me, scaring the shit out of me.

"Jesus," I yell, almost causing my chair to fall backwards.

"Hey, don't use Christ's name in vain, we work in a Catholic school." Emma laughs as she sits on one of the desks. I laugh at myself and she tilts her head at me and I raise an eyebrow.

"What?" I sit in my chair and pull out my phone.

Act casual, Victoria…

"Vic, your lipstick is all smudged." She hands me a napkin and my eyes widen in horror. That is why Michelle gave me the look that she did when I walked out of Auston's office. I look back up at Emma and she's squinting her eyes at me suspiciously. I'm just about to get up and shut the door when Hannah walks in.

"Shut the door," I say as I lean back in my chair and squish my lips together, giving them a really odd face.

"Vic, your lips." Emma stops her and states that she already told me. Hannah raises her eyebrows now too and they both turn and look at me.

"Okay, so," I begin and stop. How the hell do I begin with this when it's not even eight in the morning? "Mr. Scott called me into his office this morning to discuss the matters from Friday night." I pause to look at both of their faces. Hannah looks surprised, but Emma has a devilish look on her face.

"And?" Hannah states.

"And, we kind of had this really heated make-out session, again. This time it got way too hot though, and apparently Michelle knows it too because my lipstick is all fucked up…"

Hannah stares at me, completely shocked, and Emma starts laughing.

"Seriously, Vic? I thought we had decided we were going to avoid Mr. GQ?" Emma says while laughing.

"I know! I was trying to, but when I walked into the school he was already there staring at me, and there was nothing I could do when he told me to follow him." I continue, telling them everything that happened from the time that I walked into his office to when I walked out. Emma starts fanning herself.

"So, he has a big dick *and* is gorgeous? What the fuck? We need to move to the city." Emma paces the room as if God himself is punishing us.

"Hey, Em, I thought we weren't supposed to use God's name in vain in a Catholic high school?" I banter back at her and she flips me her middle finger. I laugh and look over at Hannah who is still thinking, a serious look on her face.

"Vic, I know this is fun and games now, but he's our boss. This can't end well, can it?" I bite my lip and shrug. I honestly have no idea what I'm doing, and I have no idea what to do about Auston. I'm a bit out of my territory with this. The girls know that, but none of us have ever dealt with anything like this.

"I have no idea, honestly. Just promise me you will keep your mouths quiet about this, it may have just been a two-time thing and may never happen again. Or maybe I'll have to crawl into my bed and hide forever, I don't know yet." I lean my head onto my hands and groan. I'm a grown ass woman; I can control myself around a man. Even if he does fit the description of a perfect Adonis.

"You know we won't tell a soul, just promise me you'll be careful." Hannah says. I nod my head in agreement.

"But, also tells us if shit gets freaky because I want all the details." Emma waggles her brows, causing Hannah to shove her while I laugh.

"I don't think it will get to that, but you guys will be the first to know, as always." I start my computer, noticing that it's almost time for students to start filtering in.

"Well, us and God. I mean, he will know as it's happening." Emma laughs out loud and I tell her to fuck off. The first bell rings to indicate that our day is about to start, and we all wish each other a good day and separate to get ready for another day of classes.

My first two classes go by smoothly. During my first period with academic grade twelve English, which is one of my best classes, the students are preparing for university so they truly try their best. Unlike my grade nine students, who are just getting used to high school. My second period is Creative Writing online which is a bit different, because I teach all the students in the Catholic district. I have a classroom where the students come to use computers, but I have no idea who the other students are because they are from different schools. I know them by name but have never become acquainted with them in-person. It isn't my preferred way to teach, but creative writing is a passion of mine, so I couldn't say no to the opportunity to teach it.

Third period is my break, during which I decide it's time to run to Tim Horton's to grab a coffee and a bagel. I forgot my lunch today with the whirlwind of emotions I experienced while trying to get ready, so buying food it is. Grabbing my bag and locking the door, I head downstairs to get to my car. The halls are mostly empty, but students still roam either on spare or skipping class. I honestly can't find any care with how my stomach is growling. I make my way down the stairs and quickly maneuver my way out the doors and to my car.

Twenty minutes later I'm sitting at my desk with the delicious aroma of coffee and baked goods. I take my first bite and moan; I didn't realize how hungry I was. I have always preferred to sit in my class and eat rather than go to the staff room. That room is like sitting in a prison cell with tables and chairs—talk about uncomfortable. The girls and I have always wanted to have it re-vamped, but Principal Hiffin didn't want to touch the chamber of sadness.

I sigh, throwing my trash away and grabbing my writing book. I set it on my desk and stare at it.

CHAPTER SEVEN

The week passed in a blur. I had an essay due in one class, and spent my week marking various pieces of work from the others. Thankfully, some of the other teachers had decided we were going to go to Kline's. I don't usually look forward to Kline's, but lately my perspective on going out has changed. I need it to get through the week's I've been having. It's a bit on the dingier side, but the alcohol is cheap, and they are televising the Toronto Geese games tonight. I stand at the mirror in my bathroom and apply a nude lipstick, so it doesn't contrast with the team's blue jersey. I look at myself in the mirror and smile. With my thigh high boots, dark wash jeans, and tucked-in jersey, I'd say I look good for a night out. I smile and shut off the lights, then head towards the front door where I know the girls will be waiting.

I hear a honk sound from outside, and I grab my cross-body bag and head out to meet the girls.

We walk into Kline's twenty minutes later and see our black half-circle booth is empty. We make a beeline for it before we even order drinks. The projector streams the game in perfect view of the booth, so to say it is the best seat in the house is an understatement.

"Oh, it has been a while since we have been here!" Emma says excitedly.

"I know, we used to come here so much back in high school. I remember the look on Joe's face when he saw us come in with our legal ID's. It was a priceless moment." Hannah laughs. We all look towards the bar and see Joe making drinks behind it. As if he feels us looking at him, he raises his head. We all put on our best smiles and wave, and he replies with a small wave and the hint of a smile on his lips. I don't think he will ever forgive us for all the times we could have gotten him shut down for being minors.

I motion to the girls that I'll grab the first round, and get up to order some shots. I put on my best smile and head over to the bar.

"Hey Joe." I smile at him sweetly, and he rolls his eyes, smirking. For a fifty-year-old guy, Joe is attractive as hell. When he's not at the bar he's working out, and he's covered in tattoos. He has that sexy, gentleman biker look that *really* works for him. He walks back over and hands me a tray with three shots and three margaritas.

"On the house, beautiful. Try and stay out of trouble tonight." He winks at me and I smile back.

"Wow, haven't changed since high school, eh? Are you sucking him off to get free drinks?" I cringe as I hear her voice. I already know this comment says more about her, than it does me. But I can't help the pain it causes in my chest.

"Laura," I nod my head at her. I will not play into her stupid games. She made me do that enough when we were in high school.

Another negative to living in a small town is that the bullies seem to always come back, and even bitchier than when they were teenagers. It's enough to deal with her sister at work, but now she's back in town. I walk back to the table with the tray and set it down.

"What did she say to you this time?" Emma glares over at Laura.

"Oh, you know, just that I'm sucking Joe's cock to get free drinks." I sit down, raise my shot in a cheers motion, and shoot it down. The girls do the same and take their shots right after.

"I mean, that wouldn't be horrible. Joe is pretty sexy for an older man." Hannah pumps her eyebrows. I tilt my drink at her, because she definitely isn't wrong.

"He is, but why does it matter to her whose dick we're sucking?" Emma motions towards Laura. She is leaning against the bar, her make-up perfectly done and her outfit fitting her like a second skin. Our dislike for Laura began when we were all teenagers and she was the rich ice queen of the school. For some reason, her point of attack was always the three of us, but mainly me. She did everything she could to make me feel like shit. She even went as far as to create a horribly-done website aimed at fat shaming me. She would take my face, photoshop it onto other bodies, and write some clever tagline at the top. The day the website went live I called home sick because everyone had seen it, and laughed whenever they saw me.

Standing at my locker after the first period, I hear laughter and moo's coming from all around me. Hannah and Emma rush up to me with pained looks on their faces, while I raise my brow in question.

"You haven't seen it yet, have you?" Hannah's lip is quivering, and I look over to Emma who has a look of pure hatred aimed over my shoulder.

"What's going on?" I shake Emma's shoulder and notice

she has a piece of paper crumpled in her hand. I grab it quickly and smooth it down, only to see my face on the body of a cow. Surrounding the page is the tagline "Moo, here comes the fattest cow of all."

Everything slows around me as my eyes fill with tears. I turn around to see Laura smirking and yelling moo, causing more people to join in with her.

I slam my locker shut and run down the hall towards the entrance.

"God, does anyone else feel the ground shaking?" Cole, Laura's boyfriend, yells while dramatically holding the wall. It only makes me feel worse and I run out the door. I continue to run until I'm out of sight from the school. I pull out my flip phone and call my mom to pick me up. I slump down on the curb and cry my heart out.

I hate high school so much.

My eyes fill with tears as I remember the first incident from that stupid website. Laura was able to come out with six more blog posts after that one until Hannah's dad, a police officer, got it taken down. She's part of the reason I work on my self-confidence as much as I do. For months, I went home to bed and cried. The mooing followed me around until the end of high school and even hearing it now causes my stomach to turn.

"Earth to Vic, you okay babe? Why does it look like you're going to cry?" Hannah grabs my hand and gives it a squeeze.

"It's that ice bitch's fault. She should fuck off back to New York and never come back." Emma growls.

"I'm sorry guys. I think having her actually say something to me just triggered all those emotions from the past and brought me back to the hallway where it began." I fan my face, shake my shoulders, and take a large gulp from my margarita. The girls sandwich me in the circular booth and squeeze me to the brink of suffocation.

"I still want to punch her pretty face in, it would make us feel much better," Emma snides and I look at her wide-eyed but with the touch of a grin. Emma's not the violent type, but she has an undying passion for protecting those she loves. It's one of my favorite qualities about her.

"Babe, it's all good. I can't change the past, but I can move forward from it. If she tries anything tonight, I will stand up for myself. I'm not the same sixteen-year-old I once was, I won't allow her to make me feel like shit thirteen years later." I state confidently and smile, trying to move on.

I need something to change the mood and it seems like Joe has felt the tension in the bar, so he starts playing "Wannabe" by the Spice Girls. He knew this was our karaoke song when we used to come here in high school. I look over at him and he winks at us, gesturing to the small square dance floor. Emma hollers and grabs our hands from the booth, and we make our way to the floor.

After a few minutes we are sweating lightly, and a few people are whistling and hollering at us. I laugh until I look up and find a smirking Mr. Scott with two other handsome men behind him. My laugh dies in my throat as he winks at me, then motions for his friends to follow him to a booth. My eyebrows draw together.

Did Mr. Scott just make a blatant hint at me? I scrunch my lips together to keep my smile hidden.

"Did Mr. Scott just fucking bite his lip while looking your way!" Emma shouts from behind me and causes me to jump. I start to push them towards our booth and motion at Joe to bring us some more drinks.

"So, my eyes weren't deceiving me? He is actually here… with two other GQ models?" I fan my face and the girls laugh. I look at the screen and notice the Toronto Geese just scored. I shout loudly, and the girls jump at my sudden outburst. I grin, a bit embarrassed.

"You ladies still put on one hell of a show." Joe sets our drinks down in front of us, "I heard what that woman said to you Vic, and I'm sorry. If there are any problems, you let me know and she's out." He flicks his thumb towards the door and I smile.

"Thanks Joe, I think we will be okay though. I'm a big girl and can deal with it." I smile at him and he nods, and heads back toward the bar. I relax against the booth and watch the game, at ease with a drink in my hand. A little cardio helps loosen up the knots that had formed in my body and my stomach.

Thirty minutes have gone by with three drinks each, and three goals for Toronto. The girls and I are laughing and enjoying our time, that is, until I catch blonde hair swaying towards Auston's table. The girls notice my body freeze and glance over to see that Laura has squeezed herself beside Mr. Scott. Jealousy seizes my body and I grip my drink tighter in my hand, trying to stop myself from doing something stupid. It doesn't help that I'm a little tipsier than I was half an hour ago.

Why am I jealous? I've only kissed him...twice.

"You have got to be fucking with me universe, haven't I dealt with enough of your shit?" I lean my head back and groan. I hate the feeling of jealousy, it's something I've never really felt. There has only ever been one circumstance that sometimes causes that trait to rise, but seeing Laura with Auston? Yeah, make that two circumstances now.

"Yeah babe, keep your head tilted back... I don't think you want to look up." My head bounces upright as soon as Hannah says that. I see that Laura has one of her arms wrapped around Mr. Scott's while her other hand has disappeared under the table.

"This chick has some nerve," Emma says as she takes a drink while shooting a glare in their direction.

"Emma, it's okay." I shrug and look up to notice that Auston's friends look super uncomfortable. I roll my eyes. Is Auston really fucking doing this here with his friends across the table? Is he that horrible? I shift my eyes towards him and he looks even more uncomfortable than the other two do. He keeps moving Laura's hands and clenching his jaw, looking over at his friends with his eyes as slits. Hmm... maybe I should stop assuming he is such a horrible person. Maybe it's just me who brings out that side of him.

"Vic, go save them. Clearly Laura can't take a fucking hint, she's trying to grope all of them. I can see her leg on his tall, gorgeous, friend..." Hannah grimaces and motions for me to go.

Fuck, Laura is seriously going to kill me; she hates me enough already. I stand up, thankful for liquid courage and force my heeled legs to move towards their table. Auston looks fucking relieved when he sees me standing there.

"Hey Laura, I don't know if you don't know how to take a hint, but these gentlemen clearly don't want your well-used claws digging into them." I grind out. I didn't think my voice would sound so angering. It doesn't even sound like me, but fuck, this woman gets under my skin.

"Hey, moomoo. How about you mind your business?" She looks up and smirks at me. I look at the men and they all have confusion lacing their faces clearly at the "moomoo" name.

"Alright, I have had more than enough of your bullshit to last me a damn lifetime. It was enough to deal with you in high school, but now too? Nope, get out of this bar and don't come back." I take a deep breath, but she notices the nerves radiating off me. She always has. She's like a cobra with emotions, except she only strikes at me.

"Oh honey…" she says sadly, "you're still the same cow you were in high school. You think by trying to dress better that's going to change how people see you? Please." My nostrils flare and I clench my jaw. Don't react Vic, you don't want to lose your job. Your boss who you have made out with is directly in front of you.

"Jesus fuck." The one friend says while shaking his head. He pushes himself out of the booth and his friend follows, and I see in my peripheral the girls waving at them to come over.

"Alright, I have had enough. I'm not sixteen anymore and your petty words do not affect me as they once did. I'm not going to take any more bullshit from you." Auston pushes himself up to stand on the booth and jumps to the other side where his friends just were. He slowly comes to stand beside me and turns towards Laura.

"I don't know who you are because no self-respecting adult talks to another person like that. I was trying to stay quiet and be nice, but this behaviour is childish." I gape at Auston and he grabs my hand, dragging me back to the booth with his friends and the girls.

"So, what did the wicked witch say now?" Emma glares at her. I slump into the end seat and rest my eyes. I acted tough back there but it brought back every emotion I had back in high school. Doesn't matter how much time has passed, that bully will always affect me and the way that I see myself. The high I had from dancing has been drained away after that altercation.

"She did what?" I hear Emma shout, which shakes me from my inner demons. Hannah has a frown on her face and I look around at the five faces around me and notice the concern.

"I zoned out for a minute there, but please can we drop it." I bite the inside of my cheek and force my eyes to stay trained forward. I didn't need Auston to hear that much baggage, but I shouldn't be surprised that Laura would try to bring my insecurities forward. She does it every time she sees me, even though we have been out of high school for years.

"That chick was crazy, I never thought girls like her existed. I used to watch them in movies with my sisters, but man, that was like seeing the real thing." Auston's friend says while making a sour face.

"Well, when you grow up in a small town, there are only so many people to bully and Vic was always her target." Hannah replies back.

"I'm going to get a drink," I stand up and make my way towards the bar and tell Joe to bring me two shots of tequila. I lean my elbows on the bar and take a deep breath. The tightness in my chest starts to suffocate me, my anxiety choosing this moment to make itself known at full force. I notice Joe drop two shots in front of me and I swallow them down in record time, trying to calm my racing heart. I lean my head back and it bumps against something. I turn around to see Auston behind me.

"Are you okay?" Auston looks at me and I nod my head and motion back towards the table. I don't want him asking questions, I don't think I have it in me not to break down and cry. I take a seat and Auston sits beside me and introduces his friends Axel and Garrett. Axel moved to Canada from Africa when he was five and has been friends with Auston since they were kids. Whereas Garrett has been friends with them since their first year at the university in Toronto.

I try to pay attention to the game and what everyone is

talking about, but I can't shake the anxiety that's wrapped itself around my chest and throat. My hands shake on my lap and I try to take deep breaths but it does nothing to help shake what happened tonight. My hands are clammy, and I feel a breakdown coming. I rub my hands together, the familiar tingling in my limbs spreading as dizziness creeps in.

I need to get out of here.

"Why are you shaking?" Auston leans over and whispers in my ear. I notice the game has only a few minutes left so I decide this is the perfect time to leave and grab a taxi home. I stand abruptly and tell everyone that I need to head home. I grab my bag quickly and rush out the door to a waiting taxi. I run towards it and fumble with the handle until it finally opens and I slide in, telling the driver my address. I turn around, looking through the tinted back window, and notice that Auston ran out after me. I watch him realize that I'm currently in the taxi moving away from the bar, and away from what could have been a good night.

CHAPTER EIGHT

I spent the weekend trying to cope with my anxiety attack that happened on Friday night. I told the girls that I needed the weekend for myself and turned off my phone. I collapsed in bed as soon as I got home and stayed in it until mid-morning on Saturday. After contemplating whether I wanted to do anything or not, I decided against sitting in bed. I ran to the craft store to grab some new frames and spent time adding new pictures to the memory wall. It was therapeutic for the time being, but sadly, the weekend came to an end. It's Monday morning, and I have to go back to my normal life.

My outfit today is geared towards comfort: cheetah print heels, black jeans, white T-shirt, and a beige cardigan. I straighten my top as I unlock my classroom door and safely close the door behind me. I don't want to face the girls, or Auston. I hate that I'm embarrassed about what happened on Friday, but I'm going to have to face all of them at some point. Hannah and Emma are used to my breakdowns, but no matter how many times it happens, I hate the burden I put on them when I have an anxiety attack.

I load up the computer and set up the slides for this morning's class. I decided to change up the regular readings on Shakespeare and instead focus on Jane Austen. Most of the academic students have read Shakespeare the past three years, so Austen is who I favoured to discuss this term. I walk up to the front of the classroom to write down our schedule for the day and hear lockers slam behind my closed door. I hear further commotion when students start shouting, and I rush over to the door. I turn the knob and throw open the door to be confronted by Brad holding Drew, a past student of mine, up against a locker. I can't make out what Brad whispers to Drew, but it seems unpleasant based on the look on Drew's face.

"Brad! What do you think you are doing?" I come up behind him. Before I get further, heavy steps come down the hall just as Drew sends his fist straight towards Brad's jaw. I gasp, rushing forward to help Drew when Auston's booming voice sounds through the hall.

"Drew, my office, now!" I jump from his tone. I have never heard Auston use that tone, but guess it makes sense from his "strict" nature.

"Mr. Scott, Drew is not the student to blame here. Brad was provoking him and—" Mr. Scott cuts me off.

"These are my hallways Ms. Mateus, let me handle this." I swear to God, I see red. After what happened last week which he clearly saw with Laura, I will not allow Brad, *the bully*, to get away with his behaviour.

"Boys, follow Mr. Scott and I. You will sit outside the office with Michelle while I discuss this with him. Now." I send a pointed look to Auston. I'm so disappointed about what happened here without him having any knowledge of what actually took place in the hallway. Drew stood up for himself. Although it admittedly wasn't the best way to do it. I think everyone has been told to fight their battles with words, not fists, but Drew clearly had enough. He reminds me of myself in high school though, always quiet and allowing others to pick on him. I'm glad he stood up for himself, but I wish it wasn't with his fists.

I motion for the two boys to go ahead of us and we follow steadily behind them. Emma and Hannah were just about to come down the hall towards my class when they see me walking with the two boys and Mr. Scott. I give them a pointed look, signalling that we will talk after.

We walk into the main office area and I point at the seats where the boys can sit, then continue down towards Mr. Scott's office. I wait for him to enter before shutting the door behind him.

"Are you for real, *Mr.Scott*?" I grind my teeth together, sending him a death glare.

"Victoria, this is my school. I will handle situations like this when they arise. I have dealt with far worse than this at my old school." He crosses his arms in front of him and leans against his desk.

"No, you immediately judged the situation as Drew being the one to blame because you saw a punch thrown." I mock his stance by crossing my arms.

"Victoria, I don't tolerate any kind of bullying—" I cut Mr. Scott off.

"Ha," I bark. "Auston if that was true you wouldn't have told Drew to meet you in your office. I have been in his fucking situation before and I won't tolerate it. I've had Drew in my previous classes and he's never shown anything other than a positive attitude. Maybe you need to pay better atten-tion to the lives of your students and open your damn eyes!" I shout at him and fling the door open and walk out. The two boys and Michelle stare at me with wide eyes, which indicates that they heard everything I just said. I frown over my very obvious meltdown and scramble back to my classroom.

I know part of the reason that I took out my anger on Auston was because when I was Drew's age, I never had anyone try to fight for me besides my girls. I lived every day dealing with nasty comments from my peers and knowing that the same could happen to Drew doesn't sit well with me. Nobody ever stood up for me, so it never put an end to it. Yes, teachers saw it and sympathized, but nothing was ever done. That's the sad truth.

The girls are sitting on some desks with their brows raised when we settle into my classroom. I glance at my watch and see we have ten minutes before classes officially start. I groan while shutting the door and explain everything from my sudden departure on Friday to this chaotic morning with Auston.

"Shit babe, we had no idea you were having an anxiety attack on Friday. You know we would have come home with you if we would have known." Hannah looks down in sadness, but I squeeze her shoulder to reassure her that it's okay.

"Don't worry please, I needed a weekend to clear my head. I think standing up for myself shook me more than I expected, and I hated that Auston witnessed her laying out my insecurities." I shrug and sit down at my desk.

"Babe, we get it. I think Auston felt shitty too at least. He went after you when you rushed out but came back looking pretty damn glum." Emma says.

"Yeah, well he clearly showed that this morning." I growl and stand up to turn the Smart Board back on. "I think I made a mess by entwining myself with him, but it needs to end now. I'm going to avoid him all week and hope that I can clear my head of this situation." I turn back towards them and they have sympathetic gazes turned my way. I roll my eyes and shoo them out of my classroom since students are going to start filtering through.

My plan to avoid Auston this week went well since I took irregular exits from the school and stayed in my classroom during the day. I think he knew better than to come up and try to talk to me after clearly seeing my disappointment with him. I spoke with Drew later in the week and he told me that Auston had listened to him and that Brad had been suspended for two weeks, but Drew still had a three-day suspension. I sighed in relief when he told me that, but it didn't dim my annoyance towards Auston's behaviour.

It's Friday night and I'm going to meet the girls for dinner at Dallas Pub. I wasn't ready to go back to Kline's just yet after last week, so we decided that DP would do.

I grab my keys off the ottoman by the front door and throw my bag on my shoulder. I decided to drive myself this time, which will both limit how much I drink and allow me to leave whenever.

Twenty minutes later, I walk into the pub and notice that the girls are already sitting at the table in the bar area, but a tall and muscular back is also seated at the table. I can't catch a break. Auston moved here less than two months ago, and he's everywhere.

I wave at them and send a scowl at both of them. Their eyes are twinkling with mischief and I falter in my steps because *oh my God*. Auston turns around, but he looks nothing like the principal I'm used to seeing. My anger slightly fades when I notice his hair is slightly messy, compared to his usual neat quiff. He is wearing black jeans with rips in the knees, a black T-shirt, and white runners.

He is the definition of a GQ model. I see the sexy, suited man at school and the rugged, causal version of him outside of it.

"Hey." I set my bag on the back of the high stool and climb onto the chair.

"I know you're probably shocked to see me, but I was about to leave when Emma and Hannah asked me to stick around for dinner." Auston looks slightly regretful. As he should be.

"Honestly I was, but I don't like to hold grudges." I'm not lying. It's more common for me to hold sadness and fear inside, than anger.

My eyes begin to trail down his body, taking in his casual appearance. I hear a cough behind me, while Emma has her head down on the table laughing.

Wow, way to be subtle Vic.

"I'm going to agree with Vic roaming eyes, I didn't recognize you when I walked in. However, I think we we're both thinking different things…" Emma snorts from her covered mouth. I send her a 'fuck you' look and glance down at the menu. I know they're all staring at me, but I have no idea what the hell to say.

"Bitches…" They started giggling again and I send an apologetic face to Auston. He shrugs confidently—he knows he looks hot as hell.

Jerk.

"Anyways, have you guys ordered yet? I'm starving." I look back down at the menu.

"We haven't, we were waiting for you to get here." Hannah smiles.

"I need to go to the washroom. If the waitress comes, I'll

get the Greek burger." He slides off the stool and heads in the direction of the washrooms. I slowly turn around with death in my eyes, aimed at my two best friends.

"You guys are the worst! You didn't think to text me and tell me that you added a plus one to our dinner? Talk about shocking me silent!" Hannah smirks and Emma laughs.

"We're sorry alright, we just saw him here alone and decided to ask him to join us. I mean what's the worst that could happen?" Emma questions, and I shrug. It's not really that bad, but I haven't spoken to him since Monday and never really discussed what happened on Friday night. There is a lot of unspoken conversation between him and I that will definitely need to happen. I don't want to feel awkward around him, mainly because I see him everywhere.

The waitress comes over and we give her our order just as Auston returns. The waitress checks him out, way too obviously, and asks him if he would like to get anything. Clearly suggesting something that's not food with the way her body leans into his, and the way she thrusts her chest out.

"Well, the four burgers clearly aren't for just the three of us women, so perhaps we already spoke for him." Emma gathers the menus and hands them to the waitress with her eyebrows raised. Auston coughs to disguise his laughter that manifests from the shake of his shoulders. He seems much more at ease when he's not at school, less daunting and serious.

"I...yeah, sorry." The waitress looks at us wide-eyed and I bite my lip to hold from giggling. She scrambles away and heads towards the kitchen to give our order.

There is a moment of silence between us when I turn my head and notice some commotion towards the entrance of the pub. There is a girl, who doesn't look older than eighteen, fighting with the hostess. She's wearing dark skinny jeans and a hoodie that covers the majority of her face. She throws her hands up in defeat and looks over at our table only to send me a heinous look. I widen my eyes because if looks could kill, that would have done it. My mouth tugs downward for a moment and then I hear Auston's gruff velvety voice bring me back to the group.

"So, I'm gathering you are the brash one of the three?" Auston questions while Hannah and I reply yes, Emma replies no. I laugh again and shake my head at Emma. She knows that she's the sassy one but doesn't want to admit it.

The waitress rushes over with our food and tries her best to avoid eye contact with both Auston and Emma. We all thank her as we watch her hightail it back to the kitchen.

"Man, you have completely ruined her. She wouldn't even look at us as she set our food down." Hannah says while shoving some fries in her mouth.

"I agree with Hannah. I feel bad about the young girl. Tip her well so she knows that we won't be ratting her out." I take a huge bite of my burger and moan. I notice in the corner of my eye that Auston shifts in his seat and bites his lip.

"Well, she doesn't know what the situation was. Imagine if one of us was actually with him. She would be in for a hell of a lot worse." Emma shrugs and I shake my head. Emma can be a little harsh at times, but her honesty is an admirable trait.

Twenty minutes later, I take that last bite of my delicious bacon cheeseburger when I notice the bartender from the other night is here and she is sending eyes to Hannah.

"Hey Hannah, that bartender from the other night is sending you some obvious glances." I wiggle my eyebrows at her and Emma flips around to confirm that she is for sure checking her out. Hannah looks over at the bartender behind the bar and receives a wink. Hannah turns back around, her face a little pink,

"Well, that is my cue to go." She wiggles her brows, "Sorry boss." She laughs and hugs Emma and I and heads over to the bar. We all watch her in her element and see the bartender reach under the bar to grab her jacket.

I guess her shift is over?

Damn, Hannah is really going to get some. Hannah reaches for her elbow as they head out the door of DP, sending us one final wink over her shoulder.

"Does that happen often?" Auston looks a little surprised.

"What? You've never seen a woman go for what she wants?" Emma questions him. He covers his discomfort with a cough, clearly caught off guard with that remark. I don't think he expected Emma to reply that way. I kind of enjoy watching him squirm, since he's usually so poised and poker-faced.

"What Emma is trying to say is that Hannah knows exactly what she wants, and when she wants it. Hence why she just left with the bartender." I laugh and Emma shrugs, accepting my vague, less intimidating explanation of her question.

"Well, I think I'm going to head out too. My mom is making me go to the mall in Hamilton, at nine in the morning." She adds emphasis to nine as she stands up and grabs her bag.

Realization hits me hard when I realize they are both leaving me alone with Auston. These two definitely had this planned all along, but kept me out of the loop on purpose. I repeat fuck in my head around twenty times before I realize Emma is gone and Auston is looking at me with his eyebrow raised.

"Look, I wanted to apologize for what happened earlier

this week." Auston's face shows a lot of guilt. It's been nice to sit and spend time with him and the girls today, but we can't act like what happened this week didn't. "I didn't have the intention to come off the way I did, but you were right. I should have listened to you, and allowed the students to express their perspective. I immediately wanted to punish Drew because I saw him throw a punch, but should have known that there is usually a reason when someone acts in violence." He scratches the back of his neck with slight embarrassment, and I can't help it as my heart pulls for him.

"Look, I get it. You're supposed to be an authoritative figure in the school, but I have found that when you actually listen to students, they behave better. There are obviously still students that rebel, but as a teacher I've never witnessed anything like I did this week with those two. Brad has always been one of the rebellious students, but Drew is an amazing kid. I've taught him before and he's extremely intelligent." I shrug my shoulders because Auston probably has more experience than me, so he may not listen to me at all.

"You're right, I just tend to forget that. Coming from the city I was always more disciplinarian due to student behaviours, but I think I need to remember I'm not in the city anymore. Students here seem to respect the staff. Not that they didn't in the city, but I came from a more prestigious school where the board could more often than not, be bought." He shrugs, "I think it will just take some time to get used to the calmer atmosphere in a small town." He smiles lightly and I bite my lip to keep my smile from waning out. His body seems to relax more now that we have both cleared the air about this week, which gives me a sense of relief. I know what it's like to be the survivor of bullying, and I think we need to bring more awareness to that at school. I stare into his green eyes, glimmering against the pub lights as my heart flutters. I notice that Auston's lips are moving, but I haven't listened to one word.

"Did you ask me something?" I ask him slowly. I lean my body back against the chair and fiddle with my fingers under the table. My heart beat picks up slightly, I have never felt this way before around a man. I mean, guys in high school made me uncomfortable, but it was for a whole other reason. Auston makes me feel exhilarated, anxious, and calm all at once. It's as if my body is bipolar around him, unsure of how it should be feeling.

"How would you feel about sharing the chocolate brownie explosion? I hear it's delicious." He smiles.

"That just shows that you've never had one. You never want to share one because the deliciousness is too good to share." I laugh and ask the passing waitress to bring us two of them.

We finish enjoying two delicious brownies and I can't help the flutters in my stomach. We flirted while enjoying our desserts and I may have wiped off some excess chocolate from Auston's face with my finger... then licked it clean. I think his darkening gaze when I did that will be forever ingrained in my brain.

I've never done something so bold.

"I was wondering if you had any plans for the night?" He leans his elbows on the table and sets his hands under his chin. I peer down at his forearms, which are heavily veined. Why are veins so attractive? They begin at his elbow and go all the way to his hands; he must have worked out today or something because they are prominent. He coughs to get my attention again, and I cover my face with my hands and breathe out an embarrassed chuckle.

"Uh, no I don't. I was just going to head home and watch some movies..." I pause, "Would you want to come over?" I stop, shock covering my face. I don't think my mouth and brain have caught up to one another because my brain now realized that I asked my boss, who I have made-out with, if he wanted to come over.

"Sure, I'll never say no to a movie night with a beautiful woman." He smirks, clearly knowing I didn't mean to let that last thought slip out. I give him a tight smile and nod my head while leaning to grab my bag from the back of the chair.

"I'll just follow behind you?" He questions as we walk out the door into the frigid air. The wind catches on my hair, blowing it away from my face. I shiver all the way to my toes. I turn towards him and nod my head again, while rubbing my hands together. I reach into my coat to grab my keys and notice that Auston gets into the same BMW I saw a while ago on the country road.

The same car that stood out to me a few weeks ago also holds the man that is standing out to me currently. Who would have thought the universe could play these games so well?

I walk over to my car and press the unlock button. Once inside, I blast the heat and turn the seat warmers on. I'm over winter already; I need sunshine and warm weather. I turn around to see that Auston is waiting to the left of my car to let me out before him. I quickly reverse out of my spot and turn my signal on for Auston to know where we are heading. We are waiting at a stoplight, so I turn the volume knob up to find out what the upcoming weather is going to be like. From the chill that's in the air, it feels as if a storm is brewing in the atmosphere.

"This weekend is going to be a cold one everyone. Prepare to blast your heaters and have your backup generators going; a storm will be hitting us this weekend!" The weatherman announces, and I scrunch up my face in disgust. I'm so happy I went grocery shopping this week because there isn't a chance I would want to leave my house during a snow-storm. I don't want to have to get my snow blower out and clear thirty meters of snow.

No thank you, not this weekend.

We drive for fifteen minutes and arrive at my driveway. I crack open my window, letting the chill flow through, to stick my hand out to motion for Auston to move up beside me.

"You can park your car in the garage. There is some snow coming in, so it will be easier for you to get out if snow isn't covering your car." I glance back up at him and he is running his thumb across his lip while staring at me. My eyebrows pull together in confusion, but my core reaction is opposite... I realize this may have been a bad idea inviting him back to my house. My mind is telling me to stop whatever is about to happen, but my libido has completely different plans.

CHAPTER NINE

I unlock the door while Auston stands a little too close behind me. Every hair on my body stands at attention as I push the door open and move forward. I throw my purse down on the ottoman out of habit, and take my shoes off as I turn around and notice him looking around my home.

"Your place is beautiful." He takes off his shoes and hangs up his jacket.

I can't help looking down to notice the size of his feet.

Nope, don't go there.

"The living room is right through there. You can find something to watch. I tend to stick to horror movies or romantic comedies, but you can choose whatever." I smile. "I'm going to grab a glass of wine, do you want one?" I show him to the living room and he takes a seat, looking way too comfortable already. He glances around the room and I can't help wondering what he is thinking. My home says a lot about me, from the pictures hanging on the walls, to the simple rustic touches scattered along the room. My couch is a large, L-shaped, grey piece that sits five people, with an emerald Sherpa blanket thrown messily atop, surrounded by pillows. It looks like a living room someone would find on Pinterest, which is exactly where I found it.

"Yeah, I will have a glass if you don't mind." I don't bother turning around to look at him as I make my way to the kitchen. I rest my hands on the counter and welcome the coolness it brings to my clammy skin.

Deep breaths.

I turn towards the floating shelves which display all my glasses. I push up on my toes to grab the wine glasses from the top shelf, setting them down to uncork the unopened red I had sitting on the counter. I planned to drink this alone over the weekend, but I don't exactly mind the company. I pour myself a hefty amount and take a large gulp from it. Setting my glass down, The hair on the back of my neck rises. I go to turn around when a hand gently moves the hair away from my neck and lips connect with my skin. I jump lightly as my arms begin to flourish with goosebumps. I take a deep breath, realizing this is my first sexual encounter with a man in years.

I decide to move my head to the side to give Auston more access to my neck. He runs his fingers down my back, grabbing a hold of my hips, and turns me around to face him. I'm biting my lip to the point of pain while Auston raises his hand to slowly release my lip from my teeth's grip. I stare into his green eyes and see myself reflected back at me.

"You're so fucking beautiful." He leans forward to nip at my lips. My shoulders relax and I feel myself lose control for the first time in years, applying more pressure against his lips. His hands start to move things behind me and before I know it, he is picking me up and setting me on the counter. I wrap my legs around his hips as he moves his lips downwards along the column of my neck, towards my breasts. My nipples harden against the cotton of my bra and push my chest forward, silently giving him access. His hands slide underneath my shirt and he looks up to get my permission to take my shirt off, I give him a small smile in acceptance.

Oh god, I have never taken my shirt off in front of a man before. Even when I had sex in the past, I always kept my shirt on. I begin to hesitate, but he swiftly removes my shirt and bra and slowly licks from the top of my collarbone down towards my nipple. Too late to worry about it now.

I lean my head back and take in the sensation coming from Auston's mouth. I moan loudly when he bites down on my nipple, the scruff of his beard heightening the sensations. I widen my stance to allow him to come closer to where I want him.

I grab the hem of his shirt as he makes his way back to my lips and it's my turn to quickly lift his shirt over his head.

"Holy fuck." I blurt, and stare at his athletic physique. He is toned in all the right places. His torso is defined and his arms bulge, which only sends another zip of pleasure to my core.

On his side, he has a tattoo. I run my fingers along it and take in the intricate design of an old pocket watch that acts as the core of the tattoo, surrounded by broken watches and text that reads *the trouble is you think you have time*.

I look up to find him smirking down at me and I grab his head and bring his lips to mine. The tattoo is for another day's questioning. I run my hands down his torso and moan into our kiss. Auston's hands sneak into my leggings slyly, slowly beginning to apply pressure to my clit and it nearly has me bucking off the counter. The fact that this man knows to treat a clit with ease has me nearly coming. He looks at me with his devilishly green eyes and motions for me to lift my hips off the counter. Sweat slowly builds at my temple as I use my arms to leverage my body upwards. He slowly pulls my leggings and panties down and bites his bottom lip while staring at my bare pussy. My face reddens - I don't think I have ever been naked with a man with light in the room. Looking back at me his eyes have darkened, and his hand slowly makes its way towards my pussy. His fingers graze along my calf, his fingernails nudging lightly at the skin every so often.

Unexpectedly, Auston grabs me behind the knees and brings my body jolting forward so it sits on the edge of the counter. I raise an eyebrow at him, surprised, only for him to lick his lips in reply as he lowers himself onto his knees.

Holy fucking fuck.

He kisses his way up my thighs, changing between thighs at each kiss. I automatically go to shut my legs when his hands grab onto my knees and force them to stay open. I lean my head back trying to control my breathing, but I can't. I haven't had a man go down on me in years and I'm not mentally, *or physically*, ready for it.

Auston's finger glides through my folds and he intakes a sharp breath, "Fuck, you are so wet." He uses his two fingers to spread open my folds and licks up my center. I moan loudly, grabbing a hold of his hair while I spread my legs wider.

I'm definitely welcoming his mouth. I've missed the sensations of having a man go down on me. His beard tickles my thigh and I let out a satisfied sigh.

"Fuck, you taste delicious." He slowly rubs circles on my clit and my core tightens. His tongue continues along my pussy. At some moments his strokes are rough and toe-curling, others soft and teasing.

"Oh my God, just like that Auston." I push his face into my pussy. I can't help it. I look down to find his eyes already staring back at me as he slowly enters a finger and bites my clit.

"Fuck!" I throw my head back, and my legs begin to quiver. Pleasure grows throughout my entire body and I'm getting close. I have never reached climax with a man between my legs. Apparently, there is a first for everything. He continues licking and fingering me when my legs tighten around his head, and I tell him I'm close. The familiar build in my core begins to spread. It begins at my toes and gradually climbs until it's reached my core, ripping through my body.

"Oh, fuck me, Auston! I'm coming." I throw my hands behind me to hold me up, so I can look at Auston. His finger goes to my right nipple and pinches it. I tighten my eyes and turn my head. I bring my fist to my mouth to bite on to keep from screaming out.

After a few seconds, I come down from my high and Auston stands slowly, licking his fingers and smirking; my arousal causing his scruff to glisten. My eyes want to roll back into my head, but instead I bite my lip and grab his hand to show him to my bedroom.

I don't usually have sexual confidence, normally I would shy away and try to find my clothes to cover my body back up. But Auston makes me feel sexy, and I love this feeling. I want to bask it in as long as I can. We walk through the memory hall and I push my door open. I grab onto his belt loops and direct him towards my bed. Before he sits down, I undo his pants, shaking slightly, and push his pants and boxer briefs down to his feet. My eyes widen to the thick cock that is now between us. I look at him and see the lust in his eyes, giving me another boost of confidence. I lower myself onto my knees, spit in my hand, and slowly begin to pump him. I bite my lip and lean forward to take his head into my mouth. It's slightly salty with pre-cum, but his moans are distracting me from the taste.

"Jesus, Victoria. I knew that mouth did tempting things,

but fuck..." He growls, using his hand to grab a hold of my hair and slowly guide me the way he likes it. After a few moments my jaw starts to become sore. I bare my teeth slightly to run along his length and he hisses through his teeth. I hold my hands around his thighs and his legs stiffen. A loud groan leaves his throat as something salty spills onto my tongue. I swallow as quickly as possible, but some drips down the side of my lip. I look up at him on purpose and slowly lick the white bead that had dripped from my mouth before standing up.

"That may have been the sexiest thing I've ever seen." He grabs me and throws me onto the bed. He leans down to grab something from his jean pocket and produces a small square foil. He puts the corner in his mouth and rips it with a diabolical smile on his face. I lean myself on my elbows and widen my legs to accommodate his body. My hips protest to the harsh bend, but I don't even care. It will be worth the pain to have Auston's cock deep inside me. He slowly slides the condom on and leans forward so his dick sits right on top of my pussy.

"Are you sure you want to do this, gorgeous? There is no going back after this..." His face is mere inches from mine, slight worry creased into his eyebrows. I lift my hand up in an attempt to rub out the wrinkles he's creating on his forehead.

"God, yes." I lean forward and suck his bottom lip. He glides his length through my folds and slaps my clit with the head of his penis. I release a moan, not expecting him to do that.

The tip of his cock slowly reaches my entrance and I stiffen. He lowers his lips to mine and slowly pushes forward. I peek my tongue out to gain access to his mouth and begin to suck his tongue just as he thrusts forward quickly.

"Fuck!" I curl my head into his neck and bite down. I

haven't had sex in a while and he is stretching me to capacity. My rabbit isn't even this big. Auston pauses, letting me get used to his size, but the pleasure begin to build so I thrust upwards seeking more. He gets what I'm saying with my body and begins to thrust in perfect measures. I bite onto his neck to keep myself from screaming.

"Fuck, you're going to leave a mark." He grits out and continues pumping in and out of me. He kisses me before pulling out abruptly, flipping me onto my knees, and slamming back into me.

"Oh yes," I moan, from this angle, his cock is so much deeper. He pumps in and out of me at the perfect speed while reaching forward and rubbing slow, light circles on my clit. I clench my eyes shut and my core begins to tighten again, I buck backwards against him, wanting, *no - needing*, more. He becomes faster and more frantic with his movements and my body finally catches up and my orgasm erupts through me.

"Yes, Auston!" I feel myself calm down just as he pumps faster and groans out his release. He falls on top of me and slowly rolls me over to lay on my side, facing him.

"That was…wow," I say, a little breathless. Auston runs his fingers up and down my sides while trying to get his breathing back to normal. He slowly turns to me,

"Oh, you are going to be addicting." His hands move around my neck and he licks his lips before capturing mine in another frenzied kiss.

What he doesn't realize is that I already feel myself becoming addicted to him. He has given me more emotion in the last month than I have felt in my entire life.

CHAPTER TEN

W e had sex twice last night and once more this morning. I bless Emma for jokingly giving me a box of condoms as a gag gift for my birthday. I don't know what we would have done if I didn't have that extra box hidden under my bathroom counter.

I'm daydreaming in the kitchen wearing Auston's shirt, stretched to hold my curvy body, but still comfortable. I'm waiting for the coffee pot to fill when I hear Auston shuffling into the kitchen. I turn around and find him heading towards me in only his briefs.

"Mmmm, good morning." He wraps his arms around me and kisses me slowly; feeling it all the way to my toes.

"I mean, it has been a pretty great morning," I blush. "Coffee?" I nip at his lips and he smiles. He reaches above me, his arm straining, and grabs two mugs and sets them down. I quickly grab sugar, and milk from the fridge, and notice him looking out the window. The kitchen and dining room are open concept design with large windows that span the entire backyard. I've always loved natural light. A majority of the house was boxed in when I got it, so when I renovated I opened up a lot to let in more natural light.

Auston grabs both of our mugs and walks to sit in the window nook that overlooks the backyard. I walk over, going to sit on the opposite side, when he hands me my mug and grabs my waist for me to sit in between his open legs.

"You're making a girl too comfortable Auston, this isn't good." I nudge his ribs and he laughs, bringing his mug up to take a sip.

"Just shut up and enjoy your coffee, and the fact that you're in between my legs." He winks down at me and I roll my eyes. I have dealt with confident men before but never any that I've had in my own bed. Usually, I'm dealing with them as they try to get into my friends' beds.

It's a surreal knowing I slept with Auston even though I made a commitment to myself that this was going to stop. I lean my head back on his shoulder and continue to drink my coffee in peace, trying to deter my negative thoughts. I stare into the backyard that is now covered in snow. Flakes are still falling lightly from the sky, but it's peaceful.

"Alright sir, I know you're all lean, built, and GQ-like, but this girl has got to eat." I say to him a few minutes later.

Coffee can only do so much for a growling stomach.

I make my way to my stainless steel fridge and grab bacon, eggs, and bread for toast. I usually have a quick breakfast on weekdays, but weekends are for fun unhealthy breakfast foods. I hum to myself when I notice that Auston is at the other side of the room going through my dad's old records.

"Which album is your favorite from here?" He looks up at me in question.

"Definitely Queen's Greatest Hits album. I used to listen to it non-stop, I'm surprised that record isn't worn thin by now." I smile and turn back towards the stove putting bacon on tin-foil and into the oven.

I hear the opening to *Don't Stop Me Now* by Queen. I turn around to face Auston with a huge grin on my face.

"What?" He shrugs, and I can't help embarrassing myself. As soon as the tune picks up I use my wooden spoon as my microphone; thank God it's clean this time. I begin to dance around the kitchen while setting up the table, being obnoxious with my movements.

I keep dancing and turn around to find Auston has his phone pointed at me, recording.

"Oh my God. How much of that did you get?" I ask in horror. This was meant to be a one-time show, and now there is evidence of it on his phone. I run over, trying to snatch his phone out of his hand, but he just holds it up out of my reach while laughing at my embarrassment.

"I got the perfect amount and no, I won't delete it, because you looked happy." He holds his phone up, nearly touching the ceiling. I huff in annoyance and give up. Auston is six foot two and there is no way my five foot five body will snatch that phone out of his hand.

"As long as you promise not to show anyone the video." I point my wooden spoon at him and mimic hitting him with it. He laughs and crosses his heart with his fingers. I roll my eyes and turn to finish breakfast before it burns. My anxiety gnaws at me with him having a video of me on his phone, but I just take a few deep breaths to calm down.

"Voila!" I set down our plates on the table and Auston places two fresh mugs of coffee.

"Everything looks delicious," He kisses me. "Especially you." He swats my ass and sits down before I do the same back to him. I sit down beside him, and we dive into our food, clearly both starving after our activities from last night and this morning.

"Speaking of… you know we can't tell anyone about this?" My heart plummets at that moment, "There isn't a policy in place at school and although we are adults, it can make the other staff feel inferior." I slip my hand from his and bring it to my lap while nodding my head.

"Gorgeous, that doesn't mean that I want it to stop." My heart flutters.

"So, what do you say we do about it?" I bring my eyes back up to his.

"I want us to keep it quiet until the end of the year. That even means keeping Emma and Hannah out of the loop, unfortunately…" He rolls his eyes playfully and I laugh. This is going to be so hard to keep from my best friends. I mean, they know everything about me. There has never been a moment in my life where I haven't told them something, and we have gone through so much together.

"Fine… only because I love what you have hidden in those briefs." I smile while getting up to straddle his lap. My heart soars when I hear a satisfied groan leave his throat.

"That's the only reason? Not my charming personality? My ability to be a GQ model, as you like to say?" He squeezes my plump ass and I smile, enjoying the playful side of Auston.

"Okay, I guess those two are also applicable reasons…" I lean forward and kiss him. It quickly becomes heated between us since we only have our underwear on. I slowly rub myself on him and my panties soak with moisture. Auston's hand slowly makes its way towards my pussy, teasing me by running his finger along the seam.

"Fuck Auston, stop teasing me." His shoulders shake with

laughter until he slips my panties to the side and glides his finger into my already wet pussy.

I'm slowly riding his hand to the brink of orgasm when I hear the door slam shut.

"So, mom cancelled our trip to Hamilton and I was wondering if you wanted to go shopping? Hannah is here too, looking all satisfied." Emma says joyously.

I gasp, halting Auston's hands. I look up at him only to find him looking amused, and a little shocked at our interruption. I hear their footsteps getting closer so I jump up from Auston's lap, wincing from the loss of his delicious fingers.

Auston stands quickly and is about to run into the hallway when Emma walks in.

"Oh fuck," Emma shouts while covering her mouth, and Hannah is standing there with hers wide open. I turn to face Auston as he quickly grabs a dishtowel to shield away his boxer-clad erection that is straining to release. He lets out a breath that sounds half laughter, half *oh shit* while staring at the ceiling.

Talk about awkward… for him. These girls have seen me naked, so I don't really care.

"You guys couldn't have used the doorbell?" I squint at both of them.

"Actually, we did ring it, four times to be exact, but remembering where you hid the key we just used that to get in. We didn't see anyone's car in the driveway so we assumed it would be safe to come in." Hannah shoots her eyes to Auston's body and he excuses himself to my bedroom. As soon as he's out of earshot both girls whip their heads to me. I can't even keep a straight face because as soon as they look at me a huge smile breaks across it.

"Okay, well Auston put his car in the garage last night-" I start but get cut off.

"Yeah he did!" Emma shouts while thrusting her hips, and I cover my eyes.

"Stop it! Go to the living room, I will be right back." I head toward my bedroom and quickly walk in, shutting the door behind me. Auston is on me in seconds flat. He has me up against the door with his body flushed against mine. His fingers drift back down to my panties and I sigh.

"Auston, they are sitting in the living room." I grab his face to look at me. He has an evil glint in his eyes.

"Then I guess I will have to be quick." He slides a finger in slowly and my head bangs against the door. My orgasm begins to build again as he applies pressure to my clit.

"Just like that, fuck yes." I hiss through my teeth. My orgasm erupts, and I grip his arms for support. I lean my head back lazily and open my eyes to look at him.

His face is way too cocky after what just happened out in the kitchen.

"You're so sexy when you fall apart." He kisses me once before walking over to the floor to pick up his discarded pants. I take off his shirt and give it to him while I get myself cleaned up in the bathroom.

I walk out to see him sitting on the bed deep in thought.

"Everything okay?" I bite my lip, worried he is about to end whatever the hell we just started so soon.

"Yes, more than okay." He smiles down at me. "I think we should go out and talk to them before they come looking for us." I agree with him because I know Emma will do exactly that. I giggle and grab his hand to follow me to the living room, hearing the women speaking in hushed tones.

We walk into the living room to find the girls slowly turning to look at us. I push Auston towards the love seat, so he doesn't have to sit between the two vultures.

"Okay, first of all, how did this happen?" Hannah twists

her hands in her lap and stares back and forth between Auston and I.

"Oh please. Don't act like you two didn't think of this when you left the pub last night." I squint my eyes at them but break out in a smile. I can't even be mad at them because I have wanted this since the moment I saw him at DP as the mysterious man in the suit. "Lucky for you two, it ended extremely well. You guys have to keep this quiet though, we decided we weren't going to tell anyone-" I get interrupted.

"You weren't going to tell us?" Hannah asks.

"As if you would be able to hide anything from us. You have that satisfied sex glow, we would have found out…" Emma smiles and I shrug my shoulders and nod. I think my huge grin would have given it away at some point in the upcoming week.

"Now that you guys know, would you please keep it to yourselves?" Auston leans forward and the girls both nod at him. I know they wouldn't speak a word of this because it could cause a lot of problems at work.

"Okay, well I'm sure you girls want to go shopping. I'll head out, but you," Auston points at me, "message me." His mouth tugs upwards in a smile and he comes over and kisses me. It's not as long as I wanted, but it will have to do since my friends are sitting in front of us.

"I'll walk you out." I walk behind him and give my friends a look that says 'behave.' Auston puts on his shoes and jacket and I open the door and follow him out, gently shutting it behind me.

"I had a really great time with you, before that ungodly interruption." I thump my head against the door and he smiles.

"I had a great time as well. I'll see you at work, but," He pauses for emphasis. "I'd love to take you for dinner somewhere this week." He leans his arm beside my head and gives me a gentle kiss.

"I think I can definitely make time for that…" I smile and give him a gentle shove. "Those two probably have their ears against the door, so I'm going to let you go. Text me when you're home safe." I kiss him hard, one last time.

He jogs over to the open garage and gets into his car. A second later he rolls out, sends me a wink, and drives away.

Nothing good ever lasts, but God I want to believe this will be the one thing that does. I have never been the girl to get what she wants, but I want Auston Scott.

CHAPTER ELEVEN

After a two-hour drive to Toronto from Simcoe, the girls and I are having a great time shopping. We've only been here for a few hours, but we've already spent too much money. Emma has been trying to get me to buy clothing that she thinks Auston will love at work, but I have to keep reminding her of what we talked about at my place.

"Oh, this place is calling our names after what we witnessed this morning. You need to make sure the goods are covered in a sexy way." Hannah tugs us into Forever Sexy, the franchise brand for lingerie clothing.

"Guys, I think my underwear is good enough. I have always made sure my goods are covered beautifully." I glance around and spot a gorgeous pink set. The underwear is a delicately laced thong with a matching bra, and I fall in love as soon as my eyes pass over the material.

"Well, you know you have to try this on. It will look so good with your complexion." Emma saw me eyeing it, and she throws it into the bag she already started for her and I. I shake my head and watch as the girls start throwing things into a bag for us to go try on.

I make my way through the store and grab a sultry red set and a foxy black set to try on with the pink set Emma grabbed for me. The girls motion towards the dressing room and I nod my head, following them. We are quickly guided to dressing rooms beside one another when my purse begins to vibrate.

Auston: How is shopping going?

I smile at his message. I've never had a guy reach out to me when I was with the girls. Even past boyfriends avoided talking to me when they knew Emma and Hannah were around. I start to type back that it is going well, but pause.

I'm still riding high on emotions from our time together and decide to have some fun with him. I undress quickly, slip on the sexy pink set, and look at myself.

Damn, this set is really sexy. As a size fourteen woman, I've never had lingerie that fit me properly. The underwear is always too tight causing an uncomfortable muffin top and hip dips. As I stare at myself in this set though, I don't feel any of the usual discomfort. My breasts are comfortable in the bra, showing off more than usual and the panties lie perfectly on my hips. Lace has never been my thing because it's usually a material without a lot of stretch, but this lace has a nice give so it fits almost like a second skin. I check out my ass and nod in approval at its plumpness in the thong. I quickly fix my boobs and turn my video on. I smile shyly at the camera and show off my body to Auston, making a point to turn around and show him the sexy lace that dips at my curvy ass. I delete the previous message I had started and type out a new one,

Vic: I think it's going pretty well. What would you say?

Without second guessing myself, I text him the video and bite my lip. I hope he doesn't think I'm being too forward.

But what if that was a bad idea? What if he hates it? Or thinks I was too much?

Slowly my anxiety starts to creep its way up my stomach and into my throat. The tight and unsettling feeling makes me start to doubt whether I should have even sent him that message. I mean, we only spent one night together... What if he never wants to do it again? What if he asked me out as a courtesy after our night together?

What if he shows that video to people? My mind drifts off to the time in high school where people laughed at my body edited onto random objects on a flyer that Laura had printed out, and my body starts to heat as my breathing accelerates. He also has a video of me dancing on his phone - what if he decides to share that too?

My throat starts to tighten painfully, tears brimming my eyes as sweat begins to bead at my temples. I take off the lingerie in a rush to hurry out of the store before I have a full-on anxiety attack in a change room. I zig-zag through the aisles in a panic until I slide down the wall beside the exit, close my eyes, and try to slow my breathing.

It has been a few years since I've had a full melt down in public. I'm usually able to contain my meltdowns to when I'm home alone, but everything happening with Auston is bringing more back to me, emotionally.

I hear footsteps rushing towards me and I open my blurred eyes to see the girls running towards me, freaking out.

"Vic, what happened?" Emma grabs a water bottle out of her bag and forces me to drink it, and Hannah is dabbing at the sweat that has collected on my upper lip with a tissue.

"I... I had an anxiety attack. I tried on that pink set and

decided to send a video to Auston, showing it off. Before I knew it, I felt as if I was back in high school except Laura was now Auston and he was showing everyone the video of me…" I lean my head back and tighten my eyes, trying to keep the tears at bay.

"Vic…" Hannah says with sadness lacing her voice. "I don't think Auston would ever do that. He doesn't seem like the type to bully someone, or want to lose his job for that matter."

"Or that thing hanging between his legs because I swear to God, I would cut it off and nail it to his head!" Emma whisper-shouts, and I grimace at the image she just put in my head.

I cough to clear my scratchy throat. "I know, I just don't think I'm used to this. I haven't had a boyfriend since the beginning of my second year of university and the thought of having one brings a whole new set of emotions." The girls join me, sitting on either side and each grabbing one of my hands.

"You have been dealt a really shitty hand in life, but maybe this is life trying to make it up to you. It's no wonder that your anxiety has been acting up lately; there are a lot of changes happening in your life, and you've never really been good with change." Hannah tightens her grip on my hand and Emma nods in agreement.

A heaviness weighing on my heart because I know they're right. I have never been able to handle change, ever since I was a kid.

My eyes well with tears as I remember the biggest and most difficult change in my life.

"Hey ladies, I'm sorry to interrupt but you can't be sitting on the floor." A security guard is looking over at us and we all just nod our heads. Emma suggests we go out to eat and I agree, shutting my phone down and trying to cope with what just happened. I've been dealing with anxiety since I was in high school; it's a vicious staple in my life. I try to avoid having to take my medication, but lately it seems as if it's the only way I'll survive.

"One second, I'll be right back." Emma rushes back into the store. She probably wanted to buy herself something, but my moment had disrupted her from being able to do so. Hannah and I patiently wait for her as we discuss some of the calming methods my therapist taught me when I was a teenager. Emma returns with two bags and hands me one.

"What is this?" I look up at her and she shrugs. I look over at Hannah and they both give each other knowing looks. I move the coral tissue to the side and see the pink set wrapped in tissue. My eyes water. "You didn't have to do this…"

"I wanted to. I'm sure it looked stunning on you. You wouldn't have sent Auston a video of yourself in it if you thought otherwise." She links arms with both Emma and I and we head off to eat.

I have no idea what I would do without these girls; they're my family.

"I'll see you both on Monday at work. I love you guys." With a heavy heart, I give the girls tight hugs.

"We love you babe, try to relax tonight and tomorrow." Hannah squeezes my hand as she gets back into the car. Emma kisses my cheek and follows Hannah back to the car. I grab my shopping bags from the trunk and wave as they pull out of the driveway. They stall on the road waiting for me to unlock the door and get into the house. I quickly do, sending one last wave out the door and I hear a honk signalling that they have driven off. Locking the door behind me, I take off my shoes and put them away in the closet.

I walk down towards my bedroom and I pause at the memory wall. A photo of me positioned between my smiling parents stares back at me. My throat constricts and my body chills as I stare at the multiple photos of them. My mom would know exactly what to say right now with everything going on. She was my go-to when I needed advice for anything in life.

My parents left my apartment an hour ago because the snow had started to pick up. They thought it would be better to leave now rather than later on when the roads would be covered in ice and snow. I suggested they stay for the night, but mom has always preferred to sleep in her own bed if she can. My mom had dropped off her chocolate cake, her secret recipe; with exam season around the corner, she knew her cake could help to relieve my stress. I smile with a plate on my desk, a mug of coffee beside it, and my computer on with the final assignment of my undergrad. My parents came to visit and my dad, being the amazing man he is, reviewed and edited my final paper. Having also majored in English, he is the person I rely on the most when I need help with school. I take my first bite and moan. This is seriously the best cake in the world.

I've told my mom thousands of times that she is making this as my wedding cake. I don't need some big, three-tier cake that will cost me thousands of dollars when I can just have my mom's delicious cake made with lots of love... and sugar. I snicker to myself as I begin one last re-read of my final paper, so I can begin studying for my finals.

I'm finishing my last delicious bite of cake when someone knocks at my apartment door. I quickly adjust my oversized sweater and peek through the hole. Two police officers stand there with their hats under their arms.

My heart begins to thump and my head spins. Who are they? Why are they at my door? With shaky hands, I pull open the door and the officers look filled with guilt.

"Ms. Mateus?" The male officer shuffles uncomfortably while the female officer puts her hand on his shoulder, taking over.

"Yes?" My throat clogs, my stomach feeling like lead. What's going on?

"There has been an accident with your parents... While on the 401 they got caught in a pileup with three other vehicles. I'm sorry, but..." She pauses. "They didn't make it." Her voice cracks towards the end.

My entire world tilts on its axis and my legs give out.

I drop to the floor with a thud. This can't be real.

"Are you sure it was them? How would you know?" My voice rises an octave, trying to understand what they are telling me.

I don't even realize I'm crying until my body starts shaking with uncontrollable sobs. Repeating "no" quietly to myself as I hear the officers talking.

"This can't be real. They can't both be gone. They were just here! It couldn't have been them, please check again. Please." I beg as I wrap my arms around my knees, rocking back and forth. "It couldn't have been them! What car was it?" I try to take a deep breath, but everything is getting stuck. It feels as if barbed wire has found its way around my chest.

"I'm sorry, Ms. Mateus. They have been declared deceased at the scene and their identities have been confirmed. If you'd like to come to the station with us, you can see them. It could help you get closure." The woman *kneels in front of me and rests a hand on my shoulder. I frown as I shake and try to keep my sobs in, but they let loose as I see the blank look on both their faces. They've probably done this a lot.*

I stand up on shaky legs. "I..." I stutter, "I can't do that right now. Please... just let me be alone." I practically shove them out the door, lean my body back against it, and slide to the floor. Tears coming full force down my face, I can't breathe.

I mourn my parents' death on the floor of my apartment, where they were standing not too long ago.

They were just here.

Smiling and laughing... Something I'll never hear or see again.

I choke out a sob at the memory of finding out my parents had died. I lean my head against their photo and cry quietly, fat tears rolling down my cheeks and onto my neck. Eight years later and the pain has not subsided. Grief never goes away; it just becomes something to cope with. It grows with me as I age. Losing my parents was the most painful thing to ever happen to me. Life can throw literally anything at me at this point and it will never be as hard as losing the two people who made me whole.

I wipe my eyes and realize my make-up is all over my face from sobbing. I drag my feet into my room with after-math hiccups. I put the bags in my closet, not wanting to deal with putting anything away right now. I strip down and grab my leggings, my Queen's University sweatshirt, and a pair of fluffy socks, and get dressed.

After I wash the make-up and tear residue off my face, I notice that my face is all puffy and my eyes are red. I stare at my reflection and can't believe the whirlwind of events that have happened today. I'm used to dealing with my anxiety and grief, but I've never had to deal with emotions towards a man on top of those. I hear my mother's voice reassuring me that everything will be okay, and another lone tear slips out. I give my shoulders a shake and take a deep breath. I look at my reflection and don't see anything different, but everything is. Maybe not physically, but emotionally I'm dealing with things I have never had to before.

I walk out of the bathroom, keeping my head down as I walk through the hallway.

The weather started to pick up on our drive home from the mall, just like the weather broadcaster had stated yesterday. There wasn't any wind, but snowflakes were falling gently from the sky.

I decide to go lay down on the bed swing on the porch while I watch the snow fall with a comforting mug of tea.

Ten minutes later, I'm laying on the porch bed with my heated blanket and cup of lavender tea. The sky is transitioning from day to night, so the countryside looks beautiful with the snowflakes falling. Some of the flakes have joined me on my blanket, but melt quickly due to its heat.

I think about going inside to grab my phone but decide against it. After what happened today at the store, I worry about what I might find in my messages. Maybe Auston said something positive, but my fear outweighs the good that could possibly be sitting in my phone. I relax my head against the pillows and stare out into the night. The snow is starting to fall heavier, just as sleep starts to take over my body.

I jolt awake when headlights flash down the driveway, coming towards the house. I sit up, yawning - I must have passed out for some time. Snow is still clearly falling from the sky, around three inches on the ground. I look back towards the blurry car and my heart jumps in my throat.

I recognize Auston's car rolling up. He pulls up in front of the garage, gets out quickly, and rushes through the snow to my porch. He reaches the steps and sees me tucked in my blanket. I probably look like a deer caught in headlights because that is exactly how I feel. Why is he here? In the snow? The plows take forever to get to the country roads, so clearly, he pushed his car to get here through the thick snow. He shuffles his feet through the snow as he makes his way towards me, concern etched on his face.

"Hi… You weren't answering your phone." Auston runs his fingers through his thick hair and emotion twists in my gut.

"I'm sorry, Auston. I can explain," I pause. "Do you want to sit?" I make room for him and lift the blanket, not welcoming the rush of cold air that joins me under my warm cover. He nods his head and joins me under the blanket. I angle my body towards his so that I can see his face while I talk to him.

I scrunch my lips, because I don't know how much I should tell him. I mean, we have only known each other for a couple weeks. I have a gut feeling that I can trust Auston, but letting someone in other than Emma and Hannah is difficult. They have been constants in my life for so long, how do I know that Auston isn't going to up and leave after this semester? My fear of abandonment swirls in my stomach as I decide to tell Auston about my anxiety. That is heavy enough for us since we are still getting to know one another.

"When I sent you that video today, I felt confident. I believed I looked good and without a second thought I sent it to you. But the moment the video read 'sent' below, my past and my anxiety clawed its way into my body. I had so many thoughts running through my head that I ended up having an anxiety attack outside the store." I twist my hands under the blankets. The only two people that know about my anxiety are Emma and Hannah, and they have been helping me deal with it since I was a teenager. My parents helped me cope through it once they figured it out, but after they left, it became slightly harder to manage alone. I look at Auston and sadness flashes across his face. His lips purse, trying to find the right words to say after that.

"You should have felt confident because you did look sexy, Vic. I went and met with Axel and Garret for lunch and completely zoned out on our conversation when I saw you." He smirks at me and I let out a light laugh, "I understand how hard it is dealing with anxiety though. My younger sister deals with severe depression and anxiety." Understanding covers his face. I had no idea he had a sister, let alone that he would understand what I'm talking about. A piece of my heart grows further for Auston. Not many are able to understand the depth of mental health, especially if they don't deal with it themselves. Hearing Auston say that he understands gives me a sense of comfort because it means he might be able to understand me, for who I really am. At least a small piece of me.

"I'm sorry to hear about your sister. It's hard to watch someone you love go through something and not know how to help." I look back up at him and he smiles down at me.

"It is, but she started seeing a doctor and they ended up falling in love. Obviously, she had to switch doctors," he laughs. "But she fell in love with someone who understands her." He rests his head back on the edge of the swing and yawns.

I have no idea what time it is. It was around seven thirty when the girls dropped me off and a lot of time has passed since I first came out here.

"What time is it? I came out here to get some peace but

haven't checked the time since." Auston lifts his wrist to check the time and states that it's one in the morning.

"What? I fell asleep for that long? Why did you come here so late?" I sit up abruptly and he follows suit.

"I tried falling asleep, but you weren't answering your phone and I was worried something had happened. I decided I wanted to check on you. That may be a little forward, but fuck, you're constantly on my mind." He raises his hand and moves a piece of hair that fell out of my messy bun. My heart does a little somersault, but my brain is telling me to slow it the hell down.

I decide to give my heart something it wants for once and lean forward and tease his lips. Leisurely I apply more pressure and our kiss becomes hypnotic. I feel nothing but his lips on mine and his hands caressing my side. He lifts me effortlessly to straddle his hips and runs his hands up my thighs. He grabs me around the neck and positions me so that he has control over our kiss. My body heating from head to toe, until a frigid breeze sweeps through the air and I shudder.

"I should probably get going, it's late and you've had a long day." He goes to stand up and panic seizes me as I grab his wrist. My blinking becomes rapid as I stare at the snowstorm that has picked up since he got here. More snow seems to be falling in the dark sky, a beauty to behold, but not to be in.

"What's wrong?" Auston raises a questioning eyebrow, and he grabs my chin to look at him. I gulp down the saliva that has gathered in my throat and give a slight shake of my head.

"My parents died in a pileup on the highway during a snowstorm…" I whisper, and his eyes widen and his posture crumples. I'm hitting Auston with a lot of baggage tonight, but I guess it's better to do it now, while I still have the strength from his comfort.

"Jesus, fuck." He wraps his arms around me, and I squeeze my eyes closed. I never know if I should tell people that my parents died, because I don't want their pity. I don't want people to think differently of me, as the girl with the dead parents.

He leans back and kisses me slowly, "I'm not going anywhere then." He scoops me up in his arms and heads into the house, maneuvering his way through. I hate when people pick me up, absolutely hate it… but after the day I've had, I can't find it in me to complain. He pauses at the memory wall, finally taking notice of the couple that sit in multiple frames. I give him a slight nod, confirming that those are my parents' faces surrounding the wall. He kisses my forehead and my body melts in his arms.

I started to see someone in my second year of teaching at Angel's and when he found out about my parents and my issues, he declared me a basket case and stopped talking to me. I have a hard time trusting people, but Auston makes me doubt everything I've ever believed.

Maybe this time will be different?

He walks us into my bedroom and lays me down, covering me up. He discards his clothing on the chair in the corner, leaving on his briefs, and gets under the covers with me.

He wraps his arm around my middle and pulls me towards him, keeping a tight and comfortable hold on my body.

"Goodnight beautiful, get some rest." He kisses the top of my head and I feel light. This weekend has been different. I've put myself on a platter for Auston and now he knows the deepest parts of me.

CHAPTER TWELVE

Monday comes in the blink of an eye after the emotionally draining weekend that passed. Auston spent the majority of yesterday with me to make sure I was okay. I assured him he could leave at any time, but he didn't budge; he seemed to genuinely enjoy being with me. We baked my mom's chocolate cake and he loved it. I didn't give him the recipe because I told him it was a secret within my family and was going to stay that way. To say he left disappointed was an understatement, but at least I gave him a plate to take home.

Auston announced last week that there was going to be an assembly this morning, and that every student was to report to class then head to the gymnasium. Students begin to filter into their seats at nine o'clock sharp, and I take attendance as announcements are made on the televisions in the right corner of the room. I quickly jot check marks by everyone's name and grab my phone to put it in the waistband of my skirt.

"Alright, let's head to the gymnasium for the assembly. Please don't be rowdy and come straight back to class after it's over. I will be taking attendance again after to make sure you come back." I give them a pointed look. Some smile and nod their heads, others laugh it off and walk out the door to the left toward the gymnasium.

"What is this assembly for, Ms. Mateus?" Maria waits for me while I close the door to the classroom.

"I'm not too sure, Maria. I didn't receive much information regarding it." I smile at her and she nods and walks ahead to her friends.

I meet with the girls at the back of the gymnasium. They're already seated in the bleachers where students are piling into the seats in the front. I rush over to them and sit at the end, closest to the door. I look up to find Auston already staring at me with a smirk on his face. A flush creeps its way up my neck and onto my face, and I dip my chin to engage myself in the conversation with the girls. How are we supposed to act normal when he stands there staring at me with a devious look on his face?

"I see things are better now than they were Saturday. Did you get a chance to talk to him?" Hannah questions. I never updated the girls on Saturday night, technically early Sunday morning because I had spent a majority of my day with Auston and didn't turn on my phone until last night.

"He actually stopped by on Saturday night. A couple hours after you guys dropped me off. We had somewhat of a serious conversation about me... and my parents." I twist my hands in my lap and gnaw at my bottom lip while trying not to make eye contact with them.

"Wow." I hear Hannah say quietly.

"I'm assuming it went well since he's still making eyes as if he wants to screw you under these bleachers." I sputter. That is not keeping it quiet, like him and I both discussed with them.

"Emma," I hiss. "Keep your voice down. You know there

are some teachers we don't get along with…" I send a side-eye to Laura's older sister. Emma's mouth turns down to one side when she realizes her mistake.

"Sorry babe, we will talk about this later." I nod my head and turn to face the front of the gymnasium when Auston clears his throat into the microphone.

"Good morning everyone," his face stoic. "Today's assembly has to do with some issues I've noticed in the school since I've arrived. We have a guest here to discuss the importance of why it is not okay to bully someone, what to do if this happens to you, and how to deal with the long term impacts it may have." His eyes shoot to mine and I feel a small smile form on my lips.

He knows how much the issue of bullying in school rests on my chest and is doing something to hopefully help the problem.

Emma bumps my shoulder and sends me a look of approval and I bite my lip, trying to keep my grin at bay. Auston introduces the individual to the front of the room and students gasp. I look at the girls with my brows furrowed, not understanding the freak out.

"That woman over there is Rachel Growlee. She is "Instagram famous" for her strength story from being bullied in high school. She helps students all over the country now, using her platform to help them deal with bullies." I widen my eyes. That is pretty impressive. I wonder how Auston got a famous influencer to our small town high school.

A pang of jealousy hits me, but I notice Auston casually walking towards us. I try to calm my emotions down a bit, not wanting to seem jealous for no reason. Those are my own insecurities showing.

"Ladies," he whispers to us, "What do you think of the

assembly?" He whispers to me while keeping his eyes facing forward, focused on the action in the front of the gym.

"I think it was exactly what this school should have done thirteen years ago." I smile at him with gratitude in my eyes. His smile tips up the smallest amount. I bite my lip and move my eyes towards the front before it becomes obvious that I'm staring at my boss. I've never attended an assembly regarding bullying as sad as that is, so the blooming in my chest is warranted. Maybe students will actually stop the unwanted bullying that happens in these hallways and focus on their education. I know that's nearly impossible, as bullying is always going to happen. But, if we can help students feel more comfortable talking to us, maybe it will help. Some-times all a student needs is someone to talk to when going through tough situations. Some events in high school can impact a student for the rest of their lives; I'm the perfect individual to prove that point.

Ten minutes go by before I jump slightly and throw my hand to cover my mouth to refrain from shouting when a hand creeps up my thigh. With Auston leaning on the bleach-ers, his hand reaches my thighs. Anyone on the right side of us would just assume that he is staring at the front, but to our left is a wall... and a door.

My face heats up and I slowly bring my hand down to hit his when suddenly it's grazing its way between my thighs, towards my sex. He is slyly trailing his hand from underneath my thigh, rather than above to be discreet.

I press my thighs together and send him a warning glare. He sends me an amused look and my body heats with lust.

"Auston," I lean down towards his head. "What are you doing? Are you trying to get caught?" I whisper.

"Maybe." He looks up at me with his eyes twinkling with deviousness. I push my hands through my closed legs and try to move his hand away before a student, or worse a colleague, looks over. I'm about to shove him with my thigh when his forefinger lands with pressure directly above my clit and a shudder racks through my body. His body is oddly crouched, but it could look like he is just uncomfortably leaning on the bleachers, while watching the guests connect with the students.

He flicks it gently and this time I twist my body away, so his hand slips out and I raise an eyebrow at him.

This is not the time for fun, even though my body is telling me otherwise. My body wants to drag him out of this gymnasium to his office and ride him on his large oak desk.

"What are you thinking right now?" Auston whispers up to me, actually looking at me this time.

I lean down close to his ear, "I'm thinking about how I wish I could drag you out of here and ride you on your desk," I whisper into his ear seductively. As much as my brain is warning me we shouldn't be doing this, my heart and pussy are cheering for pleasure.

"Meet me in the hallway in five minutes," he says sternly, his body vibrating with tension. His eyes look as if two dark holes as lust fills them, and I'm sure mine look the same. He takes his phone out of his pocket and motions to Mr. Callihan, the vice principal, that he's taking a phone call. Mr. Callihan nods back with a smile and continues to watch Rachel at the front discuss how bullying affects someone long term. I look down at my wristwatch and watch the little hand tick by until five minutes have passed.

"I'll be right back; I'm going to the washroom." Emma gives me a knowing look and I roll my eyes while my cheeks flush.

I slide off the bleachers quietly and slip my body through the doors of the gymnasium. I look down the hall towards the parking lot and see Auston leaning against the door to the janitor's room.

"What are you doing, Mr. Scott?" I rush over to him while whisper-yelling. He unlocks the door swiftly and ushers me inside, checking to make sure we're in the clear before closing the door. The smell of bleach and cleaning products hit my nostrils and I scrunch my face up.

"Well, Ms. Mateus. I needed assistance with this hard-on after imagining your luscious body on top of mine on my desk…" His eyes darken, and he prowls towards me. I bite my lip and slowly step backwards until my back hits the wall behind me. He presses his body against mine and slowly runs his fingers up my thighs.

I grab hold of his arms and squeeze his forearm as it reaches the apex of my thighs. I lean my head back and he kisses his way from my ear to my breast bone. He lifts the hem of my skirt all the way to my hips and slides his hand into my panties.

"Fuck, you're so wet." He groans and inserts a finger into my wet cunt. My arousal hits me in a rush and I undo Auston's pants to palm his thick length through his briefs. He growls aggressively and my body begins to convulse as he puts more pressure on my clit. I squeeze my eyes and reach into his briefs to stroke him.

"Fuck, fuck, fuck…" I quiver as my orgasm releases through me. I lean forward and bite his chest to keep from screaming out and hear him groan. I realize I have a death-like grip on his dick and loosen it.

"Jesus," he groans. "You're my fantasy come to life." He nibbles at my lips and I give him one last kiss before I drop to my knees. My skirt is still bunched around my hips, but I don't give it a second thought. I glance up at him and notice his eyes are almost completely black.

I lick the bulging angry tip of his shaft and slowly take him in my mouth. I continue sucking him off and bare my teeth gently, and I hear him hiss through clenched teeth.

"I love seeing your pretty lips wrapped around my cock." I start to suck faster, the tinge of pain grows in my knees. I grab onto his thighs as he begins to jerk into my mouth. His hands dive into my hair to control my movements. I moan around him; I never realized how sexy it is when a man takes over.

His groan is muffled as he bites onto his knuckles and releases into my mouth. The saltiness of his release fills my mouth and I swallow.

He gives himself one last jerk before pulling me up off the floor. He palms my face and runs his thumb along my bottom lip, "This fucking mouth…" He shudders, and I smile. Giving a man a blowjob makes a woman powerful. Even when the man grabs your head, you know you ultimately have the control over him.

"We should probably get back to the assembly…" I smile, and he nods his head, speechless. "Are you going to be okay?" I ask smugly.

"Yes. I just need to get some feeling back into my legs that you seemed to have sucked out of me." I burst out laughing and he smiles playfully. I quickly arrange my shirt and skirt back into place, ensuring everything is in place before walking out.

"You head out first, I'll come back in twenty minutes. I'm going to go to my office, just in case Callihan asks Michelle of my whereabouts." He winks at me and I give him a nod. I walk towards the door, looking back at him resting his back against the wall with his arms crossed. He has his eyes closed and looks so peaceful. The light of the room is dim, and it glows against his skin as his chest rises and falls at a steady pace.

Fuck, he's so beautiful.

I open the door an inch to peer out and see if anyone is there, and the coast is clear. I make a dash from the janitor's room and straighten myself out, again, before I enter the gym.

I pull out my phone to check my face. Although a little flushed, there's nothing too out of the ordinary. I open the gym door lightly and make my way back to Emma and Hannah.

"Damn Vic, what could you have possibly been doing in the bathroom for twenty minutes." I send her a glare to shut up and they both giggle in their seats. They are enjoying this too much. I know Hannah is worried, I see it in her eyes hidden behind the enjoyment of teasing. Hannah has always been the one to worry about my well-being because of every-thing that has happened, but right now, in this bubble with Auston... I'm happy.

Twenty minutes later the assembly is over, but students are in a frenzy trying to get pictures with Rachel. She's great and being super attentive with the students, listening to them as they tell her stories about their experiences. The girls and I are standing now, watching all the commotion as Auston enters the gymnasium, heading towards the front to the podium.

"Hello again students, I hope you learned some valuable lessons today from our guest. Ms. Growlee has agreed to take photos, but I want everyone to stay seated, so it doesn't become chaotic." His voice stern as he eyes the students. "Teachers will call you up row by row and if you decide to come up, you may, if not stay seated." His stern tone puts a fluttery sensation into my belly and I lean against the wall, trying to keep my composure.

I'm not turned on by hearing him talk to the students… not at all. I grimace to myself, really needing to keep my shit together, especially if I want to keep our relationship a secret. I don't even know if this is a relationship. The girls note the confusion on my face and raise their eyebrows.

"I'll tell you both later, I'm just having a moment." I laugh lightly to myself. That dies quickly when I see Tracey, Laura's sister, walk up to Auston with a bright and flirty smile.

"Oh, for the love of God, if it isn't one sister, it's the other." I can't help but cringe because it's so true. Although Tracey is the calmer of the two, they're almost on the exact same level.

"She's just as suggestive as her sister. Look at the way she's thrusting her chest out at him." I'm watching their altercation when Auston glances my way and I send him a small smile. He has no idea that she's Laura's sister. If he did, I'm sure he would look much more uncomfortable.

He shakes his head with an apologetic look on his face and excuses himself from Tracey. He walks over to the three of us and says hello.

"Wow boss, you're looking pretty light on your feet. Seems like it was a good phone call?" Emma smirks while Hannah chokes out a laugh, trying to cover it with a cough. I shake my head at them and mutter, "assholes" under my breath.

"The best phone call," he winks at me. "Although, my conversation with Ms. Maey took some of that feeling away." Discomfort evident on his face..

"What'd she do now?" Emma asks.

"Well, she asked me for dinner tonight and I politely declined that offer." All of our eyes widen, but then laughter finds its way out of us. "Why are you three laughing?" He looks confused, like really confused, which makes me laugh harder.

"Oh, that woman is Laura's sister. You remember her, right? The one who aggressively forced herself on you at Kline's?" Hannah replies, and his eyes widen in realization. His face screws in disgust and he shakes his head.

"I never thought to make the connection, but now that I picture the two of them they do have similarities." He says. We all nod our heads, over-exaggeratedly. Tracey and Laura are two peas in a pod, completely alike. When I got my job here, I thought that Tracey would have forgotten all about her and her sister's nastiness towards me, but she didn't. My problems were never with Tracey, but she hates me because her younger sister does.

Auston excuses himself from our little group to head back to the podium to tell the kids to head back to class. The girls and I say our goodbyes and head back towards our students to herd them back to class. The beginning of the second period has already started, so we need to take attendance and make sure that everyone comes back and heads to their next class.

An hour later, third period commences, and my break has started. Sadly, the girls have classes to teach during this period and usually I go to Tim Horton's or eat my lunch, but I'm not hungry. I grab my writing book and set it on my desk, staring at it.

Why is this damn notebook so intimidating? I grab my pencil and hit it against my notebook repeatedly, trying to think of something… *anything.*

I start to jot down some minuscule notes but am interrupted when I hear a knock on my door. I look up into those gorgeous familiar green eyes that belong to Auston.

"Hey, Mr. Scott." I smile up at him and he walks in with ease, shutting the door behind him.

"Hey, beautiful. I was wondering, would you like to go to dinner with me tonight?" He leans back on the desks in front of me and runs his hand through his disheveled hair.

"Hmm... let me check my agenda." I wink at him and he lets out a charming smile. I flip through my agenda aimlessly and tap my pencil on my lip. "I think I'm free for the evening." I draw out. He lets out an easy going laugh and quickly leans over and kisses me.

"Perfect, I'll pick you up at five." He looks down at my notebook on my desk and tilts his head to the side.

"It's my writing book. I've always wanted to be a writer, but struggle to actually get anything done." I shrug.

"Hmm..." He pauses, "maybe we can find some inspiration for you that would make it easier to write?" He has a glimmer in his eyes and I laugh.

"What makes you think I want to write a romance novel, Mr. Scott?" I lean back in my chair and his eyes go down to my legs.

"I mean, you have the perfect muse right in front of you." He stretches his hands out to show himself off and I laugh.

"You're not wrong there..." I smile, stand up, and round my desk towards him. He smiles a dazzling smile and I swoon.

Literally, he's too handsome for his own good. His pink shirt contrasts against his tanned skin and makes his eyes look even brighter.

His shirt matches the lingerie set I got over the weekend. I draw my head back and look up at him, and he smirks.

"You like my shirt? It reminds me of a certain someone. She's unbelievably sexy, even though she won't admit it herself." He grabs my wrist and brings me towards him.

"I…" I swear this guy is going to swoon me to death, "I love it Auston." His eyes light up with content and he wraps his arms around me. The bell to announce lunch rings and we pull apart from one another.

"I thought you said we needed to be careful; it hasn't even been three days and you are already breaking your own rules…twice now." I shove him gently.

"Well Victoria, some rules are just meant to be broken." He leans forward and kisses me passionately. "I'll see you tonight, gorgeous." He walks out, and my eyes follow him the entire time.

"You are totally fucked, Victoria." I mutter to myself, and grab my lunch from beneath my desk.

CHAPTER THIRTEEN

I stare at my reflection in the mirror and run my brush through my long, dark curls. I decided to style my hair into loose curls for my dinner with Auston. I put my brush down and reapply my Russian Red lipstick from Mac, pairing it with my black ribbed mock dress and black thigh high stiletto boots. Most mock dresses hit right above the knee, but on my curvaceous body, it hits mid-thigh. I step back to look at my reflection and can't believe the woman who stares back at me.

She looks happy... confident, even.

I try to push away the anxiety that creeps its way into my brain. I haven't been on a date in over five years. I twist the ring on my left hand nervously just as the bell rings. I glance down at my watch and notice it's already five o'clock. I rush to grab my clutch and keys from the front ottoman, and swing the door open.

Auston stands there in grey plaid trousers, a black button down tucked in with a few buttons undone at the top, and black Chelsea boots. I make my way up his body with my eyes and notice how his arms stretch out the fabric, perfectly showing off his immaculate physique. I look up to find him wetting his lips.

"You look stunning." He leans in to kiss me. "You take my breath away. I remember when I told you to stop dressing the way you did in the hallway when I first got to the school..." I roll my eyes and shove him backwards to lock the door behind me.

"Yeah, I remember. You really pissed me off that day." I jiggle the knob one more time to make sure it's locked before turning to face him.

"I told you that because I couldn't stand walking around with an erection every time I saw you. Do you know how hard it is to walk around a school full of teenagers with a hard-on?" He questions in all seriousness.

I didn't know I had this effect on him. I mean, he said it so rudely that I just thought he was making a jab at my body.

"Well, you sure made it seem the opposite." I grumble while walking towards his car. I cautiously walk over to the passenger door and just when I'm about to reach for the handle, I'm spun around abruptly.

I gasp in surprise at Auston's proximity.

"Not once did I doubt how fucking beautiful you are. You make me feel like a God damn teenager when I'm around you, who can't control his fucking dick," he says in my face with a growl. I smile devilishly at him and grab his collar, bringing his lips to mine. I stroke his tongue and his bulge is evidently growing on my leg.

"We haven't even made it to dinner..." I say breathlessly. "In case you're wondering, you make me feel like a teenager too." I wink, open my door, and plant my ass on the luxurious leather seats. He groans out loud and shuts the door for me, jogging around the front of it and sliding into the driver's seat.

"You make me out of control, which I'm not used to." He looks at me from the corner of his eye and puts the car in reverse, his arm laying across my seat as he pulls out of the driveway.

"Well get used to it." I smile a toothy grin and watch the snowy scenery pass us by. Auston is messing around with the stereo when I hear a familiar drumline.

"Oh my God," I look over at Auston and his lip is twitching, trying to refrain from laughing. Hot for Teacher by Van Halen starts playing through the speakers, and I can't help but burst out laughing. This was one of my favorite songs as a teenager. I mean, it's about fantasizing about a teacher; can't say I never did it.

"Got it bad, got it bad, got it bad, I'm hot for teacher." Auston says along with the song while squeezing my leg, and I laugh harder. This song is so well-suited, especially since it seems Auston has it hot for me.

I bite my lip to keep from smiling like a fool as he sings the lyrics, his gaze bouncing between myself and the road. The more time I spend with him the more he begins to open up and uncover this playful version of himself. I have a thing for eighties rock since it was what my dad and I used to listen to in the garage. The fact that every time I have been with Auston he plays eighties music resonates with me.

"So, you have it bad for a teacher, hmm?" I raise an eyebrow at him. His eyes are on the road as I take him in. His one arm has control of the wheel, while the other rests possessively on my thigh. The material of his shirt seems to strain against the pull of his movements, but it's his face that makes me melt into a puddle. His scruffed jawline is prominent from the side and his lips are begging to be kissed.

"You have no idea…" He squeezes the hand resting on my thigh and I bite my lip to keep from letting out a girly squeal. He continues to sing the song and sends me devilish looks whenever the lyrics state an underlying message. I sing along with him and he squeezes my leg when the song's lyric says, "I think of all the education that I missed, but then my homework was never quite like this." He sends a wink my way and moves his hand up my thigh only to bring it back down with a teasing smile. I groan and relax my head while I watch Auston drive us to our unknown destination. Thirty minutes later, he unbuttons his sleeves and rolls them up to drive more comfortably, and I stare at his forearms. These veiny arms may just be the death of me. As if my hormones weren't already jacked up just from sitting here, he has to go and roll up his sleeves. There is something about rolled up sleeves and pulsating veins that hits me right in the core and makes me want to jump across the console.

"So, where are we going? It's almost been an hour now." I turn my body to face him and see him rubbing behind his neck.

"Well, considering you look beautiful, I needed to take you somewhere beautiful. We are going to Langford Hall." I widen my eyes. Langford Hall is crazy expensive, it's one of those lavish places you only go once in a while because it costs over three hundred dollars for two people. The girls and I went there for Emma's twenty-fifth birthday and when we saw the bill, we almost cried. Three girls right out of teacher's college forking out two hundred dollars each was striking. I ended up paying for the three of us because I had gotten money from my parents when the accident happened and decided we deserved it for finishing undergrad and teacher's college. I never thought twice about it because I know my parents would have done more for us; Emma and Hannah were family. They always told them so.

Auston turns and drives up towards the large hall that

looks more like a mansion. It's a giant old house made of brick, with four large, white pillars framing the entrance, and other white contrast pieces spread throughout the building. It looks like a house straight out of a historical romance book. My heart flutter; I can pretend to be a modern duchess tonight. Auston smoothly navigates the car around the u-shaped driveway to the entrance and the building up close is mesmerising. The sun is setting in front of the building, its reflection on the windows giving off a glow. Auston comes to a stop a couple metres away from the entrance and quickly exits, rounding the car to my side. He walks around and opens the door for me, grabbing my hand to help me out.

"Thank you." I smile up at him as he pockets his keys and takes my hand. He guides us into the restaurant and shakes hands with the hostess.

"Mr. Scott, it's good to see you. It has been a while since you have visited us. Who is the beautiful woman on your arm?" The host reaches out to shake my hand and I blush, extending my hand to meet his.

"Jerry, meet Victoria." Auston introduces us and I smile. He walks us to our table as he raves positively about Auston.

"Please enjoy yourselves here at Langford Hall and don't take so long to come back, Mr. Scott." He gives Auston a pointed look and Auston laughs at him and promises.

"Wow, it seems you're pretty well-acquainted here." I smile at him as the chandelier twinkles in his eyes. He resembles a real-life prince out of a romance right now with the ambiance and low, twinkling lights. This couldn't be more perfect.

"I used to come here a lot with my family when I lived in Toronto." He grabs my hand and plays with my fingers. "We used to make it here once every few months, as a family tradition."

"Why did you move from the city if your family is still there?" I notice his features change immediately; something shifts in the air. His shoulders hunch, his jaw tightens, and his eyes darken intensely. He recovers quickly, though. If I had blinked, I may have never noticed the change in demeanour.

"I needed a change of scenery from Toronto. I've lived there all my life, and sometimes the setting and people can become too much to handle." That answer sounds rehearsed, like he has said it many times before. I try to ignore the tightness in my stomach, probably overreacting to his reply. I'm sure the city can get chaotic. There is a reason the girls and I only visit to shop once every couple of months. The people can be rude and impatient. It's a lot to handle, coming from a small town.

"I get that. Whenever I visit the city with the girls, I get this awful feeling because the people are so different than in Simcoe. It's as if I'm in an alternate universe." I laugh lightly, trying to lighten the mood from his initial reaction.

"Yeah, my family adores the city life, but it became too much for me recently. I needed a change in my life and when the board opened up a position in Simcoe, I knew I had to apply. Luckily, since I have five years as a principal under my belt, I was called immediately," he states, relief evident in his voice.

"I mean, they would've really messed up by not hiring a GQ model to work around a bunch of horny teenagers." I purse my lips to keep from laughing and he rolls his eyes.

"That's precisely why I'm as strict as I'm. I don't want the students to view me as their friend, I would much rather they hate me." I'm surprised by his admission. At one point he must have been a teacher, and his reaction to students is surprising. Maybe something happened in the past that has him distrustful towards students? Or maybe that's what makes him such a good principal; he's able to differentiate between business and pleasure. To me, being a good teacher is about being able to connect with students on a level where they understand that you're still their superior, but also a friend, to an extent.

Our server comes over at that moment with a bottle of wine, and completely distracts us from our conversation about work.

Two hours later, we are back in Auston's car driving home. After I *accidently* saw the bill, I told him I would pay half because I had never seen a bill so high for two people.

"Auston, I still can't believe you paid that much for dinner." I turn my head, pouting my lips. "It doesn't sit right knowing you paid that much."

"When I take a woman on a date, I pay. I could have spent three thousand dollars and it would still be worth it because you sat across the table from me." He brings my hand to his lips and kisses it softly.

I sigh, "You're such a smooth talker."

"It worked though, right?" He says smugly and I roll my eyes in a huff. A smile crossed my face because I can't help it. I've never met a man as confident, charming, and likable as Auston. He has two different sides to him that I don't think he allows for many to see. At dinner I learned that he is thirty-six, which makes him seven years my senior. I got a sick satisfaction knowing that he is older than me, and he saw it in my eyes that I liked it a little too much. For thirty-six he looks amazing, and I still have no idea how he is single.

"How are you still single?" I ask abruptly without think-ing. My curiosity getting the better of me due to the slight buzz I'm feeling from the wine at dinner. My cheeks heat in embarrassment. I put my hands over my eyes and peek over at him through the small gap, and he laughs at my embarrassment. Bringing up the topic of exes can be like opening up a can of worms, but I want to know everything about Auston, even his slew of past women.

"I met this woman named Shantel while in my first year of University, while at a house party. We hit it off right from the start. Whether it was the alcohol at hand, I don't know." he laughs lightly. "At first it was casual, just spending time together..." He pauses, clearly indicating spending time together is sex. "Fast-forward, we became official, graduated, and I felt the pressure to propose to her, so I did on graduation night." His grip tightens on the steering wheel and I have a feeling this story is about to take a turn.

"We were in the midst of planning our wedding when I had to go to a teaching conference downtown. I had planned on staying downtown to meet up with Axel and Garrett, but they both had to cancel on me. I decided rather than spending money on a hotel when I had lived twenty minutes from downtown, I'd just go home. I got home to find her being fucked on our kitchen counter by some guy." His eyes fill with anger. "Since then, Axel, Garrett, and I have just stayed single and messed around. I never dated anyone long enough to consider them my girlfriend. I had a hard time trusting a woman after what happened with Shantel." He shrugs his shoulders and I'm sad for him. I was never cheated on because I never gave a man the opportunity to get that close, but I can imagine how crushing it would feel. I don't know if I would ever be able to deal with that, especially knowing how I blame things on myself even when they are out of my control.

"I'm sorry..." I grab onto his hand and bring it under my chin, "I mean, mostly for Shantel, because she's seriously missing out on one sexy principal..." I smile playfully, and he laughs. I try not to let the creep of jealousy come into mind, thinking about what he was doing for the last ten years or so with other women.

"I'm glad you feel sorry for her," he rolls his eyes playfully. "How about you Ms. Mateus, why is a woman as gorgeous as you still single?"

I scrunch my lips together. I hate this question because all of my insecurities wind up at the front of my head, the largest being that I'm scared to care for someone and have them be ripped from my life like my parents were.

"It's always been easier to hold back on love than to have to worry about losing love at any moment." I mumble quietly.

"But isn't it better to take the chance and experience a love like your parents than to worry about being alone forever?" Auston questions and I nod.

I know what he's saying is right, but the fear of abandonment outweighs the fact that I could truly be happy, even with my parents buried six feet in the ground. The only two people I have truly let into my life are Emma and Hannah, yet somehow Auston is slowly becoming the third person.

"I understand that you're probably scared. I can't say that I understand fully because I have never lost either of my parents, but don't you want to have your own family someday? One that you love and care for like your parents did?" He squeezes my hand. There are too many emotions all of a sudden and I feel like a rock has settled in my stomach. I have always wanted all of those things, but at what cost?

We drive in silence for the rest of the ride home. Auston figured out one of my biggest fears after only knowing me for a few weeks, and I have no idea how it sits with him because we have both been quiet. Auston pulls up the driveway to my house, parks the car, and turns it off.

"I'm sorry. Maybe I shouldn't have said anything, but I don't think you should hold back, Vic. You deserve all the happiness that life brings you." He turns my way and grabs onto both of my hands. "Listen, I haven't had these kinds of feelings in years. It's hard for me to even gather my own thoughts after being alone for so long, but I want to take you to Toronto this weekend. I want to show you around where I grew up, and maybe meet my parents?" I think this is the first time I have ever seen Auston flustered. A smidge of hope gathers in my heart and I sit on a scale, trying to decide if I should take the jump with Auston or not. He looks up, a little worried since I haven't given him an answer yet, and I smile.

"Yes, I'd love that..." I lean forward and bring my lips to his. My core awakens as Auston brings his hands up to my face to deepen our kiss. Our tongues entwine with one another and I moan loudly into the quiet car.

I push myself away from Auston and bite my lip, "I think we should call it a night, Mr. Scott. It's a school night after all..." I grab my clutch and open the door, stepping out. I know I have already given my body to Auston, but I feel we have moved forward in our relationship. I have no idea if we're actually in a relationship, but I would rather us figure that out with our clothes on. Despite my body fighting with my brain, I need to make sure I'm not going to be hurt.

"Tease..." Auston mutters as he follows me to my door. I turn around at my door after unlocking it.

"Thank you for dinner, this was a first for me." I smile up at him, cheekily.

"What do you mean, a first?" He leans his arm over my head against my door while looking down at me.

"I've never had dinner with a GQ model, it was a first and hopefully not a last." I smile, with my tongue between my teeth.

"Oh my God..." He mutters as he brings his lips to mine.

"You're something else. Will I ever live down the GQ thing?" He bites my bottom lip harshly and I gasp.

"I don't think so. I mean, it suits you well…wouldn't you agree?" I run my hand down his body and he groans out loud while leaning his head on mine. "Goodnight Mr. Scott. I will see you bright and early at work tomorrow." I peck him on the lips and rush myself inside. I hear him groan a second time before his footsteps retreat to his car.

The lights to his car illuminate the front door and slowly his car rolls down the driveway, onto the road, and zips off.

I lock the door and lean back against it; maybe I can take this step. It's exactly what my parents would want for me. They would have lost it on me if they were here, knowing I have never put myself out there.

I hear my mother's voice in my head telling me that some risks in life are worth taking, and this is one of those risks. I walk over to one of their photos on the wall and kiss it, wishing they were here to guide me through this fear. Although, I guess if they were here, this fear probably wouldn't exist.

CHAPTER FOURTEEN

My date with Auston feels as if it was forever ago due to the quick pace of the week. It's Thursday evening and I'm cooking bifana sandwiches for the girls and I for dinner. This week has been busy for all of us because of work and we haven't really gotten to talk much, so we planned a dinner at my place. I stir the onions, peppers, white wine, paprika, and pork cutlets together in the pan and let the delicious aroma fill the air.

My mom and I used to make bifanas all the time as a kid. It was our go-to Sunday lunch, traditional Portuguese sandwiches with a side salad. I haven't gotten a chance to make them in months, so I drove to a Portuguese bakery yesterday to get natas—Portuguese custard tarts—to have with our coffees later. Luckily for me Emma and Hannah aren't picky eaters and love the Portuguese dishes I make. My mom was very traditional with the meals we ate, so I got to learn a lot of Portuguese dishes before she passed. She kept a little drawer with all her recipes and to this day they sit in the same drawer as when I was a kid.

I hear a knock at the door and Emma shouts that she's

here with Hannah and wine. I wipe my hands quickly on the cloth hanging on the oven and make my way to the door.

"Hi babes!" I give them both hugs as soon as they take off their shoes.

"Why does it feel like we haven't talked in forever? This week has been disastrously long and it's only Thursday!" Hannah whines. We make our way to the kitchen and they sit at the island. They don't bother trying to help me cook because after years of friendship, they know I cook alone. I don't need other people around me trying to get in my way... it's the European in me.

"I know. I feel like I have just been going to work, coming home, eating, and sleeping. Then doing it all over again the next day." I exaggerate with the wooden spoon in my hand, moving along with my gestures.

"Woman, put that damn spoon down. You are giving me PTSD." Emma grimaces and I laugh. Most European households use this damn spoon to smack a child into shape. Hannah never understood why Emma flinched so much every time I would flap around this spoon, but then we had to explain to her that our parents would hit us with it when we misbehaved.

These spoons hurt if they hit bare skin. My mom chased after me with one when I was seven because I made her break her favorite wooden spoon from Portugal; it was horrifying. I ran directly under her bed because I knew there was no way she would get me under there. I hid under the bed for an hour waiting for my dad to come home from work, and then sneaked to hide behind him when he walked through the front door. Once I made it behind him I revealed what happened with mom, the fear evident in my voice. He laughed and told me not to worry, then proceeded to walk into the kitchen. My mom's eyes lit up with love, and her whole persona changed. As if she hadn't been just screaming at me an hour prior.

"You guys should talk to someone about your spoon trauma." Hannah laughs, and I join in. Emma sends us both dirty looks, definitely having gotten the spoon more than I did.

"You guys suck… is that bifana's I smell?" Emma walks over to the stove and picks up the lid, and does a little jig of excitement. "These are the best! Last month when my period was here, I was craving one of these. I almost drove to my parents house to ask them to make me one." She grabs a spoon from the drawer to the left and dips it in, getting some of the juice before sliding it into her mouth. She moans and holds another one out for Hannah to try. She proceeds to moan in approval as well.

"You guys are too much. That's just the sauce, not even the whole sandwich. Also, why didn't you tell me you were craving them? You know I would have made them for you. God knows how many times you've come here with chocolate cake during my period." I laugh and walk over to my record player to put on some music.

"I know, I know. I think it was one of those periods where I was angry for no reason, so I didn't want to bother you guys." She shrugs while grabbing plates from the cabinet and setting them at the large oak dining table.

"Oh yeah, I think I remember this! I texted you asking if you wanted to go to the movies and you told me to fuck off." Hannah exclaims while pointing at her and she nods back, laughing.

"I love you guys." I stand in the middle of the kitchen, a sudden burst of emotion of love towards these two wild women who I have been friends with for over fifteen years. These two have become my only family, considering almost everyone else still lives in Portugal. It was hard to cope with being alone after my parents passed, but Emma and Hannah moved in for a couple months after we finished teacher's college. They didn't want me alone in the house I grew up in, so we lived together for six months until I decided they needed to find their own places. We were just getting started with our own lives and I didn't want to hold them back, so I forced them out and assured them I would be fine. Over the years, I have worked on renovating the house to make it my own. It doesn't even look like my childhood home anymore, but the love of the family that once was still flourishes between these walls.

"And we love you too, but feed us now." Emma winks at me while she finishes setting the table. Hannah grabs wine glasses from the shelf and pours each of us a healthy amount of wine.

"So, how is it going with Mr. GQ?" Emma asks while I plate our food, bringing it to the table. We all take our seats, both of them staring at me, and I giggle.

"You two are vultures, but it's going well. Our date on Monday was beautiful; however, we talked about some deep things, which I didn't think I could talk more of." I take a bite of my bifana and moan. The various flavours bursting along my tastebuds.

"I mean, you told him about your parents after only knowing him for a few weeks. I'd say you are feeling pretty comfortable around him." Emma shrugs and I shrug back. I am comfortable around Auston, but the way he thinks of students still sits oddly with me.

"I mean, yeah. I absolutely feel comfortable around him. I don't understand how I do in such a short period of time, but he gets me. Like, really gets me." I sigh happily, "I actually found out that he was engaged once, after he completed his undergrad."

"What?" Hannah gasps.

"What kind of woman would leave that man? Was she blind? Crazy?" Emma exclaims loudly, and I shake my head, just as confused as them.

"I have no idea, but he caught her having sex on the kitchen counter while he was supposed to be away for a teacher's conference."

"Jeez, well, I'm sure she regrets that now. He seems pretty successful and put together. I mean, half the guys in this town don't know how to dress in anything other than camouflage." Emma grunts and I laugh.

"God, that will never change, will it? Every guy in town looks like they are getting ready for a deer to jump in front of them, just waiting for the chance to shoot it." I laugh while Emma acts surprised and mimics shooting at something out the window, pretending to see a deer.

We all laugh. "I know, it's definitely something we aren't used to, but totally welcome." I wiggle my brows and Emma grunts.

"Says you. You actually get to welcome that man into your bed. We have to live vicariously through you." Emma rolls her eyes and I laugh.

"Hey, I'm just as surprised as you guys. I never thought these thighs or hips would attract a man like that. I was lucky to have a guy in full camo look at me." Hannah throws her wadded-up napkin at me.

"Don't say that. Any man would be lucky to have your sexy, curvy body. So, what if you have a little stomach? I know a lot of these thoughts stem from high school, but you need to start seeing yourself the way we do." Hannah grabs my hand and squeezes.

"You're beautiful and smart, babe. You're a little more-curvy than some, but your fucking personality outshines all the others." Emma smiles while grabbing my other hand.

"Okay enough, you guys are making me emotional." I stand and shake my head, grabbing their plates to put in the dishwasher. "Auston said something similar on Monday that had me feeling all mushy inside." I turn to face them and Hannah is making a 'tell me more' motion with her hands, so I continue.

"He pretty much said that I deserve happiness. He isn't used to the feelings he has for me... and," I pause for suspense. "He's taking me to the city this weekend to meet his parents." I cover my face and look at them through the gaps in my fingers. Emma starts freaking out and Hannah looks genuinely surprised.

"This man is really growing on me. I mean he is right, if there is anyone that deserves happiness, it's you babe." Emma smiles, bringing over the wine glasses, and Hannah agrees. I rinse off the dishes and put them into the dishwasher.

My brain is telling me that I deserve happiness for the first time in my life, but my heart wants me to put a wall up for fear of anyone who tries to get close. Hannah excuses herself to the washroom and Emma and I finish cleaning up the kitchen before I grab our delicious desserts from their styrofoam container on the counter.

I finish making three cappuccinos and take out the desserts, putting them on a plate. I mention to the girls that we could have dessert on the porch bed.

The weather is slowly getting better, but it's been a bit unpredictable the last couple of weeks. Tonight it's only plus five, so I grab the heated blanket and the girls grab the mugs and goodies.

"I'm so excited that you got natas." Hannah exclaims

with her English pronunciation. Emma and I laugh because we're used to using accents to pronounce our foods.

We all sit down, and I open up the blanket and turn it on. "God, I think this swing is the best thing you installed in your house during renovations." Hannah says while snuggling into the blanket and sipping her drink.

"I agree, it's so peaceful. Town is only minutes away but from here it seems miles away." Emma nods while leaning her head back onto the pillows that line the sides.

"I'm telling you guys, Pinterest was my third best friend while renovating. I would never have thought about putting something like this here. I always assumed I would put in an iron table set to sit and enjoy my coffee, but this is much better." I laugh and look out into the country. A large piece of farmland sits across the street from me, so the scenery is always beautiful; it's the best during sunsets.

The girls and I sit in comfortable silence for a couple of minutes before I remember my favorite part from my date with Auston.

"I forgot to mention my favorite part of my date with Auston. When we were driving in the car, he played *Hot for Teacher*..." Hannah bursts out laughing, and Emma's eyes light up.

"So, you're telling me that Mr. Scott serenaded you by playing a song about how he's hot for a teacher and knows he shouldn't be?" Emma wiggles her eyebrows and I laugh.

"That's exactly what he did. Not only was the song a perfect choice, but it's from the eighties. You know how much it means to me when I meet someone who can listen to eighties music without thinking it's trash. It was just something else, it made me so giddy." I hum the tune, appreciating the memory of Auston's playfulness.

"You are so smitten." Hannah nudges my leg with hers

and I scrunch up my nose. I have only known Auston a short period of time. I remind myself that we are going to the city this weekend and I will get to learn so much about him then. Anxiety gnaws at my stomach, but it's probably the jitters of getting to see where he grew up and meeting his parents.

The girls and I continue our conversation until ten when the sky had become dark with twinkling lights. We realize we all have to work the next day and should probably call it a night.

"See you tomorrow my loves," I shout as they both get into their cars and drive off. I walk inside, locking the door behind me, and set the alarm.

Walking into the kitchen I load up the washing machine with our mugs and plates and anything else from dinner before turning it on. I quickly shuffle out of the kitchen after closing all the blinds on the big windows and decide to take a bath. I pour bubble bath and bath salts into the tub and hear my phone vibrate from the charger on the nightstand.

I unplug it and bring it with me into the bathroom. I strip down and slowly lower myself into the bubbles before grabbing my phone to see who texted me. My heart does a flip when I see Auston's name pop up.

Auston: What are you wearing right now?

I let out a laugh reading that message. Seems as though someone is frisky tonight. Maybe I can take advantage of the situation.

Me: Nothing.

I take a quick photo of my bottom half covered in bubbles, but my legs sticking out looking slick. I attach it to my message and click send. I can't help the nerves that pop up when I send photos, but seeing Auston's genuine reactions to my body gives me a sense of confidence I didn't know I had. I set my head back on the bath pillow and hear my phone sound again.

> **Auston: I'm imagining all the things I could do to you in that tub...**

> **Me: Hmm, too bad you're not here. Maybe this weekend you can put those thoughts to action, Mr. Scott.**

> **Auston: Oh, I will. Get some rest, beautiful. See you tomorrow.**

I smile at his text and a zap of arousal goes to my core as I think about this weekend. I was never much of a sex fiend, I really didn't put myself out there to learn more about myself sexually. But with Auston? My inner sex goddess has awakened, and she wants all that Auston can give her.

I realize I need to get to bed before I text Auston to get his ass over here to satisfy me. I drain the tub and grab my towel to dry off. I put on my large flannel shirt and hop into bed with a big smile on my face.

CHAPTER FIFTEEN

I set my duffle bag on the ottoman beside the door and try to tamper down the nerves I'm feeling about tonight. Work went by extremely slowly, of course, since I was looking forward to spending my next two nights in the city with Auston. It's just after four thirty p.m. when I see Auston's silhouette coming to knock on the door. I rush away from the door, so it doesn't look as if I was just standing there eagerly awaiting his arrival. I hear his knock and wait a few seconds before opening the door.

"Hey, beautiful." He leans in to give me an innocent kiss and I bite my bottom lip; the guy really knows how to kiss.

"Hi." I blush. "I'm just going to confirm that everything is off, give me one minute." I rush throughout the house and make sure everything is unplugged and off...for the third time. House paranoia is definitely a thing when leaving for a few nights. I nod at him to let him know we're good and grab my purse. Auston has already grabbed my duffle bag and is waiting at the door for me. I set the alarm, make my way out locking the door behind me.

"All set?" He puts my bag in the trunk and opens the door

for me as I nod, sliding into the comfortable seats. I bite my lip anxiously as Auston tells me we will be heading straight to his parents' for dinner, then to his condo downtown.

"I never asked," the fear of the possibility of us staying with his parents worried me, "Where are we staying while in Toronto?"

"I have a condo in the heart of the city that we're going to stay at. I never sold it because as much as I love my family, while I'm visiting I like to stay in my own space. And I still go see Axel and Garrett as much as I can because I don't have any friends here." He admits sheepishly while playing around with the radio. I'm surprised to find out he still keeps a place in Toronto. It makes sense though, I can't imagine moving somewhere and leaving Hannah and Emma behind. I don't think I'd be able to do it.

After a two-hour drive to get to the city, my nerves have reached a new height, and I'm blowing out a bunch of short breaths in an attempt to gain control of myself. I've never met a guy's parents before, so to say that my anxiety could make me vomit in Auston's luxurious car doesn't seem far off.

"Victoria, are you okay?" I look up at him and his eyebrows are furrowed. I wipe my hands down on my jeans and give a slight shake of my head.

"I've never met a boyfriend's parents." I stop. "I mean, is that what we are? Oh my God." I shoot my head forward in shock, too many thoughts passing through my mind at the speed of light. I'm making myself lightheaded with all the thoughts going through my head.

My right leg begins to bounce as I try to gain control of my emotions and what's happening around me.

What if they don't like me?

What if they compare me to his ex?

The car stops and I notice that we've stopped in a beautiful suburban area with big, luxurious houses. My eyes span the road... I've never seen such beautiful homes. All of them are tall, big, and look like they belong in Beverly Hills.

I hear Auston get out of the car and I just sit here, trying to control my breathing. I try to focus on the beauty of the area to calm myself down.

The door beside me opens and Auston removes my seatbelt and turns me so that he is kneeling between my legs.

"Let's tackle this one issue at a time. First, if that was your way of asking me to be your boyfriend, you could have done it without so much panic." He smiles and I let out a mixture of a huff and a laugh. "I figured that's where we were, but I'm not the biggest fan of labels, so I never really asked. But I should have thought about it from your point of view, so I apologize." He grabs my hands and I squeeze them.

"I should be the one apologizing, I don't know why I need the label. I guess it's because I'm waiting to wake up from this wonderful dream that we're in. I struggle with loss, so I'm trying hard not to get attached..." I frown at my lap. My chest feels like barbed wires are tightening. Struggling to face one of my largest insecurities head-on with Auston.

"Babe, I get it." He pinches me on the thigh, and I yelp, "However, this isn't a dream, so you can get that out of your head immediately." He brings his hand up to my face and runs his thumb along my lips. "Secondly, my parents are genuine people. You have nothing to worry about with them. They are affectionate, sometimes too much..." I smile. I notice that the tightness and sweating have begun to fade away.

"Thank you, Auston. I'm still in shock that you're real." I grab a hold of his face and bring our mouths together. I'm doing it as a thank you, but also to make sure he really is real.

My doubt tries to creep in at the worst moments, but I want to believe that what's happening between Auston and I is real and not fleeting.

"God, maybe I should just take you back to my condo. My parents could wait…" He bites my lip and I groan, almost agreeing. Why is it so sexy to bite on someone's lip and pull? The notion seemed hot in my romance movies, but nothing will compare to the tingles that jive down my body.

"No, no. You just helped calm me down, there's no way I want to go through this a second time. Come get back in the car and drive to your parents. It's already seven in the evening and I don't want to keep them waiting." He groans his disapproval and stands up, giving me a quick peck before getting back into the driver's seat.

"How far are we from your parents' house?" I ask as he puts the car back in drive.

"About three minutes." I make a weird face because we are currently driving by more very large, *very luxurious*, houses. I stare in awe out the window, my nose practically pressed against the windows, and I utter a "wow" as I stare at these gorgeous houses.

One of them even has a gold unicorn statue in front.

Oh my God…

Auston turns into the driveway of a large beautiful home and my eyes widen.

"Fuck off…" I look at him, my mouth agape, and he covers up his laugh with a cough. He clicks the garage opener that he keeps on his visor, and I hit him so hard to keep from screaming.

"What the fuck, Auston! The garage is underneath the house. How is this even possible? Oh my God, I'm not ready for this. Is my outfit okay? My hair? Why didn't you tell me to dress better?" I fan my face and he doesn't stop laughing, which only stresses me out more.

This looks like the house I would scroll through on Pinterest that's owned by some flashy millionaire...This can't be real.

"Babe, you look gorgeous. Absolutely fucking edible." He growls and I roll my eyes, then lean over and kiss him. I look down at my outfit and I hope it's appropriate. I'm wearing heeled black booties, black jeans, and a black T-shirt tucked in with my brown overcoat. I didn't change after finishing work because I thought this was classy and modern. But looking at this house? I wish we would have stopped at the fashion outlets on the way and I could have picked up a dress good enough for this breathtaking home.

I huff at him, remove my seatbelt, and get out of the car to stretch. I grab my jacket from behind the seat and throw it casually over my shoulders and he smirks.

"Cold?" A sly smile touches his lips, grabbing my hand and kissing it.

"Oh, be quiet. This jacket makes my outfit marginally classier, let me be. You've given me enough stress today for a heart attack." I shove him away, but he brings me back and holds me. He tilts me backwards and I let out a yelp before he kisses me passionately. I swoon while my pussy clenches.

He puts me right-side up and motions for me to follow.

"Swoon-worthy kiss there, Mr. Scott..." He winks at me and we make our way out of the garage to the front of the house. The house is made of mixed brown brick and deep brown accents along the windows, and a decorative windowed door. This house screams picture-postcard worthy; the neighbourhood is probably worth millions. There is a large arch over the door and a large window above it, showing off a beautiful chandelier hanging ornately in the entrance of the home.

Auston casually walks us up towards the door and knocks. I hear some commotion inside when the beautiful solid doors swing open with gust, and a beautiful woman appears in the doorway.

"Auston! It's so good to see you. Come in, come in." She gestures us inside as she opens the door wider. I follow shyly behind Auston as we enter his parents' home. My eyes catch on the chandelier I saw from outside, and I gape. Until my gaze reaches the rest of the home. It's comforting, not at all as misleading as the outside. It's decorated with neutral hues and gives off a calming essence.

"Son, welcome home." I widen my eyes at an older gentleman who looks exactly like Auston. If this is what Auston grows up to look like, I wouldn't be mad. His parents are absolutely stunning. His dad's hair has turned silver, but his green eyes, like Auston, shine brightly against his complexion. Compared to his mom who has caramel blonde hair and brown eyes, and stands about a foot shorter than his dad.

"Mom, Dad, this is Victoria." I smile shyly at them and grant them both hellos. His mom gushes while she brings me in for an embrace, saying how happy she is to meet me. Apparently Auston doesn't bring women home often, especially after the witch who broke his heart. His mom's words, not mine.

"It's really nice to meet you too, Mrs. Scott." That feels so weird to say, especially if I have to say it to Auston's dad. I try to hold my smirk at the thought.

"Please, call us Amara and Hudson." She smiles warmly and I nod my head.

We quickly shed our jackets and shoes, walking further

into the house. I gaze around, catching pictures scattered around their home. There are random photos with Auston, their family, and even some with friends. Their smiles are infectious as I glance around the room and notice their actual faces are the exact same as they laugh around the kitchen island. I didn't even notice they moved there, having been too preoccupied staring at their family photos.

Auston waves me over and I walk into his arms, his mother's eyes twinkling as she takes us in.

A few hours have gone by, eating dinner and enjoying a few glasses of wine together on their deck in the backyard. Auston's parents are genuine. Although their home appears rich with materials from the outside, the inside is filled with love.

I'm currently standing at their gorgeous marble island, putting dishes from dinner in the dishwasher when Amara walks in,

"Victoria, please don't worry about the dishes." She goes to take the plate away from me, but I quickly put it on the rack.

"It's no problem, Amara. I wouldn't feel right leaving these dishes here." I grab a small pod from the jar on the counter and plop it into the dishwasher. Shutting the dishwasher, I click the start button. I grab my wine glass and quickly wash it while leaning my hip on the counter.

"Oh, that's very sweet of you. Your parents raised you right." She pats my hand and a small pang hits my chest.

That they definitely did.

"Thank you." I smile.

"Tell me about yourself Victoria, I would like to get to know the woman who's spending so much time with my son." I smile, not really knowing what to say about myself. I hate when people ask me this question. Do I be honest?

Or should I lie and make myself seem like this perfect woman?

I try to go with the safest reply, "What would you like to know?"

"We can start off easy," she winks. "Did you grow up in Simcoe? That's where you teach, right?" I smile at the simplicity of this question; my anxiety always makes me worry about the questions people will ask me. The questions can either be simple and answered with ease... or difficult, making my throat close up.

"Yes, I teach at the same high school where Auston works. I grew up there as well; I didn't think I would stay there, but life seemed to have different plans." I laugh lightly. I look up at her as she clears the shock that was registered on her face and replaces it with a small smile. Maybe Auston hadn't told her we work together? *Oops.*

"Do your parents still live there?" *Fuck.* My throat begins to close up, but I try to feign a cough to cover up my discomfort. I dry my wine glass quickly, without shattering it, and set it on the counter. I bite my lip because I hate saying these words aloud.

"Uhm," I look up, "My parents actually passed away eight years ago in a car accident." I give her a small smile. It's so awkward discussing this because nobody understands how to handle death or grief. Although it's part of life, it's just a topic that's never easy to talk about.

"Oh, Victoria, I'm so sorry. I shouldn't have asked." She slowly walks over to me and gives me an attentive hug, and I squeeze my eyes shut.

"It's okay, you didn't know." I whisper.

Auston chooses this moment to walk in and his brows furrow. Concern is etched across his face while he notices me in his mother's arms.

"Vic, ready to go?" Concern is still evident in his eyes and I nod, his mother letting me go.

"If you ever need anything, you can call me, okay sweetie?" Tears line my eyes as I mouth a thank you to her. Hudson walks inside from the deck and looks between the three of us, and Auston puts his hand on my lower back and leads us to the door. I take a deep breath and stare into the bright light, finding that it always helps to dry my eyes out quickly.

"Thank you for dinner, it was a pleasure meeting you guys." I slip on my booties and smile at them. Amara leans in to hug me and whispers, "My door is always open, even if Auston isn't around... we can have a girl's night." She gives me an extra squeeze and I thank her quietly with a giggle.

Auston grabs my hand and leads me down into the garage. We're both pretty quiet as we get into the car. He's probably wondering what happened between his mom and I, but wants to give me a moment to gather my thoughts.

"Your mom asked about my parents. I didn't really know how to explain it, so I just told her. You walked in right after I told her." I shrug and twist my hands in my lap. I never saw myself as the type of person who held a lot of baggage, but having another person in my life romantically shows me that I might be that person. I rest my head against the headrest and think about how much my life has changed since Auston came into it. I thought that I would have been by myself forever if I'm being honest. I never imagined the turn my life would take when the new principal arrived.

"I'm sorry, Vic. I wish I could've stopped her prying." He grabs my hand and sets it in the center console, rubbing his thumb back and forth. We're driving the inner city streets to the highway and it's so different from Simcoe. There is a vibrance in the air that I can't explain.

"She didn't pry, she just wanted to know a little more

about me. It's not her fault. I don't spend much time with people outside of Hannah and Emma, so I usually don't have to explain myself." I take a deep breath, "I haven't been with anyone in a long time and if I'm being honest... I never thought I would be again. I'm just trying to gather self-understanding towards how much you have changed my life in such a short time." I turn towards him. "Changed it for the better."

"You're so beautiful Victoria Mateus, I wish you saw yourself the way I did." He glances at me, the city lights twinkling in his eyes. "You are the complete catch." He winks and I smile.

I think I'm slowly allowing myself to believe him. I rest my head, still facing Auston, but catch the twinkling city before us as we drive on the highway heading towards the heart of Toronto.

"This is beautiful." I admire how all the skyscrapers take up the skyline of Toronto and how beautiful the CN Tower stands in the dead center of it all. "Wait, your condo is right downtown?"

"Yes. After everything that happened with Shantel, I purchased a place downtown. I rent it out sometimes when I know I won't be in the city for a while." I feel giddy; I've never stayed downtown Toronto before. I continue to stare at the city in awe. It's stunning at night. During the day it's nice, but at night the city twinkles and becomes mesmerizing. As we are driving on the highway, I notice something in a condo window.

"Oh my God, Auston!" I say breathlessly as my eyes widen in realization. "Those people are having sex against their window." I gasp and Auston moves forward over the steering wheel to look and smirks. A pang of arousal hits me, and I bite my lip. I've never done anything like that before, but can't stop wondering if Auston's condo has huge windows like that too.

Auston pulls off at the next ramp and I can't keep the dirty thoughts out of my head after seeing that couple take part in exhibitionism. My nipples harden as I imagine Auston holding me by the neck, my breasts pressed against the cool glass windows. I shiver and Auston looks over at me with desire hooded in his eyes,

"What are you thinking about, gorgeous?" His voice is deep, vibrating all the way to my toes. I bite my lip and press my thighs together.

"I'm thinking about you fucking me against the window of your condo..." I say shyly but hear his groan and acceleration on the gas. A thought comes to mind that's rather daring of me, but this weekend is about exploring myself, and our relationship. I slowly reach my hand across the console and run my hand up his thigh.

"I'm thinking about what it would feel like to have your hand wrapped around my neck," I pause. "And my nipples pressed against the cool glass of the window." I palm his hardening length through his pants. I squeeze his cock as we take a sharp turn into an underground garage and he throws the car into park with a growl.

"Let's bring that fantasy to life, babe." He opens his car door and rushes to the trunk to grab our duffle bags and slams it shut in a rush. My panties dampen as I get out of the car and close the door behind me. Auston guides me to the elevators with his hand just above my ass. The anticipation is killing me, I just want the relief of pressure on my clit. The steel elevator doors open and we walk in, mirrors all around us, making me take note of the flush that is clear on my cheeks. He drops our bags on the floor of the elevator and he looks at me like I'm his prey. His eyes are hooded and his hair is messy from running his fingers through it. I bite my lip as he stalks towards me and traces a single finger down my torso. We both shudder out a breath.

The elevator ride takes forever, but once we reach Auston's floor he smirks at me, takes a step back to grab our bags, and motions for me to follow him. We walk to the end of the hall and he enters his key to unlock the door, and gestures for me to walk in first. I take in the beauty of his condo. There are floor-to-ceiling windows along almost the entire room. He has a corner condo, so his view captures the entire city.

The door clicks behind me and the air shifts from calm to a storm. I turn to look at Auston and he roughly grabs my face and brings his lips to mine. Our teeth and tongues are clashing together. I relent when he growls and I lean my head back in a moan. He takes that as an opportunity to lick between my shoulder and ear, which causes goosebumps to scatter all over my body.

"Fuck, Auston…" I moan as he walks us backwards, and realize the city is right behind me.

"Do you want this city to see how beautiful you are?" He slowly undoes my belt and tugs my shirt swiftly off my body, throwing it over his shoulder. I move my hair out of the way and leisurely run my fingers under his shirt. I have never been with a man as confident as Auston, and that thought alone sends a ripple of pleasure to my core. I remove his shirt and lean forward, swirling my tongue around his nipple. I feel it tighten underneath my tongue and decide to give it a little bite.

I hear Auston inhale.

He works at getting the rest of me naked as I kick off my boots, allowing him to peel off the rest of my clothing. I look up at him through my lashes and slowly lower myself to my knees.

Auston looks up in a frenzy and whispers a "fuck" into the air as I undo his belt and bring his jeans and briefs down to the floor for him to step out of. His cock hits his belly button and I slowly grab it, and bring the tip between my lips.

"Mmm," I hum, flattening my tongue along the length and licking upwards. I wrap my hand around the base where my mouth can't reach and use my other hand to massage his balls. He wraps his hands around my hair and begins to take control of my movements.

He picks up the pace of his movements and I gag a little from his cock hitting the back of my throat. He continues his assault as my eyes rim with tears, but I don't stop. I lightly graze my teeth along his shaft as he moves it through my lips.

"I'm going to come in that pretty mouth of yours," he groans out loud and tightens his grip on my hair. I would feel the pain if my clit wasn't throbbing so hard it might pop. Just when I'm about to reach my hand down and begin to touch myself, Auston grunts and his salty-bitterness lands on my tongue. I moan around him as he repeats "fuck" to himself a couple times, trying to manage the shudders running through his body.

Once I feel his body relax, mine becomes hyper aware of his movements. He swiftly stands me up, spins me around, and shoves my legs apart. Grabbing the base of my neck he leans me forward, so my breasts lay pressed against the glass with my ass thrusted out. The rational part of my brain is telling me to move our position because people can see us, but my arousal is telling me to keep going.

I'm about to turn around and tell Auston that I don't know

how I feel about this when his tongue lies flat on my mound. A jolt spikes up my core and I press my head against the glass. I moan out loud and push myself onto his tongue, wanting it deeper.

"You're so wet, Victoria." He slowly slides a finger inside me as he flicks his tongue over my clit. "Imagine all the people that could be watching you fall apart." A shudder racks my body. This feeling is intoxicating. Not just Auston's foreplay, but the thrill of someone possibly watching us.

He quickens the pace of his finger and his tongue on my clit. The wetness of him thrusting his fingers in and out of me is the only sound in the room. My throat closes up as I try to moan, my core tightening, and my orgasm bursting intensely through me as I try to hold myself up against the glass.

Auston gets up and on weak legs, I turn around to face him. He looks at me while sucking his middle finger right into his mouth and I swear electricity flows through my body. I grab his neck and bring his face down to mine as he grabs my legs and lifts me off the ground, pressing my back to the glass.

In one swift movement, he thrusts himself inside me.

"Fuck!" I press my forehead to his while he thrusts inside me. The glass against my back sends a cool shiver up my spine, a stark contrast to the heat radiating off the rest of my body. I scratch down Auston's arms as he quickens his pace. His arms bulging as they hold my body up against the glass, vibrating from the strength of his pounding.

"Victoria." He hisses. I smirk, until I feel him biting down on my nipple and I arch from shock. I have never had my nipples bitten during sex, but I think I like the roughness of it. I grasp onto Auston's arms and lean my head back.

He reaches his hand between our bodies and swirls his finger on my clit. He has become pretty accustomed to my body, so his pressure is perfect. I bite his lip before gasping at his increased thrusts. Sweat beads above his brow and his body is tense from holding mine, every muscle looking like it was sculpted by Michelangelo himself.

"Auston," I gasp. "I'm coming!" My body tightens and a pressure relieves from my clit. I gasp and squeeze my eyes tight as Auston continues thrusting into my body.

He shockingly pulls his cock out of me and flips me around, grabbing my neck and forcing my front up against the glass. He pushes my legs apart.

"Is this what you envisioned, baby?" He growls into my ear, nipping it as he goes. I groan as my nipples pebble against the glass. I look down and see cars speeding by on the highway below.

Fuck.

He thrusts himself back into me and I scream. This position makes it seem like his cock is in my stomach.

I reach my hand backwards and run it along his side as he thrusts in me. He leans his body forward against mine and kisses my shoulder.

"What do you think the people driving by are thinking? How fucking sexy you look, pressed up against the windows? Being fucked mercilessly?" Auston's thrusts become rougher as I push back towards him.

He releases a satisfied groan, and my body shivers. An orgasm begins to build again and bring my hands down towards my clit to finish myself off.

"Fuck, I want to be the one to bring you to orgasm, but you touching yourself…fuck." He breathes against me.

We both begin to move faster and harder and before we know it, we are both releasing at the same time.

"I'll never get enough of you." He grunts into my neck while I try to bring my breathing back to normal.

"I mean, if that's what it's always like, I don't want you to." I reply breathlessly. I'm so used to giving myself pleasure that I never knew how exhilarating it could be to have sex with someone you care about. He laughs and slowly slips himself free, suddenly missing his thickness.

"Well, I think we may be in trouble then." He winks as I laugh and grab my bra and panties, slipping them on. I turn to face Auston and he is staring at me with hunger in his eyes, *again*. I look down and realize I'm wearing a black lace number that doesn't leave anything to the imagination.

Auston walks over to me and lifts me up, which he makes look easy for a woman who is two-hundred and ten.

I guess we won't be getting much sleep tonight, I smile to myself as he throws me down on his bed with a devilish gleam in his eyes.

CHAPTER SIXTEEN

I hum as light shines brightly into the room through the floor-to-ceiling windows. Auston lays beside me asleep, looking delicious as always with his hair a mess from our late night activities. He has one arm thrown over his head and another resting on his toned stomach. I got to admire his beautiful body more than once last night, and enjoy licking him from lips to cock.

I slowly lift myself from the bed and look around the room. His room looks extremely well lived-in for a guy who doesn't live here full time. He has his bed centered with the largest wall against raised, stark grey panels. I rise off the bed and continue to admire the gruff masculinity that his room radiates. He has a black carpet that takes up a majority of the room, with a small live-edge wooden table and two brown leather wing chairs. There are two doors opposite the bed, which I assume are his closet and bathroom.

My feet paddle quietly towards his dresser, to find myself a T-shirt of his to wear. Our bags are still out in the living room and to be frank, I'd rather wear something of his. I luckily open the second drawer and find a couple t-shirts, grabbing a black one, I slip it on over my curves. I didn't get to admire his place enough last night, since he had me pinned against the window as soon as we walked through the door.

I make my way towards the window in the living room and shake my head; this view is breathtaking. Since it's a corner condo, the view of Lake Ontario and the CN Tower are both visible from where I'm standing.

I never got a chance to experience city life, but if I knew it looked this good maybe I would've made more of an effort. I turn back around to admire the rest of his apartment and smile. He has a wall lined with bookshelves; a guy who reads for pleasure is such a turn-on.

I glance around and notice how big of a fan he is of black furniture. His couch looks like it's black suede with a grey shag carpet underneath, accented with another live-edge wooden table. His apartment truly portrays the word masculine, but it suits him.

I continue my wandering into the kitchen and notice that it's simple, with black cabinetry and stainless steel appliances. I walk to the fridge and start to pull out some ingredients for breakfast. It's already nine thirty and I have no idea what Auston has planned for us for today, but breakfast is a must.

"Good morning, gorgeous. I take it you're a morning person?" He wraps his arms around me from behind and kisses the top of my head, and I swear I melt into a puddle. I turn to look at him and his hair is a rumpled mess.

"I'm, I don't like to waste a good day in bed…" I pause when he raises an eyebrow, "sleeping." I wink at him and he laughs. I lean back and stare into his mesmerizing green eyes; they look like they are shining thanks to all the natural light streaming in from the windows. He quickly pecks me on the lips and joins me in the kitchen, helping me to prepare breakfast so we can start our day.

Auston and I are walking around the Eaton Centre in downtown Toronto before we head to lunch at a restaurant he loves to visit when he's home. I stare around at all the people carrying shopping bags. There's so much going on from the amount of people talking, laughing, or even yelling as they walk through the mall. I've only been to this mall once before because it's in the heart of downtown, and has three levels of temptation. I try to refrain from going to a mall this large because I admit I have a small shopping addiction. The clothing just calls my name, especially if it fits me right. Being on the curvier side, if I find a piece that fits me and I love it, I buy it. In Simcoe, stores are limited and finding something that fits me right can be like finding a needle in a haystack.

I'm trying to balance myself on the escalator when Auston mentions that we should leave soon before we're late for our reservations. I nod my head in agreement and we walk out the revolving doors into the crisp, polluted air of the city. I refrained from buying anything at the mall because I didn't want to carry anything around. I have no idea what Auston has planned for today and if it involves a lot of walking, the last thing I want is to be carrying around shopping bags. Auston purchased something while I was in the washroom but won't let me see what it is. The mystery is gnawing at me, it's even in a brown paper bag stapled shut. What store gives out brown paper bags nowadays, and staples them? Bags are part of marketing, so I'm a little lost as to what Auston could have hidden in that bag.

He drags me forward through the hustle and bustle of the city until we're at this cute little Italian restaurant called Rosa's. It's tucked away on one of the side streets, which I never would've seen unless I was actually on the hunt for the restaurant. We push through the large wooden doors and my mouth drops. The restaurant's atmosphere is very traditional with Italian music playing, jars of decorative oils on the wall behind the hostess table, and wooden tables scattered around. The aroma is mouth-watering as we stand here; Italian comes in second for my favorite cuisine, just after Portuguese. A beautiful young hostess calls Auston's name and escorts us to a booth against the far wall. The booths are a deep scarlet velvet which feels so plush against my bare legs.

I decided on wearing my black faux leather skirt with a white shirt tucked into it, with my brown overcoat and booties. It was the perfect outfit and luckily, I brought my shorts to wear under my skirt because chafing is every thick girl's nemesis. I laugh, remembering when Auston tried to move his hand up my thigh in the Uber, only to find out I had shorts on. It was hilarious explaining to him what a girl with thick thighs has to go through to wear cute outfits.

"What are you smiling about?" He grabs my hand under the table and raises an eyebrow at me. He looks genuinely curious about what's going through my mind. I usually go through all my inner thoughts alone, and it's warming to have someone to talk to on an emotional level.

"I was remembering how disappointed you were when you found my shorts in the Uber, and then explaining what chafing was to you." I smile and look down to the menu and realize everything on the menu looks delicious. From the fresh mozzarella balls, to the bruschetta, to the homemade pasta… I want to order a little of everything.

"I knew chafing was a thing, I just didn't know you had to wear shorts under all your skirts. How do you wear dresses and skirts to work all the time?" He asks while scanning the wine menu.

"I usually wear nylons, so I don't have to worry about wearing shorts. But when I don't feel like wearing nylons because of their restriction on my stomach, I go with the comfort of shorts." I shrug. It's cute that Auston is actually questioning these small things that are just part of my regular life.

My gaze travels back to the menu and I ask, "What's good here? Everything I'm eyeing looks delicious, and I'm struggling to choose." Auston leans his head down towards my ear and whispers,

"You're definitely the most delicious thing here, but I'm assuming you're talking about the food?" My face heats up and I bring my hands up to press them against my face. He sends me a suggestive smile and I bite my lip to keep my huge grin at bay. Auston leans forward, like he's going to kiss me, but instead uses his teeth to remove my lip from between my teeth. He licks my lips and the hair rises at the nape of my neck, and my nipples tighten. I've never displayed any sort of public affection before, but this feels extremely erotic for a public setting.

I slowly bring my hands down towards his thigh and slyly bring my hand to feel that he's hard underneath his jeans. I smile down towards my lap; I can't believe that I give a man this handsome such uncontrollable lust.

"Don't hide from me Victoria, I want to be able to see that beautiful face and read what you're thinking." He brings his hand to my face and runs his thumb along my bottom lip. His eyes are penetrating mine in a dark and lustful gaze, and I can't help the shiver that runs through me. I look into his eyes and a burst of different emotions: desire, excitement, and… love?

Oh God. I break our eye contact at the realization I may love Auston, but am nowhere near ready to admit that aloud. His gaze piques with interest at my sudden change in demeanor.

I cough playfully. "Auston, you're quite dangerous, you know that? I mean, I shouldn't want to straddle you in the middle of a restaurant right now… but that's exactly what I want to do." Auston bites his lip and rolls his head to rest it on the booth.

"And you say I'm the dangerous one…" He brings an arm to lay on my shoulders against the booth. "I have a hard-on that isn't going away anytime soon, because you had to mention straddling me." He laughs as he adjusts himself in the booth. We're interrupted by our waitress.

"Welcome to Rosa's. Is there anything I can get you two to start with?" She has a thick Italian accent that I immediately fall in love with. I have always had a thing for Italy. I mean, the country, food, and art are out of this world, and definitely appreciated in my eyes.

"Hi, yes can we get a bottle of the *Dea Chardonnay 2000*," he glances down at the menu, "and also the bruschetta?" He smiles up at her and you can visibly see her become a little frazzled by his charming smile.

I feel you, girl.

"Absolutely, I'll let you both decide on your entrées. I'll have the kitchen get started with your appetizer." She nods and walks away towards the kitchen. I glance down at my menu, realizing I have no idea what I'm going to eat. I look between the carbonara, the truffle lasagna, and the chicken alfredo. I bounce around the dishes in my head and decide on the truffle lasagna because damn. I've had many Italian dishes before, but never one that mixes truffles and lasagna. I close my menu and set it on top of Auston's, his already closed.

"What'd you decide on?" He looks down at me with a smile playing on his lips. I remember when I first saw him at Dallas Pub and couldn't believe how a man could be this handsome. I also remember making a fool of myself and then realizing he was my new boss. That time feels like it was years ago, yet only a few months have passed since that day I walked in late to the staff meeting.

"Everything on the menu looks good, but the truffle lasagna has piqued my curiosity."

"You're going to love that dish, it's delicious. That was the first thing I'd tried here as well." He nods his head in approval and I smile. The waitress arrives back at our table with our bottle of wine and gives a small sample to Auston to try. He does the typical swirl, sniff, and taste, which looks erotic from my point of view.

The waitress widens her eyes as she takes in Auston's movements and I smirk watching her. I've never been much of a jealous person; up until recently.

The waitress shoots her eyes to me in panic thinking I'm going to call her out for getting flustered watching Auston, but I smirk and mouth "I know" to her and she smiles back at me. I don't like meaningless nastiness towards others. Unless they deserve it, I prefer to act with kindness. Completely opposite to Emma, who called out that waitress at Dallas Pub when she was eye-fucking Auston. I mean, someone has to balance out our group.

"This is very good, thank you. Can we also order two truffle lasagnas?" Auston asks with his deep, sultry voice.

He finishes his erotic show for us and glances up to the wait-ress to confirm our order. She nods her head a little too quickly and dismisses herself to the kitchen, and I laugh because this poor girl is totally flustered by Auston. He's so clueless too, because he just went back to people watching after getting both us women all riled up with his natural sexuality.

"Are you laughing because I flustered you and the wait-ress?" I snap my head back; I honestly didn't think he knew he was doing it. I thought Auston was just naturally sexy all by himself, not because he had to try.

"Wait, you did that on purpose?" I widen my eyes at him, a little shocked at his confidence. Being insecure myself for so long, it's taken some time getting used to a man so confi-dent in himself. I would love one day to be as confident as Auston because it would help minimize my anxiety the slightest bit, but it's a slow process for me. I start with my outfits which help me boost my confidence, but there always seem to be things that shake me and cause me to feel like I have to start all over again.

"Of course, you don't think that I didn't feel you both watching me with your mouths salivating?" He smiles and I playfully shove him.

"Oh whatever. I didn't want to peg you as cocky, but you definitely are." I roll my eyes at him and he laughs. Even his fucking laugh is intoxicating, I seriously can't handle this man. How is he ever going to stay with a woman like me? I try to tame the self-doubt that's making its way up my chest, because I don't want it to ruin the beautiful day we have together.

Our bruschetta arrives and the aromas that perfume the table are exquisite. I can smell the mixture of fresh bread and tomatoes, which is unusual for a restaurant. Most produce comes from mass farms, but this has that home-grown tomato smell.

I grab my phone from my bag, wanting to snap a photo of the appetizer so I can replicate it at home. Just as I'm about to put my phone back, Auston snatches it out of my hand and turns the camera so it's facing us. I look at him a little bewildered, but he puts his arm around my shoulder and smiles at the camera. I relax my shoulders and smile at the camera, and Auston takes the photo. He brings it close to us so we can see the photo, and it's beautiful. We look so happy...I look happy.

This is definitely going on the memory wall.

I smile to myself and put my phone away. I grab a slice of bruschetta and take a bite, moaning at the flavours on my tongue. Auston watches me and I quirk an eyebrow at him.

"How loud did I just moan?" My face heats and his grin deepens further, proving I moaned a little too loud for a public place.

"I love it when you blush." I smile and shield my face a little bit and continue to eat my bruschetta. I'm horrible at receiving compliments.

Our lasagna arrives just as we finish off our plate of bruschetta and I swear a little drool travels down my chin. This lasagna looks out of this world, and the cheese on top is calling my name.

"Okay, I'm probably going to moan again, so plug your ears." I wink at him and he smirks while shaking his head. He can't say I didn't warn him. I cut a piece of gooey pasta and stab it with my fork, bringing it to my mouth. "Oh my God..." I melt in my seat as the lasagna melts in my mouth. It has the perfect ratio of truffle, pasta, and cheese. I sit back and lean my head against the booth— I'm going to feel so bloated after this dish. Auston tries to continue our conversation as we eat, but honestly, I just want to devour this lasagna. Screw savouring something when it tastes this good. He laughs at my curt conversation and admires me as I eat. I can see in his face that he loves that I'm genuinely enjoying my meal. Once I finish my second glass of wine, and the last bite of lasagna, I realize my bladder is ready to burst.

"I'm going to run to the ladies' room quickly." I kiss him on the cheek and shuffle my ass out of the booth after finishing a large square of lasagna. I try to look poised as I make my way to the bathroom to relieve myself. I push on the large glass doors and stop in place; this bathroom is stunning. There is a multi-colored terrazzo composite flooring with bright blue walls, glass bowls for sinks, and large mirrors to bring it all together. This is probably what a bathroom in a small villa in Italy would look like. There's a mixture of pictures of Italy on the wall as well, and I take a moment to admire the small history the bathroom holds.

I finish relieving myself and wash my hands as I continue to admire the little pieces of history this bathroom is holding from pictures to knick-knacks; it gives it a special and personal feel. I dry my hands off on a towel and throw it into the bin they have set aside, and walk out the door. My steps begin to falter as I notice a woman sitting a little too closely to Auston at our booth. I don't like the jealousy and anxiety that begin to twist in my gut; these aren't feelings I'm used to at all. I was just telling myself I'm not a jealous person, but man… this woman is gorgeous, and way too comfortable around Auston. I slow down my steps to watch Auston's body movements and I can tell he looks uncomfortable. He looks the same as he did when Laura cornered him at Kline's. His shoulders are tight, his lips are pressed together, and he has a little frown line marring his forehead. Although Auston is outspoken, it seems that when he is around women who are slightly aggressive, he shuts down.

I see him push the bank machine towards the edge of the table after paying and he attempts to shift his body away from this woman. I square my shoulders and fake the confidence I know I don't have much of before walking back to the table. Auston sees me and looks visibly relieved that I'm back. He quickly shuffles away from the woman and gets up. I look at her just as she looks at me, and I'm taken back by her beauty. She looks athletic with beautiful blonde hair and sparkling blue eyes. I get an uneasy feeling when she shoots daggers my way as Auston grabs a hold of my hand.

"Shantel, this is Victoria, who I was telling you about." Oh, fuck me. Of course, his ex-fiancée *had* to show up on our day together. She looks me up and down with a look of disgust on her face and my confidence shrinks.

"Hmm, nice to meet you, Victoria." Her voice sounds catty and it reminds me of Laura. How the hell was Auston ever with a woman like this? First, she is the complete opposite of who I'm and second, she looks mean. Like, really mean.

"You too." I say uncomfortably, and Auston reaches to grab my bag and both our jackets from the booth.

"Auston, you can't seriously be leaving me for… that?" I shake my head and give her an "excuse you" face because did she really just refer to me as *that*? I said I don't like meaningless nastiness, but this time, it has meaning.

I'm completely over allowing other people to belittle me to my face and make me feel less than them. I may not be the standard beauty, but I know that somewhere in me, I'm my own form of beauty. I'm just as worthy of Auston's affection, if not more, due to our contrasting personalities.

Fuck this.

"Excuse me? Look, I'm sorry you lost your chance with Auston, but all this is mine now." I motion down Auston's body. "Maybe you should've been grateful when you had a sexy, thoughtful, and humbling man in your arms, but instead you opened your legs for another. Right now, the only legs opening for him are mine, and I'm sure to pleasure what's *mine*." I growl, the unnatural feeling of possessiveness washing over me. I grab Auston's hand and practically drag him out the restaurant doors. Not before he makes a quick remark towards Shantel,

"I'm grateful you cheated on me because otherwise I never would have met this gorgeous, *real*, woman." With one final smirk her way, we both rush out and push our way through the heavy wooden doors. My heart beats in my throat when we make it outside into the cold air. I can't believe I said that to someone I don't know. I feel shaken, but also a little... badass? I've never stood up for myself before, usually because I get overwhelmed with worry, but standing up to Shantel felt good. Really good. Especially since she wanted to try and claim him as still being "hers". Then Auston having the final word? That was definitely sexy.

"I'm sorry." I bite my lip, looking up into his dark green smouldering eyes, "I shouldn't have said that to her, but the look she was giving me made me small and I-" I'm cut off when Auston grabs my arm and hauls me against the wall beside the restaurant, smashing his lips to mine. I immediately wrap my arms around his neck to deepen the kiss and his growl vibrates from his chest to mine.

"That was sexy, Victoria." He bites my lip and pulls outward, which sends tingles straight to my clit. "You were confident and possessive all at once." My cheeks heat and he brings his lips back to mine hungrily. His fingers lightly trailing their way up my leg towards my sex and I quiver, knowing what is about to happen… in public.

When we had sex against the glass that was as far as my exhibitionism has ever gone, but this is going to take it to another level because people are walking beside the alley consistently. My mind halts when Auston's finger slides into my shorts underneath the lace of my panties and I lean my head back on the brick behind me.

"God, you're so wet, Vic. Does standing up for yourself turn you on?" He slides his finger between my folds and lightly circles my clit. I buckle slightly, wanting him to relieve the pressure that's building in my core. I thrust my hips slightly to motion him to continue and he smirks, knowing he's got me right where he wants me. He shields his body in the direction of people passing and raises my skirt a little more to gain better access. He slides two fingers into my centre, and I groan. He continues to slide them in and out while also applying pressure to my clit and the familiar buzz begin in my lower region. The orgasm that comes feels electrifying. The heat from my body and the chill from the air have me breathing heavily as I come down from my high.

"Oh God Auston," I sigh heavily while he licks his fingers clean. I groan again because fuck, a man licking your juices is sinful.

"Your lucky our day isn't over yet. I'd love to have you in my bed right now." He smiles while shaking his head, clearly disappointed with us having unknown plans.

"I mean, I don't think I'd mind…" I bite my lip and a laugh leaves him, while he opens the mysterious brown bag from earlier.

"Once you know what we're doing, you'll mind." He leans down to the bag and pulls out a jersey that belongs to the Toronto Geese and another for the Montreal Beavers.

"We're going to a Toronto and Montreal hockey game and if we don't leave now, we're going to be late." He shrugs on his jersey and I squeal as I snatch the other from his hand and put on my Toronto jersey.

"I can't believe we're going to a game! I haven't been to one in forever." I state excitedly as he grabs my hand and orders an Uber to the arena. Although I'm still feeling the high from having just had my first orgasm in public, knowing I'm going to watch a live Toronto game has me feeling a different kind of high.

"I know you haven't. I asked Hannah and Emma what they thought about it and they squealed just like you did a moment ago." He looks down at me and smiles. I can't believe he confided in the girls about his weekend plans, and I'm surprised they kept quiet all this time. When they were over the other night they acted so surprised we were going away to the city, yet they knew all along. He apparently had pulled them aside after leaving my class one morning and spoke to them about surprising me. They weren't hesitant at all when he asked, agreeing that this was the best surprise he could give me.

I'm giddy our entire drive to the arena; I can't believe I'm going to watch a live game. It's been over eight years since I got to enjoy this, especially since the girls aren't huge hockey fans. This was something I always did with my dad before he passed, but after, I was never able to come alone. I couldn't stomach it. Being here with Auston though, I'm excited to create new memories.

We arrive at the arena and people are buzzing around like madmen. The smell of fried food and beer fills the air and it makes me excited all over again. I used to come to a game around three times a year with my dad, so this is surreal to be back. I smile as Auston tugs on my hand and starts directing me towards the hall that will lead us to the seats. I stay close to him as it starts to get busy, as people start to make their way to their own seats. I hesitate when I notice that Auston is bringing us down to section 109.

"Auston, are you sure this is where our seats are?" He continues to tug me forward with a secret smile on his face and I feel like I'm dreaming. The closest my dad and I ever got to the rink was the two hundreds, and right now we are right in front of the plexiglass.

Auston waves at someone in the row and I notice that Axel and Garrett are both sitting there, with two empty seats beside them. I look up and see the Toronto team training directly in front of me. I know I have the most gorgeous man beside me, but hockey players are a whole different kind of sexy.

"We were thinking you guys weren't going to show." Axel laughs as we take our seats after exchanging pleasantries.

"I mean, we almost didn't." Auston winks at me and I scrunch up my face because I hear Axel and Garrett laughing, which indicates they knew exactly what Auston meant. I notice that both Axel and Auston are both wearing Montreal jerseys, and Garrett and I are wearing Toronto jerseys.

"So, Garrett, seems like we're the only two with taste in teams?" I smile playfully at him and he laughs loudly.

"I knew I liked her." He nods at me and I smile. Usually I'm intimidated being near such attractive men, but they make it feel easy with their playful banter. Thank God they're cocky, but not in the asshole-ish way.

"We'll see which team is better after tonight." Axel exclaims and I can't help but catch a hint of an accent when he speaks. I didn't get to talk to Axel or Garrett much when I met them at Kline's, so I never picked up on it. The three of them continue with their banter over which team is going to win tonight while I admire the beautiful men that are currently skating in front of me. I can't believe I'm this close to the rink.

I'm trying to hide my giddiness because one of my fantasy men is right in front of me. The girls and I all made a list of famous people we love to fantasize about and mine is right here, in front of me, stretching his hamstrings out on the ice.

Cole Anderson.

I take out my phone and sneak a picture to the group chat between the girls and I.

Me: OMG, OMG. Look who's in front of me. I know I have a sexy man beside me, but I'm freaking out.

Hannah: Cole fucking Anderson! You're so close to your fantasy man.

Emma: Ditch Auston for a little, hehe.

Me: Haha, no way. Auston is definitely at the top of the fantasy man list. However, Cole is a close second...

I turn my camera on and snap some pictures of the players, and a couple selfies with the ice behind me, because it's the closest I will get to a photo with Cole. I poke Auston, wanting to get a photo with him, and the boys photobomb the photo by sticking their heads in at odd angles to get in the frame.

The national anthem begins, which means the game is

about to start. I get comfy in my seat once the anthem ends and Auston laces our hands together to watch the game.

Nearing the end of the third period, the arena is buzzing with excitement.

"Come on, Come on!" I shout. There's only one minute to go in the game, and we're currently tied three-three. The four of us are all shouting at the players as the countdown to zero begins.

I shout at Hutchinson because he currently has the puck. He swiftly glides himself between opposing players towards their net and makes a quick pass to Cole.

"Go, go, go!" I start hitting Auston's arm as the entire arena starts to scream for Cole to score the winning goal. Cole raises his stick and shoots quickly towards the net, and the puck enters between the goalie's knees. The goal alarm sounds, and we all start to scream as Cole does his signature move by jumping in the air and landing on both knees with his hands up.

"Fuck yeah," Garrett screams and high-fives me. Auston and Axel both look slightly sour as Garrett lifts me up and spins me in a circle. I laugh and the slight discomfort from being lifted, but it passes when Garrett sets me back on my feet.

"Okay you two, enough." Auston huffs and I laugh. We wait for everyone to exit the arena since we know thousands of people leaving one place is never a fun thing to maneuver through.

"This was awesome. How did you guys get such amazing seats?" I ask as we wait to leave the rink.

"Garrett's company owns these seats. He usually allows staff to use them for games, but he made a special considera-tion." Auston smiles down at me and I'm grateful as hell. Auston really went out of his way to make today happen and it was amazing. Besides the minor hiccup with Shantel, it turned out to be the perfect day. I can't wait to update the memory wall with all the beautiful photos from the weekend.

The four of us walk outside into the chilly air and decide to head to a bar that's only a block over from the arena for some drinks. I'm not used to being the only female in a group, especially a group of GQ models. I giggle lightly to myself, imagining if I actually called them that. I know the girls would laugh if they were here because they'd agree. This nickname for hot men came out of nowhere one night while tipsy in our dorms, then it stuck with us.

I found out a little bit more about Garrett and Axel during the game in between periods. Axel's family moved from England when he was young due to his dad's work, then he studied Nutritional Sciences at the University of Toronto where he met Garrett and Auston. Garrett grew up in a small city north of Toronto called Barrie, went to the University of Toronto for Chemical Engineering, and started his own company. Axel is six feet and five inches of pure gorgeousness, and Garrett is six feet of pure pretty boy. I don't even know how women handled themselves while in school with these three, I would've been totally intimidated by them. That girl in the back avoiding any possible interaction with them? Yeah, that would be me.

Like I'm right now. We just walked into the bar and I've already noticed the multiple women who have turned their heads at them.

I feel uneasy as we're escorted to a high booth that perfectly fits the four of us. I think the host knew to give us a booth with more room because of these large men. Women are visibly staring, and I find myself shrinking down a tad.

"So, Victoria, we didn't really get a chance to talk when we first met at that bar in your town. Auston told us you work with him?" Axel has a mischievous look in his eye, probably because Auston is my boss.

I laugh a little before answering him, "Yeah, I'm one of the two English teachers."

"Have you always wanted to be a teacher?" Garrett pipes up. I bite my lip and look down because no, being a teacher isn't at all what I wanted to do with my life.

"No, not really. I always wanted to be a writer." I smile lightly and notice Auston's eyes on my face, because I'd never mentioned to him that writing was the end goal for my career.

"Really? I would've assumed a photographer with all the pictures you have hung up on your wall." Auston rubs his hand gently on my thigh and I laugh.

"Oh God, never. I just take photos to have memories of important days that have happened in my life."

"What. I guess that means we need to take a photo because this, I would assume, is a pretty important day." Garrett says charmingly as he takes out his phone, and Auston groans at his friend's charm. Garrett snaps a photo of all of us smiling and shows the table. A flutter in my stomach.

"What's your number, Vic? I'll send the photo to you to add to your wall." He winks at me and I laugh while giving him my number.

"I'll even send you a photo of it in its frame to confirm it's there." I smirk, and he nods over-enthusiastically, which has Axel laughing and Auston shaking his head. Garrett is extremely friendly and charming; I adore him already. He keeps us laughing almost the entire night. Seriously, I had my drink coming out my nose at one point. Which was super embarrassing, but Auston kissed me right after that and I couldn't even remember being embarrassed.

"God, Vic, you're cool. I see why Auston is smitten with

you, you're a breath of fresh air compared to the tart we used to have to spend time with." Axel says while Garrett's eyes widen slightly, thinking I don't know about Shantel.

"Oh, you mean Shantel? Yeah...." Auston smirks, clearly remembering what I said to her earlier and by the guy's confusion, Auston repeats word for word what I said to her today.

Not my best moment, but it led to a fantastic orgasm which I'm not going to complain about. The guys are howling after hearing what I said to her and I shake my head playfully while trying to keep my smile at bay.

"That was the perfect thing to say to her. I always waited for the day someone would speak up to that witch." Axel says with laughter still evident in his voice.

"Well Vic definitely spoke up, and it was hot." Auston smirks and I lean my head back while exaggerating my eye-roll, as if I was mad about it.

Again, I'm not because the orgasm was great.

After a couple hilarious stories of the boys during their university days we decide to call it a night. I glance down at my watch and am shocked to see it's already two in the morning. Axel and Garrett gush about how we need to do this again either in Simcoe or in Toronto, and I agree because obviously these guys are humble, down to earth, and a joy to be around.

We hug goodbye and I can't help but get a good feeling blossoming through my chest. On our walk to Auston's condo, which is only twenty minutes, Auston points out places from his childhood and teenage years. His family apparently used to live downtown, so he got to experience a lot of interesting places here from the restaurants, to activities, and even stores.

I continue to listen as he tells me memories from places

we walk by and some of them are pretty wild. I never knew that you could attach a handcar to streetcar tracks, but Auston, Axel, and Garrett made it happen in university and were arrested. I can just imagine driving down the street only to find three men pumping a handcar through the city; it seems like something out of Looney Toons. I laugh as Auston tells me more stories about his wild past and it makes me realize I may have really fallen for Mr. Scott.

CHAPTER SEVENTEEN

Our weekend in Toronto has come to an end.

After getting back to Auston's condo last night we crashed, not even able to enjoy ourselves because we were exhausted from the day we had. I can't even complain though because last night was probably one of the best nights of my life.

After a good night's sleep, I decided to wake Auston up with a surprise. I have the image of his face imprinted in my mind when I wrapped my warm mouth around his cock. His face was one of pure ecstasy, his hands tangling in my messy hair. I rub my thighs together remembering how he flipped us over and turned what was supposed to just be morning head, into heated, passionate sex.

I smirk to myself as I finish drying all the dishes from breakfast and putting them away. Auston emerges from the bedroom with our two duffle bags in hand, setting them down beside the door.

"I'm going to take out the garbage quickly while you finish getting everything in order." I go on my tippy toes and kiss him slowly. He groans, and I pull away smiling at him.

I walk down the hallway to find the door that indicates a garbage chute. I reach the end of the hallway and find the door to the garbage, finally.

I push it open and am startled to find a girl with a grey hoodie pulled over her head standing inside the claustrophobic room. I smile at her, but her eyes turn to slits as she looks back at me.

"I'm sorry, I just need to put this down the chute..." My words come out slowly as she makes her way past me, not taking her eyes off of me. Unease crawls up my spine as I slide past her and shove the bags down the chute. I turn around to see she is standing by the door, still staring...

"Are you okay?" Slight concern for a random girl standing alone in a garbage chute.

"I will be..." She whispers, with a malicious smirk coating her face. My eyes widen, trying to dissect that statement. My stomach tightens as I squeeze my way past her body that's attempting to block the exit. I quickly maneuver my body and walk down the hallway back towards Auston's place.

I quickly look back and frown as she hasn't moved from her spot, her stare still directed my way. I pick up my pace slightly to Auston's door and rush into the condo, slamming the door shut. I don't know why that interaction spooked me so much, but it was eerie having her watching my every move. Her statement was what really shook me.

"Everything okay?" Auston looks concerned as he looks at me with one eyebrow raised. He was shrugging his jacket onto his shoulders when I rushed in and slammed the door, breaths spurting out of me.

"Yeah... There was this girl standing in the garbage chute and it was super uncomfortable. She didn't move much and just kept staring at me. I felt like I was in the middle of a horror film." I laugh lightly but see something flash in Auston's eyes. His jaw tightens briefly.

"That's strange. The city has a lot of different people, maybe it was just some kid trying to scare you." He smiles tightly, and something is off. He grabs our bags off the ground and throws them over his shoulder. I nod in agreement but can't help the unease that sits in my gut.

Auston walks into the hall with our bags and looks down the hall to see that it's now empty. I shrug to Auston and he turns to lock the door before grabbing my hand to head towards the elevators. I look back down the hall just to make sure and see that clearly, nobody is there. I look forward and smile down at Auston and I's linked fingers. After a quiet ride in the elevator, we're in the garage loading our bags into Auston's car and getting ready to head back to Simcoe.

"Thank you for the beautiful weekend." I lean my head against the headrest and turn my head towards him.

"Anytime, beautiful." He brings my hand to his lips and kisses it softly while starting the car. I get comfortable in the seat with our hands laced on my lap.

I don't know if I'm ready to head back to Simcoe. Now that I have gotten a taste for Auston outside of our normalcy, I want to be selfish and stay in our bubble.

I bang my head against the staff room table as I hear the girls talking about going to Kline's this Friday. After Auston and I got back into town, he dropped me off because he had some work to do to prepare for the week and I had laundry to do from our weekend together.

"Earth to Vic! Do you want to go to Kline's on Friday?" Emma shakes my shoulder and I lift my head up lazily.

"Yeah, sounds fun." I nod while taking a bite of my bagel, courtesy of Hannah who ran to Tim Hortons before lunch and brought us back some goodies. Auston walks in at that very moment and Hannah calls him over,

"Hey, boss. I brought you a medium coffee and a bagel." She tosses the bagel his way, he catches it effortlessly and unwraps it, taking a huge bite.

"I definitely needed this, I didn't have time to make lunch this morning." He smiles gratefully. "Thank you for thinking of me." He still uses his professional principal voice with us when in the school, even though he knows they know everything about what's going on between us.

"You could've…" I stop, realizing I was about to tell him he could've texted me and I would've made him something. First of all, this would have made it obvious that we are closer than simply boss and employee. And secondly, Tracey is sitting at the table next to us and I don't trust her or her sister at all. Emma's nostrils flare noticing my almost fuck up while Auston takes a seat, smirking at me.

I think he gets a little thrill out of knowing there's a chance we could get caught together somehow. He has a great reputation among the board, so they probably wouldn't care, but I don't want people thinking I'm sleeping with him to advance my job. I know that's a thought that would pass through people's minds, but there isn't any position I would want to move up to.

"So, how was your weekend?" Auston asks no one in particular, knowing very well I was with him all weekend. He knows I had an amazing weekend and evidence of that shows in my house. Once Auston dropped me off, I spent half an hour printing the photos from the Italian restaurant, the photobomb hockey game photo, and the photo with me and the GQ gang to hang them up on my memory wall. I was up a little later than usual waiting for the laundry to finish, so I decided to update the wall with our weekend adventures. Seeing Auston's face up on my wall with some of the most important people in my life leaves me with flutters in my stomach.

"Actually, pretty relaxing. I binge-watched Netflix shows and then went to my parents' for Sunday dinner." Hannah shrugs.

"I spent the weekend with my sister, she's here visiting from England." Emma smiles, and the two girls look at me and I know I look like a deer caught in headlights.

Every single one of them knows exactly what I did this weekend and they're still trying to get me to fess up. My anxiety tingles in my palms and I wipe them down on my pants.

Why does my mind go blank when being asked a simple question? I mean, most of my weekends consist of me being home. I should've been able to say that, but I just sit there frozen in my seat.

My mouth opens, but nothing comes out…

"Well, I better head back down to my office. Have a good rest of your day." He winks casually, and I put my head in my hands. Auston put me on the spot on purpose, knowing I would get flustered with my response to our weekend.

Mr. Scott likes to play games.

"Okay seriously though, how was your weekend?" Emma whispers and I laugh. I feel myself relax as I inch closer to the table, because I don't want anyone to overhear. I give them the details of the weekend as quietly as I can, since there are still a few teachers sitting within the premises. I don't mention Auston's name at all just in case *someone* is listening and Hannah swoons as Emma fans her face.

"Yeah, Friday night and Sunday morning were pretty exhilarating." I laugh.

"God, I'm sure, getting hot and heavy in the car that leads to window sex? Our baby is growing up and experimenting in exhibitionism." Emma pokes me, and I laugh. I can't disagree though because Auston really has brought me out of my comfort zone. I'm not the most confident sexually, but Auston makes me feel like I am when he worships my body and acts like he needs to have me the very moment he sees me.

It makes me sexy and confident which are two words I would've never used to describe myself. Fashion was usually my shield against everyone, but the presence of a man who worships me? Yeah, that definitely can add to a woman's self-esteem.

I tell the girls I'm going to the washroom quickly, but really, it's because I want to send a sultry photo to Auston. I decided to wear a button-up blouse today with a pencil skirt which is pretty tame for me, but I feel different; more confident today. Not needing my usual shield to take on the day.

I quickly undo some of the buttons on my blouse and fix my boobs in my lace black bra to take a photo that shows off my breasts with my shirt straining underneath.

Me: I hope this helps you get through your busy day, Mr. Scott

I attach the photo to the text and send it. Just a few weeks ago, I couldn't handle the thought of sending a photo to Auston, worrying that he'd spread it around. But I've quickly realized that isn't him. I mean, his ex-fiancée cheated on him, and he never says anything horrible about her.

I quickly put myself back together and rush back to the

staff room to sit down with the girls. We have another ten minutes before lunch is over. My phone vibrates in my lap and I look down to a text from Auston,

Auston: See me in my office after school, Ms. Mateus.

A shiver down my spine and my panties moisten at the strict message. I bite my lips and clearly, I'm not being as discreet as I thought because much to my dismay, Emma snatches my phone out of my hand and the girls both squeal when they see the recent string of texts.

"Oh, Ms. Mateus, you're in trouble," Emma says in a sultry voice, and I laugh because shit, I'm definitely in trouble. The best kind of trouble, though.

The bell rings a few minutes later. The girls and I hug and promise to have dinner tomorrow night at Dallas Pub, but not before they make me swear to text them after my "meeting."

Two and a half hours, a fresh reapplication of lip gloss, and an empty hallway later I'm making my way to Auston's office. My heels click down the hall as I walk into the almost empty main office and smile at Michelle.

She gives me a knowing look and I roll my eyes at her. Michelle has been here since I was in high school and she was always one of my favorite people in this building, and still is. She clearly knows something is up since I left here last time with smudged lipstick, but I made sure to wear a clear gloss this time... just in case. I quickly walk down the short hall that leads towards Auston's office which sits at the back, very private compared to all the offices in the front. I knock three times to get Auston's attention.

"Who is it?" I hear through clenched teeth and a quiet

groan. I bring my eyebrows together and reply that it's Ms. Mateus.

"Come in." I slowly open the door to find Auston sitting at his desk with his cock in his hand and my photograph from earlier on his phone. I gasp and quickly slither myself through the door, shutting it behind me.

I click the lock in place and turn back towards the beast of a man, looking sexier than ever in his undone sapphire button up and grey slacks sitting open, his cock sitting between his legs. I slowly make my way over to him and lower to my knees in between his thighs.

"Do you need help, Mr. Scott?" I lick my lips and stare at his engorged tip, precum gliding down the length.

"Fuck, Victoria..." He bites his bottom lip and grabs my neck, bringing it forward towards his cock. I slowly bring my tongue out and lick the precum that's beaded at his tip. I bring my hands up onto his thighs and slowly lower my mouth down on his cock and begin to suck, grazing my teeth gently against his shaft.

He hisses and brings his head to rest on the back of the chair as I grab a hold of his dick and pump it as I take him as far as I can into my throat. I begin to choke a little but keep going, knowing he's close since his hand is tightened on my throat.

"Fuck, fuck, fuck..." he breathes as his release lands on my tongue. It's thick and salty, I swallow and bite my lip as I look at him through my lashes.

I stand up and Auston slowly runs his finger up my leg towards the hem of my skirt and teases the edge. I put my hand on his shoulder and lower my eyes to look at him, his fingers continuing their journey upwards towards my heated center. I begin to clench my thighs together, not able to handle the teasing that he's toying me with, and he stops to look up at me. He slowly brings his leg between mine, keeping me from being able to shut my legs, and he continues his journey towards my nylon clad legs.

In one swift moment, I'm gasping as he tears my nylons right from the center and a growl escapes him.

I think my pussy quivers.

"Jesus…" I stop as his finger slowly traces my lips over my panties, "Auston please…" I beg him. I can't take the teasing right now, I've been thinking of this since I sent that damned picture to him.

"Please what, gorgeous?" He continues his slow journey down my body onto his knees and right when I'm about to tear my own panties off, he lowers his mouth and sucks my clit over my underwear.

I gasp and jolt from the pleasure that has rocketed through my body.

"Please make me come." I beg and rock my hips into his face as he glides his fingers underneath my panties… *finally*. He inserts two fingers slowly inside me and I groan from the pressure and begin to ride his fingers to my own release because he's torturing me with this slow pace.

"Someone is needy today, hmm?" He releases his mouth from my clit and I pout, knowing his mouth isn't working its magic. His fingers continue their leisure pumping and I throw my head back in annoyance because the pleasure building, but not enough to tip me over the edge.

With one hand Auston raises my skirt to my hips and motions for me to straddle his hips. I immediately oblige because I need him.

Now.

I rise up on my knees and Auston grabs a condom quickly, puts it on, and angles himself for me to lower right onto him. I begin to lower myself onto his shaft and gasp; I will never get over the fullness I get from his cock being inside me. I continue lowering myself until he is fully seated inside me, and I look down at him. He grabs my neck aggressively and smashes his lips to mine. I begin to ride him as we continue to battle for dominance and I pick up our pace because fuck, this feels so good.

Auston slaps my ass and I gasp from the sudden pain that shoots through my behind, which quickly becomes intolerable pleasure.

"Oh, fuck Auston, keep going, just like that." I continue to ride him, quickening my pace. The sounds of our heavy breathing and the smacking of our bodies together are the only sounds to be heard. I tighten my thighs around his hips as he applies pressure to my clit with his thumb, causing me to reach my peak and I scream out in pleasure.

Auston takes control of my hips and slams me down on him with a bruise-inducing grip on my hips as he releases into me. He groans loudly, and I think if anyone is still in the offices, they definitely just heard his roar from release. I bring my head to lay against his and smile down at him.

He loosens his grip on my hips and slowly runs his hands around towards my ass. He grips it lightly this time and smirks at me.

"The next time we have sex in here, it's going to be you leaning over this desk." He brings his hand up to my face and kisses me softly, and I shiver.

"Do you think anyone is still here?" I turn to face the clock and see that it's only four thirty. I slowly rise off the chair and feel him slowly leave my body; I miss the fullness already.

"I want to say no, but I have a feeling Michelle is going to be looking pretty smug when we walk out of here." He grabs tissues from his desks and cleans me off first before cleaning himself, then throws the tissues and condom into the garbage.

"Why do you say that?" I question as I slide my nylons off, tossing them in the garbage since they are ripped all the way down to my knees. I straighten my skirt and lean myself on his desk as he finishes arranging himself as well.

"Oh, you don't know? She's been making very subtle hints about me asking you out. Tells me about how she tried to set you up with her sons," he pauses to make a displeased face, "and how you're the perfect woman, just not for her sons." I gasp at her bluntness, especially since she knows he's my boss. I mean, it didn't stop us regardless, but she doesn't need to know that.

"Oh my God, I'm so sorry. I've known her since I was a teenager and she has always tried to treat me like a daughter after she heard what happened to my parents. I mean, she tried to make me her daughter-in-law but that didn't go well because I grew up with her sons. Nothing against them, just not my type." I shrug as Auston puts his jacket on and walks over to me.

"What is your type?" He brings his hand to my neck once again and I smirk.

"I would say tall, sexy, GQ-looking principals that go by Mr. Scott." I purr, and he kisses me. Clearly that was the right answer.

"Alright, let's go beautiful." He rests his hand on my lower back and I unlock the door slowly.

"Want to come over for dinner tonight?" I question as I open the door and peak my head out, noticing that the coast is clear from what I can tell.

"Yeah, why not." He winks at me and nudges me out because I'm stalling, in case someone is there and heard us. I walk out slowly, confirm that the coast is clear, and walk out to the main area. I jump like a kangaroo when I see Michelle standing at the other side of the room, printing something out.

She turns around and is smiling way too much, which indicates she definitely heard us in Auston's office.

"I knew I had the right feeling about you two. I didn't even have to work any of my matchmaking skills between the two of you," she says sweetly, and I roll my eyes.

"Well thank goodness for that, right Michelle?" I wink at her and she laughs, as does Auston.

"My lips are sealed about you two, but maybe try not to fornicate on school premises because there are still some nosy people that stick around after hours." Michelle sends me a pointed look and I know she's talking about Tracey, Laura's older sister. Michelle witnessed a lot of the things I went through in high school and has always hated how horrible my high school experience was.

"Thank you, Michelle." Auston pushes me lightly on my back, "Well see you tomorrow." We walk out of the school together and act casual, as if he is not heading to my house right after we leave the parking lot. I smirk at him and he winks at me as he slides into his car, and we both head off in the same direction.

CHAPTER EIGHTEEN

Auston came over last night for dinner. We ended up ordering pizza and watching movies on Netflix. It was the perfect night, and I wouldn't have asked for anything else. I never imagined myself sitting on the couch with a man since I kept myself pretty closed off to the opposite sex, but somehow, we just happened.

I'm becoming more and more attached to him as we spend more time together and it's unsettling because I still doubt this is real… or lasting. My abandonment issues have been strong lately, which has caused my anxiety to be at an all-time high. I've had to take some of my medication for anxiety a few times this week, which I only use when life is really testing me.

I miss my mom and her heartfelt conversations that would give me a different perspective. She taught me so much, but it's like everything she taught me left as soon as she did.

I take a shaky breath. I hope some time with the girls at Dallas Pub will help to dwindle the anxiety that's growing in my chest, and the ache for my mom's presence.

I pull into the parking spot beside Emma's Volkswagen

and grab my black crossbody bag before hauling my ass out of the car. I walk into the pub and immediately get hit with the smell of french fries, which brings an odd sense of relief to my uneasy stomach. I look into the dining area and can't spot my boisterous friends anywhere, which means they're in the bar area waiting for me.

I turn around and walk towards the bar and I can already hear Emma talk-shouting to Hannah over something I can't quite catch. Emma shakes her head but smiles when she sees me walking over to them.

"Hello my dear, *loud*, best friends." I smile as I throw my bag over the tall wooden bar stool and use the ledge of the chair to pull myself up.

"Hi, babe. How are you doing?" Hannah smiles.

"I'm… honestly, I don't know… I've been dealing with a lot these last few days." Concern flashes in their eyes as I pause to take a sip of water that was already waiting for me. If anyone is going to understand the attacks that I have, it's the girls. They have been here to help me with my highest highs, and my lowest lows.

The nagging anxiety reaches its claw around my chest and whispers my worst fear of abandonment, but I shake it off quickly because now is not the time.

"I think I'm just struggling to accept what is happening with Auston. It's too good to be true… I think it's my fear talking. He hasn't made me doubt anything, but in my mind, I've created this worry he's going to leave…" I blab on and realize I just word-vomited to them because I have to heave in a breath after finishing. I hate doing this to them. They always have the right thing to say, but I hate being a burden to them.

"I feel like we have a conversation quite similar to this often, babe." Emma sadly smiles, and I roll my eyes because

I know we've talked about this before. Even when I feel myself taking two steps forward, there is always something making me feel like I've only really moved forward a smidge.

"I think you're being too harsh on yourself Vic. I mean, Auston seems to be completely smitten with you." Hannah smiles and I bite my lip because it does seem like he can't get enough of me.

But what if that's just my body, and not my personality?

"Stop it right there, Victoria Mateus. I saw your facial expression change. You're amazing, and yes you have some stuff you are working through, but who doesn't? Nobody in this world is perfect. We're molded into who we are because of the experiences we go through." Emma grabs my hand.

"Yeah, exactly. The three of us all have our shit, as does Auston. I mean, have you seen how he treats us faculty versus how he treats the students? He may be all sultry GQ model with us, but he becomes similar to Ms. Trunchbull when talking with students," Hannah says as Emma snorts at the referral to the movie Matilda.

"I know. I just get in my head when things get too intense… and I don't want to sabotage what I have going with Auston because fuck, I like him. A lot." I admit, "As for his treatment of the kids, it's strange. He becomes this strict, still very hot, principal when the students are around…" I never really gave it *much* thought about how his personality changes when students are involved compared to when we're in the staff room teasing one another. His demeanour changes abruptly and he loses that compassion and playfulness I usually see in him. Besides the one time he helped coach the hockey team, he's always curt with the students.

"Maybe something happened to him in the past? I have heard some horror stories about principals that are that beautiful," Emma says sarcastically with a wink and I grimace. I really hope that isn't the case...

"Oh God, don't even bring that up. That would completely ruin Auston's GQ status." Hannah groans and I laugh, agreeing with Hannah.

"I really don't think that's the case, although Hannah, in high school you totally had a crush on Mr. Bryon." I wiggle my eyebrows at her, reminding her of one of the math teachers from when we were in high school. He was charming, he slicked back his dark hair, and looked kind of like a greaser from The Outsiders, minus the leather jacket. He always looked put together, but with a little roughness around the edges.

Yeah, he was definitely one of the reasons why I didn't hate math as much as I thought.

"Oh man... Mr. Bryon, I forgot about him. I wonder if he's still single?" I cough out a laugh. Only Hannah would be curious about our past teacher's relationship status.

"He was one of the younger teachers when we went to Angel's, so who knows? Maybe he's a silver fox now?" I shrug and Emma points at us.

"See! We have no idea what happened with Auston, maybe he had a fangirl!" Emma exclaims, but I just shake my head. I think Auston just genuinely loves his position as an educator and wouldn't want to risk it by getting too friendly with students. I explain this to the girls and they nod, even though Emma wants to be convinced he got down and dirty with a student.

"Okay, moving on from this horrendous topic that is making me nauseous, how're you guys doing?" I ask. I deter our conversation into another direction because as much as I love Emma and Hannah, this conversation is churning my stomach. I'm unsettled, but I can't exactly pin what part of our conversation freaked me out most.

Our waiter interrupts us to take our order, relief fills me. Nothing takes away bad thoughts the way delicious food does. I go with quesadillas today, rather than my usual burger. The quesadillas are cheesy, gooey goodness here. Just the thought of dipping the crunchy triangle into sour cream and salsa has me salivating.

I look up after fantasizing about quesadillas and notice Emma's giving us this really goofy look that I don't know how to interpret.

"Emma, what is it? You look like you're holding in a fart with that smile you're doing..." Hannah nudges her to stop and she laughs.

"So...I started a Tinder account on Saturday night while under the influence of tequila and my sister." I make the motion for her to go on with obnoxious hand gestures and Hannah does the same. There has to be a reason that she is telling us this.

"Well, I matched with this God, who seemed familiar but I couldn't exactly place why until we started talking..." she pauses, and I get antsy because she is taking forever to explain who the hell she was talking to. I love Emma, but sometimes her stories drive me crazy. She really likes to build emphasis. Her stories can usually be told quite quickly, but she loves to build some tension with Hannah and I.

"Then as we got talking... and sending photos," she gives us a pointed look because she means dirty photos. "I realized I was fucking sending dirty photos to Auston's friend Garrett..."

"Oh my God!" My jaw drops.

"Why didn't you start dinner with this?" Hannah says while her mouth hangs open as well.

"Because you two are lunatics, with your mouths open so wide you could fucking catch flies. Shut your mouths!" She laughs while we both sit there in shock. I totally wasn't expecting her to say Auston's friend. One of her exes? Maybe. There have been times when Emma has gotten so intoxicated at Kline's, she didn't even realize she went home with one of her exes. The best time was when she couldn't find her panties and had to call me to pick her up. Her walk of shame was hilarious, until her ex started to text her non-stop for weeks. He assumed her forgetting her panties was a sign she wanted him back.

Which obviously it wasn't, it's just that drunk Emma has no shame, which is what makes a night out with her the best. She's the rowdy friend that gives us the best laughs and helps me to break out of my shell.

"So, while we were talking I kept asking him questions about himself because I was trying to figure out where I knew him from, but nothing was adding up because he said he grew up in Toronto. So, we kept on talking and he asked me what I was doing, and me being me, I snuck off to the bathroom in my cute as heck nightie and sent him a photo." She shows us a photo of her in this black velvet nightie. The neck dips deep into her cleavage and the seam hits just below the apex of her thighs. It's definitely a nightie made for seduction.

"He clearly liked what he was seeing because he sent me back a photo of his dick hard, with his sweatpants on! That was a total bonus because if he would've sent me a dick pic, I would have unmatched him immediately because dicks aren't sexy." Hannah and I both laugh at this because she isn't wrong. There is nothing worse than getting an unwanted dick pic... although I think about Auston's and how much I wouldn't mind a photo of that for night time fantasies.

"It was a test I didn't consciously know I was giving him,

but he passed with flying colors. I figured our conversation could continue, since he passed the invisible test. I asked him a little more about himself before our conversation turned into full-blown sexting." She huffs a laugh, "He asked me about my friends, so obviously I told him about you two, then he tells me about his best friends Axel…" she pauses for emphasis, "and Auston." She starts laughing again, either about the irony or the idiocy that she didn't remember Garrett. Both of his friends are just as handsome as he is, all in their own unique ways. They are also great guys; spending time with them at the hockey game allowed me to get to know them a bit more than our first encounter at Kline's. Which wasn't my best moment.

"How did you not recognize Garrett from when we met him at Klines?" I ask, genuinely confused because these guys are so distinct, I would never forget them.

"I honestly don't know. I think I drank a bit too much that night and it became a blur. I never put two and two together from your photo with them from your weekend away with Auston." She shakes her head but shrugs, not being able to understand herself for forgetting such a beautiful man.

"Are you guys still talking?" Hannah asks, smiling. We all get invested when there is any type of romance in each other's life because it doesn't happen too often. I laugh to myself because seriously, we haven't had any type of romance in forever. We're all so focused on one another that we never really take time to go out and meet people outside of Dallas Pub and Kline's. Hannah, of the three of us, is the only one who has had any type of sexual relations recently.

Before Auston that is, I think as I smile to myself.

"We are…" She giggles like a schoolgirl. Hannah and I both look at each other with wide eyes because Emma hasn't giggled over a guy since university.

Shit is getting *real*.

"You know what the best part is?" We both answer "what," as she continues, "He knew who I was the whole time. He knew and didn't say anything!" Emma exaggerates as I snort. Totally not ladylike, but whatever.

That sounds like something Garrett would do from the time I've spent with him. He's definitely the joker of the three of them. A tall, blue-eyed, visionary joker.

"Well imagine if the poor guy would have mentioned that he knew you and you had no idea who the hell he was? That would be so embarrassing for him." I rattle off as I take a bite from my fries. I defend Garret only because we had such a great time at the hockey game.

"Exactly! He would've been un-matching with you quickly, that hurts a man's ego to get embarrassed." Hannah shrugs, and I nod in approval.

"Okay, I guess you have a point... but still, I was embarrassed for not knowing it was him! And he just let me send photos of myself as he sent photos without his face." She puts her head in her hands and I can't help but laugh. Garrett knew exactly what he was doing by not mentioning it was him, it was all a game to see how long it would take for her to figure it out. I'm going to smack him for that next time I see him... but I'll high five him first. I continue to smile as we talk about how their conversation went and eat our dinner, which is going to be cold soon if we don't shut up.

An hour and a half later, we finally finish eating and decide it's time to call it a night now that it's almost eleven. We all have to work tomorrow and if we don't get some rest, we're going to be some grumpy ass teachers.

I definitely woke up on the wrong side of the bed this morning because as soon as lunch hits, I'm exhausted and grumpy. My shoulders ache, my head feels heavy, and I keep yawning. I roll my chair back and stretch after doing some marking on my spare period. My morning class had a test on Shakespeare's Romeo and Juliet, and I was surprised to see how many controversies these students came up with. They're pointing out things that, at their age, I wouldn't have taken notice of. It's impressive to me and gets me excited, knowing they actually care about what they're learning. And starting constructive arguments? A sense of pride fills me.

Hannah is helping some students during lunch with their art for some contest that is coming up, so I need to find Emma to eat with. I think that we're all out of it today because none of us met up this morning, and we're exhausted from yesterday's dinner shenanigans.

The halls have some students collected in groups, but most of them are either outside or in the cafeteria. I walk slowly down the steps towards the gymnasium, so I don't trip in my heels. I don't know why I thought it was a good idea to wear heels on a day when I felt so tired. Flats would've been a smarter choice.

I walk into the gymnasium and notice it's completely empty, which is weird because usually if we want to meet in the staff room, we text one another. I walk to the equipment room and find it empty too, minus all the equipment strewn around the little room. Next place would be the weight room, which usually needs to be monitored because there have been some minor accidents in the past. I pop my head in and just see a bunch of boys from various sports, so I tightly smile and shut the door behind me. The stench of sweat follows me out of the room and I gag. I don't think that room has enough circulation, because that smell wasn't pleasant. I wonder if

Emma still has her sense of smell after being in that room for hours at a time.

I continue my hunt for Emma, pausing to think about where she may be. My eyes shift from the weight room door to the two doors that indicate the girls' and boys' change rooms. Maybe she is in there? It's worth a shot to check. The school isn't that big, so I don't really know where she could have run off to. I pull my phone out of my back pocket and begin to text Emma as I slowly open the door to the girls' change room.

I halt my steps as soon as I hear it.

Are those fucking moans I'm hearing? There is no way... I walk further into the change room and catch two students going at it against the wall. A male student is holding up a female student and thrusting into her like a piston.

"Oh my God!" I cover my eyes and both the students scream. Okay, I have been a teacher for quite some time, and even I have no idea how to handle this. I stutter for a few seconds before I tell the students to put themselves together immediately. I keep my eyes covered as I hear their clothing rustling around.

Oh shit, I'm going to have to bring them to Auston's office. I feel guilty doing that, since Auston and I have done the exact same thing in the school... but we're supposed to be authoritative figures, so I can't exactly let this go.

Fuck, I feel like a hypocrite. I know I'm an adult and so is Auston... I groan out loud as the students finish putting their clothes back on.

"Really, on school property? Did you really think you were going to get away with this?" I cross my arms, trying to give them my disapproval, but I'm most likely feeling just as shaken as they are.

"Well, we've been doing it for months and haven't gotten

caught until now." The guy states smugly and the girl whacks her arm into his chest. He groans, and I roll my eyes. How the hell was this happening in Emma's changing rooms? She can be strict when she wants to be, and I think she would be pretty pissed knowing some students sexed up her change rooms... multiple times. She's going to have to sanitize the crap out of them now.

"Well, you know I can't just let this go. Especially now that you have admitted to doing it for months..." I motion for them to follow me, "we're going to see Principal Scott, let's go." I open the door for them to pass by me and the girl, I want to say her name is Isabel? Is gnawing at her lip from what I can only assume is nerves from being caught. The boy however, is totally smug and walking with way too much swagger.

"Tone it down Mick Jagger, this isn't exactly a prideful moment." I say behind him and he smirks. I clench my jaw because I still dislike teenage boys. It's as if they haven't changed at all from when I was in high school.

I follow behind them through the hallways as we make our way to the front office. The boy opens the door and I grab a hold of it, giving him a pointed look to go in ahead of me.

"Hi, Michelle. Is Mr. Scott in his office? I need to speak with him about these two." I point at the two standing behind me. Michelle picks up the phone and speaks with Auston briefly before nodding at me to go ahead.

As reality comes back to me, my anxiety starts to gnaw at my chest. I never liked getting in trouble when I was a teenager, having always gotten red in the face. I'm embarrassed and I wasn't even the one caught going at it, but I still somehow feel the impact. I seriously need to get a grip on myself. These students are sixteen or seventeen, they shouldn't be going at it during school hours or on school property. I know I'm being hypocritical but I can't let shit like this go, or every student is going to treat me like a softy, as they already do...my head is spinning with too many inconsistent thoughts, and it's giving me a headache.

I knock on Auston's door, peek my head in, and notice he's deep in principal mode. His hands are resting on his desk, his back is straight, and his face is emotionless. He's much better at hiding emotions than I'm; I feel like I would puke and faint at the same damn time if I were a principal. Sweat starts to appear on my eyebrow and I try to slyly wipe it away. My sweat knows no bounds when my nerves are shot.

I open the door wider to allow the two students to follow behind me and take a seat in front of Auston's desk. I quickly shut the door, not exactly knowing how this conversation is going to go. The last time Auston and I had to deal with students, we kind of got into our own heated argument. I wipe my palms on my pants and try to straighten my back; I need to feign confidence.

"I caught these two students in an inappropriate situation in the girls' change rooms..." I widen my eyes at him and jut my chin out. I hope he gets what I'm saying from that because I'd really rather not say I caught them having sex. I inwardly groan at myself. How am I even an adult?

There's a moment of silence in the room as Auston's nostrils flare.

He stands up, crossing his arms, "Mr. Johnson, you do realize that Ms. Bernard is fourteen years old and you are eighteen, which makes this a case of statutory rape?" My eyes widen in shock; I thought they were the same age.

The boy turns white as a sheet of paper at that moment; he kind of looks like he is going to pass out from finding out that information.

"I consented to it," Isabel says with a loud, shaky voice. Auston seems visibly annoyed by these two, just by the expression on his face. He shakes his head,

"Ms. Bernard, you are fourteen years old. You cannot *legally* consent to sex until the age of sixteen, especially when you have sex in public places. This may not have been an issue if you had done it in privacy, but because you have done it on school property, charges can be laid. If you two had known that, maybe you wouldn't have been caught doing such activities on school property." He picks up the phone and calls Michelle, telling her to call their parents and have them come to school immediately. He sets the phone down with a slam, making myself and the students flinch.

"Since you are still a minor Ms. Bernard, your parents are going to have to deal with the legalities of what Mr. Johnson has done to you. As for your education, you are both suspended for two weeks, and if you come back," he gives a pointed look to the boy, "you are not to be near one another. Don't think that I won't know what's going on in my school from this point forward. I do not deal with this kind of disobedience well. Both of you will wait out by Michelle as we wait for a response from your parents. You are not to leave the office under any circumstances." His voice is gruff as he tells the students what to do. It comes out low and guttural, which shouldn't be sexy, but fuck, it is. The jury is out with my body and his strict attitudes.

I shake my head to eliminate the sudden lust and realize how high the stakes are for these students. This boy can be charged. I didn't even think of all the legal shit that could happen when I caught these two students. However, it does make me less guilty, because what if this guy is just using these poor girls?

Their self-esteem?

Their self-worth?

I'm nauseous knowing there could be more girls being impacted by this one kid, who thinks he's making them feel precious for 5 minutes, only to leave her and jump to the next.

"Are you okay? You look like you're going to be sick." Auston whispers, as he puts his hand on my shoulder and I realize I've been standing here for a while in shock. His body language has completely changed since the students left his office; he's more concerned about my well-being than the real issue at hand.

"Uh yeah, I guess I just never thought about any of those things you brought to light. I was feeling guilty about bringing them here because, you know…" I look down at my feet, slightly embarrassed.

"Vic, you and I are adults. That is not the same as those two students. He most likely holds power over her because she's in grade nine and he's in grade twelve, and she wants to feel some kind of value being with an older, popular student. I don't deal with lying or illegal actions well, so it was good that you brought this to my attention, rather than sending them to lunch." He lifts my chin with his finger and I nod.

"I know. As much as I feel guilty about it, I think I feel worse knowing there are probably other girls who have had their self-worth impacted by some guy who has given them attention for five minutes, only for the girl to be a joke the next…" Auston wraps his arms around me, giving me a sense of security over what just happened. I bask in his warmth and rest my head on his chest.

"Why do I feel like you're talking from first-person experience?" I roll my eyes; am I an open book? Is it that obvious that I may, or may not, have had a guy in high school give me minor attention, only for it to have been turned into some kind of joke because of Laura's antics?

"Is it that obvious?" I say into his chest, squeezing him slightly tighter.

"Gorgeous, you don't hide guilt well." He pauses to kiss my forehead. "I have a feeling this has to do with that woman from Kline's, but I don't want to bring that up right now. I just want to make sure you are okay, so I can go deal with those two and their parents." I smile. I love when he goes back to being normal, sweet, and sexy Auston. As much as I love principal Scott, his demeanour changes a lot when he goes into principal mode. It's almost as if he's two different people.

"Yeah, I'm okay. Thank you." I quickly kiss him, before anyone interrupts us. "I'll talk to you later." I smile, and he smirks, nodding his head in agreement.

I walk out of the office, while giving Isabel a small smile. She gives me a small one in return and all I can think about is how I can help girls in the school build confidence in themselves, so they don't get pegged down by some boy. Maybe I can talk to Emma and Hannah about creating some sort of safe space for students to come and talk to us? Both boys and girls can be impacted by bullying, insecurities... the list doesn't end.

I'm thinking as I walk down the hallway towards the stairs, when I hear Emma's squeaky shoes coming towards me.

"Hey babe, where have you been? I have been looking all over for you!" Emma starts walking with me and I give her a sad look.

"I had to go to Auston's office with two students because they were having sex in your change room. I was looking for you everywhere and decided to check there, when I caught them." I shrug because honestly, I still don't feel a hundred percent after witnessing all that I did in the last half hour. Not only am I worried about Isabel, but I also caught two students having pistol sex, which wasn't exactly pleasant.

"What? Which students?" She asks, and I shrug because I don't really know these students too well. They have both never been in any of my classes. I only know Isabel because other English teachers have raved about her for her progressive concepts on literature.

"I'm not too sure, but Auston seems to have an inner list created for all students because he knew exactly who they were. All I know is that she's fourteen and he's eighteen... which is statutory rape, which I also didn't know."

"I thought that there could be a five year age difference between teenagers?" Emma questions. Clearly, she must have some first-hand experience with this but I sure as hell don't.

"I thought so too, but I think because it happening on school property and not in privacy is what fucked them over...according to the law, if a sexual activity takes place in a non-private setting, it can be statutory rape." I open my door and allow Emma to enter first as I shut it behind me.

"Shit, so I take it that Auston wasn't too happy about that then?" Emma hops onto a desk and takes a bite from the turkey sandwich she brought with her. I'm not feeling the best, so I don't bother eating my lunch. My stomach is still rolling from all the events that took place. I didn't think being a teacher would come with all these emotions.

"Well, I think he kept his cool for the most part, but his facial expression is just a blank slate when he talks to students. I could tell he was angry, but he didn't blow up on the students like I expected. Compared to the debacle with Drew and Brad, he was very calm." I shrug and rub my temples with my fingers.

In my four years of high school I never had any interest in boys, besides the one who used me to play a part in making me feel worse about myself. My mom always told me to focus on my studies while in high school because I would have time for boys later. However, I definitely spent my time with boys... not men. I smile slightly to myself because I think the first real "man" I've been with is Auston. Most guys in university cared more about their own pleasure than mine, which is why I had an array of battery-operated boyfriends.

"Earth to Vic, where are you?" Emma claps her hand in-front of my face and I lift my eyes to hers.

"Sorry, I zoned out. What were you saying?" Emma starts re-telling her story about how her conversation, and sexting, has been going with Garrett, and that's how we spend the rest of our lunch period. She may have shown us some photos Garret sent, and I have to admit, he is as fine as Auston is. He took a photo of himself where his jawline was extremely prominent, his lips were pouty, and his sparkling blue eyes were zoned in on the camera. He was also showing off his healthy six pack which was just an added bonus. I high five Emma as she walks out, because she deserves someone too.

The rest of the day goes by fairly quickly and before I know it, I'm sitting in my car and waiting for it to warm up. Auston had some meetings today after school, so he told me he would text me later.

I'm walking into the grocery store fifteen minutes later when I feel someone's eyes on me. I turn to find none other than Laura, her narrow-eyed gaze filled with distaste. I try to ignore her and continue my stroll through the snack aisle when I get jostled by someone's cart hitting mine. The clang of metal bounces in the isles, causing some glances in our direction. Before looking up, I already know who it is. The smell of Miss Dior Blooming hits my nostrils. *Fuck, not today.*

"Years later and still spending too much time in the snack aisle, hmm, Victoria?" Laura sneers and I take a deep breath. It's funny, my mom always said that people grow out of their bully phase, but it seems Laura's failed acting career has made her even worse than when we were teenagers. I try to take a few deep calming breaths.

"I don't see why that would be any of your business. Can you not just keep walking when you see me? Why do you need to corner me like you did when we were teenagers?" I try to move my cart to pass her, but she moves to stand in my way. Anger slowly easing its way into my body.

Her demeaning smirk is in place, "Well, Victoria, you're just such a large target. It's so easy to feel a sense of satisfaction when I speak to you, it makes me feel better about myself." She gloats while resting her hands on her athletic hips.

My anger rises. Not only did she call me fat, but she also tried to take a hit at my life. I nod my head slowly, coming to my own realization.

Oh my god, Laura bullies me because she's so insecure about herself, that she thinks it will make her feel better. How has it taken me years to see this?

"Well, aren't you going to say something, moomoo?" Laura steps forward into my space. She has a few inches on me since my Portuguese genes don't exactly translate to height.

"No Laura, I'm not. You are trying to tease me for being a size fourteen, but it shows how insecure you are about yourself. I'm not going to let your meaningless words impact me because I know I'm worth more. I'm also not the insecure teenage girl you once knew. I've grown up, and fuck, maybe you should too." I smile widely at her and push my way past her, a tad aggressively. It's about time I start to treat myself better than I have been, and sticking up for myself is high on that list of achievements.

Wow, I've had a lot of major epiphanies these last few weeks and it feels like pressure releasing from my shoulders.

Although I definitely need a professional to talk to about my problems, I think life has given me certain people, at the right time, to help show me that I'm worth it. These last few years the only consistent people in my life have been Emma and Hannah. And maybe that's because I always held myself back and never allowed anyone else in. My years of trauma have played a huge part in me holding myself back and thinking I'm this sad and lonely person, but I'm not. All it took was some new principal kissing me in our staff room, to have me second guess my entire life. He's helped show me that I'm beautiful and that my size doesn't mean shit... just like my girls have always been telling me.

Just like my parents always told me.

I finish my grocery shopping with a smile on my face because I needed to finally stand up and put my foot down with Laura. From the look of shock that was on her face when I said those things, I would say I did the right thing. I didn't say anything as bad as she would, but I still stood up for myself and that's enough for me. I can't wipe the smile off my face while putting the groceries in my car. I roll the cart back into its little covered cubby and feel my phone vibrate in my pocket,

Auston: I miss you.

Okay, now I feel even better. I assume Auston's meetings

must be over since he's texting me. Unless he's just sneaking in a text.

> *Me: I miss you too. Are your meetings all finished?*

> *Auston: Yes, they are, what are you doing?*

> *Me: I just finished grocery shopping. I ran into Laura, the girl from the bar, and had a bit of an epiphany.*

> *Auston: Want to tell me about it over dinner?*

> *Me: Absolutely, why don't you come over? I was planning on making Portuguese chicken and potatoes.*

> *Auston: See you in forty, gorgeous.*

My heart somersaults as I start my car. Forty minutes gives me just enough time to get home and put groceries away. Luckily, I marinated the chicken last night, so I can just throw it on the barbecue. I reverse out of my parking spot and head home to make dinner for my man.

CHAPTER NINETEEN

I finish prepping the potatoes into glassware when I hear a knock at the door. I try not to run over to it, feeling like a teenager seeing her boyfriend. My actions from today have me feeling giddier than usual. I swing the door open to a smirking Auston. He swoops in, grabbing my neck and brings me towards him for a very possessive kiss. *Jesus*, my pussy clenches. Talk about being possessive and manly.

"I missed these…" He groans as he bites my lip and I squeeze my legs together. I shut the door behind him as his grip on my neck tightens, making me groan. The frustration vibrating off of him, which could only mean that his meetings today were a little rough. But I'll ask about that later; right now, I want his cock.

I tighten my grip in his hair and he lifts me up and taps for my legs to wrap around him. He carries me to the couch and sets me down. He quickly undoes his button-up as I throw my T-shirt over my head. I changed into sweats and a t-shirt when I got home because comfort is key for me while cooking. I bring my eyes back to Auston and realize he is already sheathing himself with a condom when he grips my sweats and takes them off me, along with my panties.

I widen my legs for him and he groans while lowering himself above me. He runs the tip of his cock along my seam and I whimper. Slowly, he enters two fingers in me and I arch my back and grab onto the couch cushions. He curves his fingers upwards hitting the right spot, and leans down to take a nipple into his mouth.

"Fuck me, Auston." I say as I lean up to kiss him. "I'm ready, God please." I beg. He bites his lip while smiling and grabs his cock. He runs his tip through my folds again before thrusting himself into me. I moan loudly and wrap my legs around him, encouraging him on.

"Fuck, you're so sexy when you moan." He grabs a hold of my hair and forces my lips to his as he pumps himself in and out of me. I scratch my hands down his back and feel the familiar pressure in my core building as Austin reaches between us and begins to circle my clit.

"Auston, I'm going to..." I arch my back and throw my head back at the ecstasy that hits me. He brings his lips to my collarbone and travels upward to suck the sweet spot under my ear. It's the most sensitive spot in my body and I can't handle the hard bite he's placing there.

He's marking me.

Auston continues his assault on my body and I finally let go. My legs tighten around him as my pussy pulses and tightens around his length. My climax gives me an electrifying feeling that begins at my toes and travels up to my neck. I shudder after my release as he pumps faster until I finally feel him freeze. The vein in his neck juts out and he groans loudly into my neck. My body loosens as he breathes into my neck, trying to get our heart rates back to normal.

"I will never get sick of you." Auston mumbles into my neck and I laugh,

"Yeah, I think you decided that for yourself when you decided to mark me." I sigh dreamily, I've never had anyone mark me before.

"Hmm, that's because you're mine." He leans down and licks the hickey and another pulse goes straight to my pussy. If I didn't have to cook right now, I would be flipping us over and asking for round two.

"As much as I loved what we just did, it's almost five thirty and I have yet to start dinner." I grab his face and bring his lips to mine sweetly as I loosen my legs from his waist. He rolls his eyes at me, but smirks as he pushes himself off the couch and grabs my sweatpants and T-shirt from the floor.

He hands me my clothing and I quickly dress, still not fully comfortable strutting around naked. I walk into the kitchen and turn the stove on so that I can cook the potatoes first, since the chicken will only take about fifteen to twenty minutes.

"Whatever you are cooking in here smells amazing." Auston walks in having just finished buttoning up his shirt.

A blush creeping up on my cheeks, "Thank you, I'm making potatoes and chicken on the barbeque, Portuguese style." I wink at him as the stove starts beeping behind me to let me know it's heated to its proper temperature. I turn to grab the potatoes and slide them into the oven. I shut the oven and find Auston bringing me a glass of wine, and I graciously accept it from his hand.

This man knows me well.

He leans me against the counter capturing my body in between his arms.

"I feel like you are always the one cooking for me. I think

our next dinner should take place at mine." He leans down and kisses the space between my neck and shoulder and I feel goosebumps rise on my arm. I haven't been to Auston's place, but I genuinely enjoy having him here. This house is pretty big for one person, but I love it because it was my mom and dad's. I can't even imagine where Auston's place is in Simcoe; maybe he lives in the new development in Port Dover, a nearby tourist town.

"I would love that, I feel like you're an enigma to me Principal Scott," I smirk as I play with his shirt. "I got to know your childhood in the city when we walked around the city, and your past relationships, but I feel like there is more to learn." I bite my lip. When we were walking around the city after the game, Auston told me about how his life was very different than it is now.

He grew up low-income and struggled with being made fun of because his clothes were always slightly tattered, and he didn't have lunches like the other kids. It wasn't until he was in high school that his father's business took off and they quickly went from low-income, to high-income. He told me about how his life changed overnight. People wanted to be friends with him because his family was moving towards wealth, and girls were falling all over him. However, he told me about how he peaked in university and that's when he really grew into himself and felt confident. I can't help but put myself in his place, I'd never be able to trust anyone. If I had people only like me because of my parent's wealth, I think I would have struggled more with letting people in. That doesn't seem to be much of an issue for him though.

"What do you want to know?" He mumbles into my shoulder, while nipping at the skin there. I giggle and push him away,

"Tell me something nobody knows about you." I turn

around to move the potatoes around, giving him some time to muster up an answer.

"Hmm," I hear him thinking behind me, "I dress to impress every day because of how I was treated as a child when my parents couldn't afford new clothing." He admits, fidgeting with the collar of his shirt. He looks slightly uncomfortable sharing that, probably never having shared that information with someone else.

"Wait a second, so the reason you dress like a GQ model is because of your past? So, you use your fashion as a form of armour?" I quirk an eyebrow because we both use our clothing for similar reasons, just different forms of trauma.

"Yes, I guess so." He questions himself, never realizing that he uses clothing as armour due to his past.

"I use my clothing as my armour because it makes me feel confident." My voice raises a slight octave because someone else uses fashion as a crutch, like I do. He laughs slightly, making the connection himself to my excitement.

"So, does that make you my queen in shining armour?" His eyes twinkle and I roll my eyes.

"Shut up, I'm just saying... It makes me feel better. I was a little worried you may be a little too normal for me..." I wink at him and he throws his head back laughing. My heart does this weird pulsing thing, almost like a stutter, looking at him with his head thrown back.

"You don't give yourself enough credit. When you walk into a room, you fill the space with sunshine. Not only because of how beautiful you are, but because of how caring and kind you are. When I first saw you making eyes at me in Dallas Pub, I couldn't help but notice how beautiful you are. You looked shocked seeing me, thinking I was the most beautiful thing you had ever seen, but you were the most beautiful woman I had ever seen." He finishes and meets my gaze. My eyes began to water as soon as he called me sunshine, and now tears are trailing down my cheeks, a weight of emotion landing on my chest. Only my parents ever referred to me as sunshine, and it's as if something clicks into place when he said that.

I love this man. I really do love him.

Love has no limit, timeframe, or age... it just happens, out of the blue, in the most unexpected ways.

I take a deep shuddering breath, deciding if this is the right moment to tell him. My chest tightens because when else can I tell him? This moment seems perfect to me, but what if it's too soon for him?

Just as I think I'm about to tell him, he interrupts me,

"I love you too, Victoria." He smirks down at me, knowing that's exactly what I was going to say. I hiccup as tears continue to trail slowly down my face. "Stop crying, gorgeous." I laugh as he grabs my face and brings his lips to mine. The saltiness in between our lips but we don't stop.

I never want to stop.

"I love you." I whisper, and he smiles while pecking my lips one last time. I hug him closely and take a deep breath while wiping underneath my eyes.

This really happened.

"I should probably check the potatoes and turn the barbeque on..." I mumble as I lean back away from his chest and fan my face, trying to get it to cool down.

"I'll turn on the barbeque, you just get everything settled in here." He smiles at me, his eyes filled with an emotion I now know: love.

I finish plating our dinner as Auston takes the plates to the table, and I remember his meetings from today.

"How did it go with the students' parents today?" I fill our glasses back up and bring them to the table where Auston has just finished taking a seat. I sit down and notice the somber look cross his face.

"The parents got into a really heated argument. I'm usually the one who's doing the arguing," he pauses to throw me a smirk and I laugh. "But they immediately began pinning it on the opposite child. It was a disaster; I've never seen parents get so riled, and I come from a city school." He rubs the back of his neck, clearly stressed with the situation.

"I'm sorry." I can't help but feel a little nag since I'm the one who brought this problem to his office.

"Don't apologize for something you are meant to do, gorgeous. As educators, we need to always put a child's emotions and safety first and you did the right thing. Doesn't mean the parents agree though…" He eats a piece of potato before continuing. Moaning as it hits his tongue and I squirm in my seat watching him devour the food I made. It feels domestic, I've never cooked for anyone aside from Emma and Hannah and the pride that fills me is welcoming. Maybe this is why my mom enjoyed cooking for my dad so much?

"You are never getting rid of me when you cook like this." He smiles, and I can't help but smile back.

Thank you mom, for teaching me your skills in the kitchen.

"In the end, both parents decided to veto charges. Since there was no arrow indicating who started the relations, they let it be. Although, Ms. Bernard's parents weren't happy. They believe their child was seduced by an older boy and that it traumatized their little girl." He clenches his jaw quickly but releases just as fast. The emotions that swirled through his eyes weren't good ones. I can't help but feel like Auston has a deeper connection to students than he lets off. Maybe when he was a teenager something happened to him? I mean, it wouldn't be a surprise considering he came into money while in high school. Teachers probably realized he was eighteen and had his father's fortune coming, and wanted to sink their claws into him. That's a question for later though, because I don't want to ruin our night with something I know would upset him further. These emotions I see flashing through his face tell me there is something more to Auston, but he doesn't feel comfortable talking about it. I know better than anyone, not to push someone about something they aren't comfortable talking about.

"If I were a parent, I think I would understand better. However, from the perspective of a young girl? This could definitely be traumatizing. I know sex has become super progressive and people don't need to be in relationships anymore to do it, but young girls are still learning who they are." I pause as Auston nods along while stuffing his face with food.

"Actually, that reminds me… I was thinking the other day that Emma, Hannah, and I could start some sort of support group that allows students to come and talk to us if they are having any problems in school? When I was a teenager, I lacked so many resources for things that took place in between those walls. I had the girls and my parents, but as you can see, that didn't stop the trauma from seeping into my adulthood." My cheeks heat. I hate that my child-hood impacted me so much and pretty much ruined what was supposed to be a great time in my adulthood. Everyone was always ten steps forward, while I was always ten steps back. I watched people in university and teachers college enjoy their lives. I was too preoccupied with losing my parents, my insecurities, and my mental health. I never got to fully enjoy being careless and having fun. After my parents passed, I became a robot. I finished university and teacher's college because I knew I had to make my parents proud. Once I had finished those things and gotten a job, I became a little lost. I spent my days like a robot, going through the motions of teaching, eating, going to Kline's, and sleeping. Until Auston came into my life, I had never really lived. I mean, I had sex with him in his office. I had only ever read about that in books, and now? I have stepped outside my normal and partaken in a real-life fantasy of mine. I feel like I'm living my own romance story; I just hope it ends in a happily-ever-after. Auston shakes me from my thoughts,

"I think that's a great idea. I noticed the school doesn't really have many resources for students regarding bullying, mental health, and more. I think you, Emma, and Hannah would be the perfect individuals to start something like that. Emma being the gym teacher is beneficial because it can help with boys feeling more comfortable to talk to her, compared to someone who's never interacted with them." He takes his last bite of chicken and leans back. I love his brain.

"Yes! That's exactly what I was thinking too. I need to talk to the girls about it because I hadn't really discussed any of this with them. I thought about it while I was walking out of your office because of my anxieties for Isabel." I exclaim as I swipe one last potato into my mouth. I grab our plates and quickly pad into the kitchen to rinse them off. Auston begins to clear the table as I set everything into the dishwasher.

I turn around just as he wraps his arms around me.

"How about we go watch one of those dirty romance movies you like so much, and then re-create our own dirty romance?" Auston leans his head down and kisses a path up my neck, towards my ear.

"I like the sound of that Mr. Scott." I smirk and grab his hand, dragging him away from the kitchen towards the living room for the dirtiest movie I can find on the streaming platform.

I stretch my body, leaning over to turn my alarm off. A groan sounds beside me, and I laugh as Auston's legs are entangled with my own. After our dirty romance movie last night, Auston and I definitely re-created some of those scenes. I would judge that ours were more passionate, though I may be a little biased. I snicker to myself and turn to face Auston.

"Good morning, gorgeous." He leans over and kisses me, and I can't help but stare at him. Sunlight is shining into my bedroom and directly hitting his body, giving him a bronze glow. His green eyes are glimmering from the sunlight and his lips are begging to be kissed. His hair is tousled from my fingers and sleep which is giving off morning sex vibes. We need to get out of bed though, or else we are going to be late for work.

"Good morning handsome, how did you sleep?" I lean over and kiss him one more time before trying to get up. Emphasis on try, because Auston wraps his arms around me and drags me back against his body. I let out a girlish giggle as I try to unwind myself from him.

"We need to get ready for work! You still need to head home and change. You can't wear yesterday's suit to work today, that's almost as bad as the walk of shame." I giggle as I kiss his nose and he smirks up at me.

"I may have been a bit presumptuous yesterday and left a

duffle bag and suit bag in my car in hopes that this is how our night would end." He laughs and sits up as I gape at him. It's a feigned surprise because he knows he can stay here anytime he wants; I don't mind at all.

"Well, I guess we should grab your stuff and get ready. I'll even let you shower with me… to save water." I wink at him as he throws himself back and laughs. I walk into the hallway and grab some towels as Auston exits in only his slacks. He swats my ass as he walks to the door to go to his car and grab his stuff. I look down and notice I got out of bed and walked around naked, in broad daylight, without even thinking.

I close my linen closet door and smile because damn, it seems like things are on the up and up. I look at my memory wall, at the first picture of my parents and I back in high school. I kiss my fingertips and bring it to their faces.

Sending up a thank you.

An hour and an orgasm for each of us later, we finally arrive at school minutes apart. We've been doing a pretty good job at keeping our relationship out of anyone's ears; only the girls and Michelle know what's going on. Some days it's thrilling to be hiding something from everyone; our secret glances and touches that oddly occur. Other days I just want to grab his face and kiss him, but I know that's not professional, so I refrain.

He shoots me a wink as he gets out of his car and I try to hide my smile as I walk into school. Auston salivated at my outfit today when I came out of my closet. Clearly his earlier comments about my outfits not being appropriate for a school setting were because of his attraction towards me, not because I don't look good. I decided to go with an outfit that was a little out-there, but still conservative enough for work. I wore my big grey sweater dress that hides my body, while still looking flattering, and paired it with grey faux snake patterned thigh high boots. Auston loved the boots, and he promised to fuck me in them later.

I make my way up the stairs as I pass a few students going towards my classroom.

"Hey Ms. Mateus, nice outfit!" A student I had last term tells me in passing and I can't help the surprise that passes across my face. I quickly recover and shoot her a smile and thank her. I make my way down the hallways, and today feels different. The usual grey lockers and white tile floors look brighter. Maybe it's just my mood, but regardless, I'm feeling good.

I get to my large grey door and shove the key in, waiting to hear the clink sound from the lock. Once it clicks I push the door open and set my bag on my desk, and I take a deep breath. Everything is so good right now.

So good.

I bite my bottom lip and do a little happy dance as I draw open the window covers. I'm so busy daydreaming, I don't even notice the girls come in.

"Did I notice Mr. Scott and you arrive only minutes apart from one another? Either you guys texted one another before leaving or…" Emma wiggles her eyebrows at me and I laugh, turning around and heading toward them. They both pause and squint their eyes at me and I stop.

"What? Why are you both giving me that look?" I cautiously walk around them to my desk and grab my laptop from my bag.

"Babe, you look fine. Like you always look fine, but today's outfit is just perfection… and you look like you're glowing?" Hannah questions. They both sit down on the desks across from me and I bite my lip.

"We told each other we loved one another last night…" I say quietly, and all hell breaks loose.

"What." Emma shouts. She jumps off the desk as it skids behind her from impact.

"Holy fuck, tell us everything." Hannah exclaims, and they start screaming. I laugh while telling them to shush… multiple times. There are students beginning to roam around the hallways and I don't need them hearing these two gush.

"Don't you fucking dare tell me to shush woman, this is huge!" Emma starts bouncing and I laugh leaning my head back on my chair. I recollect everything that has happened in the last twenty-four hours to them, including Laura. They sit there a little stunned and I lean my head back up to look at them and see a gleam in Emma's eye.

"Fuck yeah." She jumps up from the desk and fist pumps, "My girl's got it. Babe, we are so happy for you!" Emma runs around and pretty much tackles me in a hug as I laugh.

"Seriously, Victoria, this is amazing. You stood up to Laura and found the man of your dreams. Your parents would be so proud of you, I know we are." Hannah reaches over and grabs my hands as my emotions get the better of me. Tears begin to rim my eyes and I sniffle.

The girls round my desk and give me a hug and I try my damn best to keep my tears at bay.

"You guys… you're going to make me full-blown ugly cry. Thank you, for everything." I squeeze them tightly before letting go and they sit back on the desks. Emma straightens the one she shoved with excitement back into place. "Anyways, what is going on with you guys?" I quickly load up my computer to get ready for today's class, which is continuing our discussion on Romeo and Juliet.

"My dad is deciding to retire as chief at the police station." Hannah says. I cannot believe those words just came out of her mouth. Her dad has been a police officer for as long as I can remember. He has an absolute passion for it and has always said he's never going to retire.

"Really?" Emma asks.

"Yeah, he decided he wants to spend more time with my mom. He says that his years are going by quickly and before he knows it, he won't have enjoyed any free time with mom." She smiles. Hannah loves her parents so much, she's an only child and she has so much love within her family. When my parents passed away, they took me in as their own and I will forever be grateful to them.

"Good for them, they deserve it. I hope they take all those trips they have been planning since we were teenagers. They haven't been on a trip in years and they should spend their time adventuring and enjoying life." I smile and Hannah nods.

"I agree, your dad has always been a workaholic. I'm sure it's killing him having to retire, but he's going to enjoy himself so much more now." Emma exclaims.

"Yeah, I know. He has a few more months until it's official, so I'm sure in that time, he's going to be working his ass off." She laughs, and we join in because it's so true. Hannah's dad did one of the largest drug busts in Simcoe's history. There were over three million dollars-worth of drugs and weapons, which is a lot for our small town. It was insane when it happened too because SWAT came to town and the news reported it. We had just started working at Angel's when it happened too. It was all anyone could talk about for weeks. Her dad won an award for his work in identifying the raid.

The bell warns us that we are ten minutes away from classes starting and I groan.

"You guys down to go to Kline's this weekend? I think

some others are going but we haven't had a night out in a while. You can tell Auston to come too." Emma winks at me, and I laugh.

"You know what? I'm totally down for that!" I smile and round my desk, walking them to the door.

"Who is this woman, and why do I love her so much?" Hannah gasps and I hug them both as they make their way down the hall to their respective classes. I stand outside my door watching as students start to move about, making their way to their classes. They start to filter into my class, saying good morning as they pass, which puts another smile on my face. This is my controversial class and I cannot wait to hear their opinions on whether they think Romeo and Juliet is a romance or tragedy. Once the final bell rings, I make my way into the classroom and shut the door. I quickly take attendance and then make my way to the front of the class.

"So, who wants to argue with me as to why Romeo and Juliet is a tragedy, and not in fact a romance?" I smirk as arms shoot into the air. A sense of pride fills me as I start picking students to share their opinions.

My morning period was awesome. It's classes like that one that show me how amazing it is to be an English teacher. Students got into heated arguments over our discussion and honestly, it filled me with a thrill. It's been so long since my students have actually immersed themselves into my classes, and it made for a productive class. I even assigned homework to them to put their thoughts onto paper about what we discussed. They look ready to start the papers in class and it makes my heart swell. It's moments like these that remind me why I wanted to be a teacher. I wanted to help mold young brains and hearts. I wanted to help them find their passions, whatever they are.

People like to belittle English literature, but it brings

thought to so many different arguments that can branch in different directions. No one person reads the same book, everyone has a different perspective after reading which is the beauty of the written word. I write down my thoughts from this morning's class before grabbing the piles of tests from the second period. Just as I'm about to start marking some students' essays on satire, my phone vibrates in the drawer beside me. I open the wooden drawer and notice a text from Auston. I shove the drawer shut since it gets jammed sometimes from the old wood.

Auston: Meet me at my car in five minutes.

I stare at my phone with bewilderment obvious on my face and send him a quick okay. I shut down my computer and grab my keys to lock the classroom. Lunch is next period, so I don't have to worry about being back until my last class of the day. I make my way quickly down the closest stairs at the rear, near the staff parking lot. I quickly glance around and see no sign of anyone nearby and make my way to Auston's sleek BMW. He must not be here yet because I don't see any sign of him. Just as I'm about to lean against his car, the back door shoots open and he grabs me. He manoeuvres my body to straddle his lap and quickly shuts the door behind me.

"Auston! What are you doing?" He runs his hands teasingly up my naked legs and a shudder racks through my body.

"I kept thinking about you all morning, I told you I was going to fuck you in these boots." He runs his hands all the way around to the front of my pussy and drags a finger slowly over the fabric of my panties. He leans his head back against the headrest with a smirk and hooded eyes.

"I thought…" I gasp and groan at the same time. "I thought you meant after work." I put my hands on his shoulders and lean down to gently press my lips to his. He moves aside my panties and teases the outside of my pussy by running a finger through my folds.

"I couldn't wait that long for you, gorgeous." He latches onto my neck and I groan as I grind myself down on his hardened length. He stretches the material of my dress off my shoulders and pulls the cup of my bra down and sucks in my nipple. I groan out loud and quicken my grinding; I've lined up our cores so the pleasure racks through both of us.

Auston finally slips his fingers into my wet core and I run my fingers through his hair. I pull his head back forcefully and hiss as his teeth grind against my nipples.

"I need more Auston." I breathe heavily. As much as I love his magic fingers, I want his cock more.

"Mmmm," he murmurs. "Do you like the thought that we could get caught? Any staff or student could just walk out and see the car moving?" I widen my eyes in realization and a devilish gleam crosses Auston's face. He doesn't give me much time to process as he presses his finger perfectly onto my clit and starts circling it. I lean my body back against the seat and moan his name. The familiar build starting in my toes. Either that or my body is cramped up. "More baby, more." I grind out as the build heightens and I climax all over his hand.

"Fuck, I love watching you orgasm." I open my eyes as he pulls his fingers out of my wet pussy and slowly brings a finger into his mouth. He sucks them slowly and his eyes roll to the back of his head at my taste. I bite my lip as I watch him, and I can't take it.

I use my knees to push myself up and unbuckle his pants to shove them down his legs as he helps me. I grab the condom he has in his hand and sheath him by rolling it on and pinching the tip. I rise on my knees and look at him as I slowly lower myself onto his cock.

The fullness is perfect, exactly what I needed.

I begin to move slowly as he grabs onto my hips and hisses out a groan.

"You're so tight." He groans out as he grabs my neck forcefully and brings our mouths together passionately. I begin to quicken my slams and feel the car moving with us. I don't even care, too lost in the moment of Auston's body under me.

The build in my core begins and I reach down between us and start circling my clit as Auston begins thrusting up into me faster and harder.

"Fuck gorgeous, keep doing that." He brings his fingers up to tweak my nipples and the overwhelming spasm throughout my entire body. I groan out my release as Auston does the same. His arms tighten on my hips and the veins in his neck jut out as his release consumes him. I take a deep shuddering breath, just as we notice a car pull up beside Auston's.

We both freeze and try to calm our bodies down from our car fucking, when Tracey steps out of her car. My eyes widen, and I say a silent fuck. I want to hide my face into the crook of Auston's neck, but I'm too scared to move.

"My car is tinted, she can't see in here unless she comes close." He groans out, still seated deep inside my warm pussy.

In that moment, Tracey does the strangest thing ever, and leans over to look into the front seat of Auston's car.

"What the fuck?" He grits out. I sit completely still as her face is pressed up against the glass, looking in the front seat. I pray that she doesn't look back here because if she does, she is going to get an unwelcoming surprise.

Auston brings his finger back to my clit and I gasp and try to push his hands away. He presses down further, and I bite my lips to keep from moaning out.

"Auston," I half hiss, half whimper through clenched teeth. He only smirks with an evil look in his eye. He presses further into my clit and it sparks another wave in my body. The build starts again in my core and I try to rise up on my knees, but he holds me down with his other hand.

Tracey backs away from the car and turns around back towards her car to grab something. Auston picks up speed on my clit and I fucking explode for the third time.

"Auston," I breathe out. "We could have gotten caught!" I whisper-shout at him and he laughs. I glance outside and notice that Tracey has decided to make her way back into the school.

"I love you; I don't care who knows anymore." He gently grabs my neck and brings my lips to his.

"I love you too." I smirk into his kiss.

CHAPTER TWENTY

"I cannot believe that you had sex with Auston in front of the school yesterday! Who even are you?" Emma giggles as she straightens her hair. We're all over at my place getting ready to go to Kline's for a night out. I have my makeup bag skewed on the floor in front of my body mirror. A curling iron is sitting atop my night table, beside Hannah on the bed as she parts her hair, and Emma is laying out the four different outfits she brought with her.

"Guys, he takes away any of my common sense. I mean, we were so close to getting caught, and by fucking Tracey of all people!" I giggle as I finish applying some mascara. Tonight I decided to wear some black ripped jeans, black thigh high boots, and one of my dad's old Motley Crue T-shirts. It's got a couple holes along the seam and is a tad faded, but it gives off this authentic rocker look. Kline's is a casual bar, so we really don't have to dress up or put any effort in, but the girls and I don't get to dress-up very often. Although I love wearing my classy teacher outfits during the week, I really enjoy being able to channel different styles.

My dad had a myriad of band T-shirts, and I kept every single one. If there's any way for me to channel my relationship with my dad now that he has passed, it's by wearing his old T-shirts and looking like a badass.

I glance over to Emma and see that she's decided to wear a black t-shirt dress with red thigh high boots. I look in the mirror and notice Hannah standing, slipping her feet into a pair of classic wedge boots. Hannah went classic with her outfit for tonight with dark wash skinny jeans and a satin spaghetti strap top. I admit we all look hot as hell tonight, and I love the vibes we are giving off. We have always been in sync with our outfits. We don't even discuss them, but we always look like we did. That's what years of friendship can do. I apply some red lipstick and pucker them in the mirror.

"Fuck yeah, we look hot tonight. We're giving off these sexy alternative vibes and I'm digging it." Emma shakes her ass behind my head in the mirror. We have The Weeknd's *Starboy* playing in the background to get us in the mood for tonight. I'm not usually one for more modern tunes, because of my oldie heart, but this man gets me going. His voice is smooth and angelic, not to mention seductive.

I walk into the kitchen to grab us some shots to get us ready for the night. We really missed out on going to clubs and parties when we were in university. We were all so preoccupied with our grades and other things that we never really got to experience university life. We're making up for it as adults though, because there have been many times in the last few years that we have gotten drunk and ended up back at my place with wicked hangovers.

With three shots in my hand, I make my way back to my room and hand one off to each of the girls.

"I guess tonight's poison is tequila because it's all I had in the cabinet." I twist my face, because this isn't usually my drink of choice.

"To a great night filled with lots of good music," Hannah begins as Emma interrupts.

"And hot sex!" Emma cheers our glasses together and we laugh as we take our shots. The familiar burn of tequila slides down my throat; I squeeze my eyes together and shake it off. Tequila calls for bad decisions. I mean, is there really any other reason it was made?

I grab my phone and see I have a text from Auston saying he will meet us tonight and I get excited. We're still keeping our relationship on the downlow, however, the sneaking around has grown on me. As nerve-wracking as it sometimes is, I also get a thrill from sneaking around with Auston.

I hear the doorbell ring, which indicates that our taxi is here. The girls carpooled with me home after work so that they didn't have to bring their cars here.

I quickly grab my crossbody bag and throw it over my leather jacket, then give myself one last look.

I pause while looking at myself.

My eyes look brighter, my lips are tilted in a subtle curve, and I feel good in my skin. It has taken me almost thirty years to feel good in my skin. I never thought this time would come, when I would be secure in my body and feel genuine happiness, but I do. Tingles radiate across my chest, a sense of content ravishing itself through my body and causing the tilt to my lips to become a full-blown smile.

"Let's go, my beautiful friends." I nod my head at Emma and follow behind them and shut off the lights to my bedroom. Our heels click down my hallway and we reach the door. I grab my keys from the tray on the ottoman by the door and turn to look into my home.

I have a good feeling about the future. Maybe optimism can be my new thing…

We open the door to Kline's and immediately the smell of liquor, grease, and sweat greet our noses. Booths are packed, people are dancing to the music blasting through the speakers in the corner, and people are enjoying the start of their weekend.

"I hope Joe is serving wings tonight. I want wings and more tequila." Emma shouts and we both follow behind her towards our booth.

"My three favorite girls." Joe has his arms out and we laugh. Each of us giving him side-hugs. "You're lucky I was able to save your booth, people are vultures tonight. I don't think I've seen it this busy in months." Joe motions for us to sit and we do.

"Winter is slowly starting to pass, so people are getting out of their winter funk. Which just means more money for you, so that's a good thing." Hannah winks at Joe and he gives a hearty laugh.

"Joe, are you serving up wings tonight?" Emma gives Joe puppy eyes and he shakes his head, but I can see the laughter in his eyes. Joe only does wing night every so often, but his wings are the best in town. By the sticky grease smell swirling around the bar, I think Emma knows her answer. I can almost guarantee that as soon as Joe saw us walk through the door, he had put in an order for two pounds of wings.

"You know the order is already in, darling." He smirks. "You girls want your usual order?" He nods his pen towards us.

"Actually, can we get some beers to start with our wings?" Hannah requests and I raise my brows in surprise. We aren't usually beer drinkers, but they do tend to pair best with wings.

"Absolutely, I'll even give you the good stuff." He winks.

"You're too good to us, Joe." I smile, and he shoots us a boyish smile and walks away.

"I'll never know how he's single. Honestly, for a guy in his fifties, he's a fox. The tattoos? Silver hair? Muscles? Like I honestly don't understand it," Emma says. I glance over and watch Joe interact with his workers. He's definitely a silver fox. For a guy who lives and breathes his bar, he looks good.

"I agree, but my dad has told me some wild stories about Joe." Hannah has heard some wild stories about most people in this town. With your dad as head chief of police, it's bound to happen.

"The bike gang stuff? Come on, that's cool... and I can see it." Emma leans her elbows on the table and Hannah proceeds to tell us the story about how Joe used to be in a motorcycle gang. He spent his early twenties tied to a gang until it took a dark turn and Joe had to move to a small town in Canada after growing up in the U.S. Hannah's dad had dug around on him when he first moved to town and bought the bar. He was relatively young, and people began to talk about this rugged biker walking around town. Joe has never caused any problems in town, but from the stories we've heard, I'm curious to know about his past because it seems interesting. Although we've known him for what feels like forever, we never asked him about his previous life, the one before the bar. It seemed inconsequential, since he was clearly trying to keep that part of his life locked up.

"Alright here we are ladies. Two pounds of wings and

three beers," He sets down the wings and my mouth salivates. The wings are shiny with sauce, and the aroma of fresh fried barbeque perfumes the air. "Let me know if you need anything else." Someone shouts his name from across the bar and he rolls his eyes at us, while going to his next customer who keeps shouting his name.

I'm in the middle of my eighth juicy wing when Emma shoves her elbow into my ribs,

"Would you look at what the cat dragged in, it's our very own GQ eye candy for the night!" Emma smiles at what I assume is Auston. I take a sip and look over to see Auston approaching, and almost choke on my beer.

I lightly tap my chest to help the beer pass through the tunnel as Hannah's arms shake against mine from laughing. Auston approaches our table and I can't help but fawn over him. Even after the time we've spent together, seeing him still causes butterflies to erupt across my lower region. His aesthetic is the complete opposite of his traditional principal attire. He's wearing light wash ripped jeans, a baggy grey t-shirt, and black sneakers. He's thrown a flannel overtop which has seriously caused some tingles down below. For a guy who grew up in the city, he makes modern country look good. He removes his flannel and sets it on the back of his chair, and my eyes widen at his arms. I don't think I will ever get over the way the fabric clings to his arms, looking like the seams are about to bust.

"Auston, you've made Victoria blind and deaf. She hasn't heard a word that any of us have said." My shoulders hunch in embarrassment. They were talking? *Oops.*

"I just…" I take a sip of beer to moisten my all of a sudden dry mouth. "I zoned out… what did you guys say?" The heat rises to my cheeks as Auston sits in front of me and sends a cheeky smirk my way. I can't help but let my gaze roam his body again, taking in his... *everything*.

I think one of my favorite qualities of Auston is his fashion sense, much like mine, is extremely versatile. Neither of us allow our professions to dictate what we should wear or what we should look like. We wear whatever we want, and on him? Yeah, probably one of my top five favorite qualities.

"I was asking how long you've been here for." He smirks, and I roll my eyes. He knows exactly how long we've been here. I texted him while we were in the taxi on the way here.

"Oh, come on guys. You don't need to act like you guys weren't texting each other while we sat in the taxi." Hannah grabs another wing, while shooting me a look that says *really?*

I motion to Joe to bring one more beer to the table. Luckily, through the throng of people that crowd the bar, he glances up at me and catches my movements. I look around the bar and notice there are so many more people here than usual. I see a lot of people I went to high school with and other locals.

I pick up my glass and finish off what's left of my beer. The girls are talking with Auston about something, when I notice Laura and Tracey walk in. After our encounter at the grocery store, I hope she keeps her distance. The familiar clench around my chest as I try to remember that I stood up to her, and I'm not the same person I was in high school, or even a month ago.

Joe walks over and sets a beer in front of Auston and he gives his thanks. Luckily, Joe also brought us three margaritas.

"We need to start going somewhere else, you know us too well Joe." I smile, and Emma nods her head and wiggles in her seat after taking a sip of her new drink. Although we enjoy beer with our wings, we will always be fruity drink girls.

"Nah, you wouldn't be treated as good as you are here." Joe laughs and walks away. I look up to find Auston looking at me and I lightly nudge his leg with my boot while smiling.

Conversation starts to flow, as do the drinks. Before we know it, the bar is thumping with beats and we all have had a bit much to drink after only having been here an hour...or two? My brain is a little fuzzy as I try to think about how long we've been sitting in the booth talking and laughing.

"Let's dance." He stands up and puts his hand out for me to grab. I look around because I don't exactly know if dancing with my boss is a good idea. The girls notice my hesitation and shove me out of the seat.

"Go dance, who gives a fuck. It's a Friday night and I don't think anyone is paying attention. There is already a crowd out there, go enjoy yourself." Emma wiggles her eyebrows suggestively and I roll my eyes while putting my hand in Auston's. His grip tightens on mine as the familiar strum to *Do I Wanna Know* by Arctic Monkeys starts pushing through the speaker. The sensual strum shakes the floorboards of the old bar and I can't help but the familiar buzz arise. Auston tugs my hips backwards so that my back is to his front. He moves his hips to the tempo of the beat and my heart lurches.

Holy fuck, this is sexy.

He slowly glides his hands along my neck and moves my hair away and plants a wet kiss on my neck.

"You look sexy tonight..." He whispers in my ears as goosebumps rise along my arms. I lean my head back on his shoulder and move my body with his. His hands are roaming my body and the heat building in my core.

"I want to feel you..." He slyly runs his hands in front of

my jean clad pussy and I gasp. He quickly spins me around so that we're now face to face. His hand rests above my ass, holding us together as we sway. He leans his head down and slowly bites my lower lip, stretching it outwards. My eyes flutter closed at the sensations sparking through me. His hardened length rests against me and I can't help but put more pressure against him. He growls in my ear, and I can't take another second of this taunting. I grab his hand and start to drag him towards the men's room.

It's not the cleanest place, but fuck, I need Auston's cock in me now. As soon as I drag him through the door, he grabs a hold of me and lifts me, slamming me back against the door. I fumble with his belt loop as he trails kisses up my throat.

"I need you, now." I gasp as he bites down on my neck and I thrust forward against him. He groans out and gives me space to release his shaft. I awkwardly pull it out and start to move my hands up and down, rubbing the tip to collect the moisture that has collected.

"Fuck…" Auston groans out as he captures his lips in mine. Our mouths battle for dominance and when I suck on his tongue and that's his tipping point. Auston quickly releases our connected mouths and leans down to remove my boots and jeans. It takes him a minute to figure it out, but once he has them off, he hoists me back up and rubs his cock along my clothed pussy.

"I can feel the heat radiating off you." He smirks and I breathe out a smile. "How bad do you want me, baby?"

I bite my lip, "I want you to give it to me hard and deep…" Auston throws his head back on a groan and I can't help but lean my head forward and lick the nerve that's jutted out on his neck. His skin tastes a bit salty from the sweat, but I latch my lips onto him and begin to suck while moving torturously slowly against his cock.

"Fuck this…" He grabs a hold of my panties and tears them from my hips. The fabric rub against my clit roughly and I gasp and bang my head backwards against the door. He's already looking at me with a dark smirk on his face and I bite my lip as he shoves my ripped panties into his pockets. He's about to reach into his other pocket when I remind him I'm on the pill and he roughly grabs my neck and brings his lips to mine.

He leans me back against the door and holds me up with one arm as he positions himself at my entrance. I look down and see the strain in his arm as he holds me up, veins lining his arm aggressively. Usually I'd be insecure due to my weight, but I'm in a lust-filled haze.

"Ready, gorgeous?" He looks into my eyes and I lean down and bite his lip. He slams into me and I throw my head back as a scream gets stuck in my throat. The air has been completely knocked out of me.

Holy fuck, I don't think I'll ever get used to his size after being empty for so many years prior.

Auston holds my body up as he begins to thrust aggressively into my pussy. Our moans and the beat of the music outside are all we can hear. My one hand sits around Auston's neck, but I slowly drag my other hand down towards my clit. I start to rub at the perfect tempo as Auston thrusts, and his eyes turn almost black seeing me touch myself as his dick is in me.

"Fuck me Vic, I'm not going to last long with you doing that." He grunts as he quickens his pace. Our bodies move together in sync and I begin to feel the crescendo building in my core. I put more pressure against my clit and throw my head back,

"Don't stop… don't stop." I press out as the intensity peaks in my core. A sense of euphoria hits me as my climax rushes through me,

"Now, Auston." His pace becomes brutal until he stills as his body releases his own climax. His hands have a death-like grip on my thighs, not that I can feel it much with the alcohol and lust in my system.

"Holy fuck…" I breathe out. I never thought I would have sex in the men's washroom, especially at Klines, but fuck… that was good.

"You are my vixen, Vic." Auston leans his head forward into my neck and I smile, giddy with feelings.

"I love you." I smile down at him as I rub his neck. My legs are cramped from being around his waist, but I don't want to break this delicious moment.

"I love you too. I never thought I would be having sex in a small-town bar with the most gorgeous woman I've ever seen, but I guess there's a first for everything." He laughs, and I bite my tongue to refrain from giggling.

He slowly releases me onto my feet and grabs my jeans from the floor, sliding them up my legs. As he fixes himself, I rush into the one stall to clean up as best as I can after having sex in a bar bathroom. I walk out of the stall to find Auston leaning against the wall, looking freshly fucked.

"I have never gone commando, so I guess there really is a first for everything." I laugh. My legs feel like jelly trying to stand in high heel boots after wicked wall sex. I grab some paper towels and laugh as I clean the lipstick that coats Auston's lips. Red suits him.

"Don't touch the marks on my neck. I like having your print on me as we go back out there." I smile, nodding my head. I fix my lipstick as best as I can without having it in here with me. We both open the door and Joe is leaning against the wall beside it, and I jump nearly out of my skin.

"I had to keep about ten people from trying to go in there

with you two doing your business." Joe gives me a pointed look, but I see the playfulness in them. Joe knows all about my past and has always wished I would let go and live a little. I'll never forget the day he told me that I needed to live my life as I wanted because before I knew it, it would all be over. I knew for a fact how right he was; I saw it first-hand with my parents. I can see the pride in his eyes because as bad as it is what we just did, he's also seeing how happy I'm.

"Sorry, Joe, it won't happen again." I giggle, and he shakes his head.

"I'm just happy to see you living a little, girl." He smiles and nods his head to Auston. Auston nods back and Joe goes back to work like nothing ever happened.

"I'm happy Joe was keeping a look out; I don't know what I would do if someone else saw what's mine." Auston growls as he pulls me back towards the booth where the girls are still sitting.

"Well, would you look at that. You two look freshly fucked." Emma says, a little too loudly. I hold my lips together to keep from laughing with her because none of this seems real. Auston slides in beside me, and puts his arm behind me along the booth. It reminds me of when we were back at that delicious Italian restaurant in downtown Toronto.

"Well, don't you two look awfully cozy." The chalkboard cringing voice sounds from beside us. I look up to see Laura standing there with a smirk on her face. I try to take a deep breath; she really knows how to ruin my euphoria.

"What Laura, never been friends with a boss? Probably not. You're always trying to get forward by opening your legs rather than your mouth to build a relationship with them." Emma growls out. Laura rolls her eyes, trying to seem unaffected by the shot Emma just took. I see the embarrassment that passes through her eyes though.

"Save it Laura, just mind your own business and enjoy your night. We..." I direct a look at Emma. "Will not be playing your games tonight." I smile and take a sip from my margarita that has not moved since we went off to dance and rendezvous.

She's about to say something else, but I send her a pointed look because I'm actually enjoying my night. I don't want anyone, especially her, ruining it. My legs are still feeling the brutal sex I just had against the door, as is my pussy.

I don't need anyone ruining that.

"Look at this." Hannah does a little happy dance before grabbing her phone to show me something. Laura takes the hint and scoffs as she walks away from our table. I look down at Hannah's phone and stop.

Oh wow...

"You guys looked so hot out there." Emma giggles, and I just stare at the photo. Auston and I are on the dance floor, our fronts to one another, in a passionate kiss.

"This totally has to go on the memory wall. It will be a memory when Vic finally became who she was always meant to be..." Hannah smiles and I nod my head. This is definitely going on the wall.

Auston leans over my shoulder to look at the picture and he smiles, love glimmering in his eyes, "send that to both of us, I want a copy for myself."

I smile inwardly because I think my cheeks are already starting to feel the pain from my happiness. The last time I got to add to the memory wall was when Auston and I went to Toronto for the weekend. Looks like I will be adding this weekend to the memory wall as well; I might just have to take a trip to the store to buy some more frames.

I lean into Auston's shoulder because I'm happy. Finally,

I'm truly happy with where I'm in my life. I have my two best friends, and a man that I never expected, who's now a huge part of my life. Although my work life isn't exactly where I want it to be, I know I have time to get it where I want it. The puzzle pieces are finally starting to come together. I just hope I can find that missing piece.

CHAPTER TWENTY-ONE

The sunlight is streaming into my bedroom, the curtains slightly ajar. I roll over and face Auston who is asleep beside me. One arm is thrown behind his head, the other is resting on his abdomen. He looks completely relaxed, and delicious even this early in the morning.

Last night was something I'd never experienced, ever. The euphoric feeling from naughtily dancing with Auston and then proceeding into the bathroom for sex still leaves me with flutters in my stomach. Although we may have drank a bit too much, I still remember everything. The way his hands roamed along my body as we danced, the passionate kiss on the dance floor, and finally, the way he held me up against the bathroom door and brutalized my body. I've never enjoyed being picked up; I don't think many curvy women really do. But last night I felt weightless in his arms.

I bite my lip as Auston groans beside me. He turns his body to face mine and grabs me by the hips to nudge me closer.

"Good morning, gorgeous." He mumbles. His morning

voice, which is groggy, sends shivers all the way down to my toes.

"How long have you been awake?" I lean forward and gently press a kiss to his lips.

"I opened my eyes a minute ago, but you were deep in thought while staring at my body... what was going through that beautiful mind of yours?" He quickly turns my body so that I'm straddling him. That shouldn't have been as hot as it was, but apparently anything he does to me causes my nerves to go haywire.

"I was thinking about last night... It was so out of the ordinary for me. I really liked it. I like who I'm with you." I look down at him. His normally perfectly styled hair is a little messed up, his eyes bright from the light shining in the window, and his lips quirked... he looks perfect.

"Don't move." I stretch my body over his to grab my phone from the bedside table. Once I grab it, almost dropping it on the floor, I lean back and take a photo of him. He rolls his eyes playfully, trying to act like he doesn't love me taking photos of him.

At first he tries to look grumpy, but then a look of yearning passes through his eyes and he grabs a hold of my thighs. My pulse picks up and a tingle of awareness spread along my thighs where his hands lay. I snap a picture of this look.

This picture says a thousand words.

"I love you, Victoria." He moves his hands under his body to lift himself up. One hand holds him up, while the other grabs me around the neck and brings me to his lips. Our tongues tangle together, not in a lustful way, but in a loving way. This kiss is full of love and passion, and my mind becomes fuzzy with emotions.

We break apart and I feel like a silly love-struck teenager, but I wouldn't ask for anything else at this moment.

"I love you too, Principal Scott." I smile cheekily at him and he laughs. "Let's go make breakfast, handsome." I rise off him and set my feet down on my plush white carpet.

I grab a scrunchie from my dresser and throw my head down to collect my brown locks into a messy bun.

"Vic, if you don't stand upright, I'm going to maul you." Auston says from the edge of the bed. I bring my body back up and notice my reflection in my body mirror. I'm wearing a loose white T-shirt and black panties. My pear-shaped body is still evident in this T-shirt due to its slight strain along my hips.

"Sorry, Auston." I giggle as he shakes his head, his teeth playfully dragging along his bottom lip. I give him an exaggerated smile and make my way out the door and down the hallway, towards the kitchen. I flick on the coffee maker and try to think of what I have in my fridge. I went grocery shopping this week, so I should be able to whip something up. I open up the curtains in the kitchen as I think. Maybe I have enough to make a quiche? It doesn't usually take too long to put together. I open the fridge doors and notice I have eggs, ham, green peppers, onions, and cheese. I grab everything from the fridge and set it down on the counter.

"What can I help you with?" Auston walks in wearing his black boxers and I smirk. I see the game he's playing.

I guess my facial reaction is evident because Auston smirks back at me with a playful gleam in his eyes.

"Could you cut the vegetables while I prepare the pastry and coffee?" I grab the cutting board and knives and pass them to him. We both begin to prepare breakfast like we've done it millions of times before. Our bodies move in sync, exchanging little touches and glances of adoration every here and there.

Thirty minutes later, we're both sitting at the table with a fresh slice of quiche and steaming mugs of coffee in hand.

"Have you always enjoyed cooking? You seem completely in your element while in the kitchen." Auston asks as he takes a sip from his mug.

"When I was younger, my mom and I spent a lot of time in the kitchen. She absolutely loved cooking and baking. I have about twenty of her go-to cookbooks sitting above the fridge. If you open them up, you'll find little pieces of paper written in Portuguese that will say if she liked the recipe or not. If she didn't like them, she would modify them herself and write what should be changed in the recipe." I laugh, thinking about all the time mom spent in the kitchen.

"Every once in a while I would help her. She would explain why a certain ingredient should be changed, or maybe she would hate the recipe altogether. My mom grew up in a traditional Portuguese home, so my grandma always made traditional meals. My mom wanted to be able to cook a wide variety, so she would buy these books to help expand her cooking." I smile as I take a bite of my quiche. I may have gone a little cheese crazy on top, but I'm not too mad about it, and neither is Auston it seems since he's almost done with his piece. "What about you, do you have anything you do with your parents?"

"My dad was usually busy working. As a kid he was constantly trying to make something of himself, so I didn't see him much. Eventually, once his business took off while I was in high school, he started being around more. By that time though, I was more preoccupied with friends and girls, rather than family. If I could go back and change that, I would. I spent a lot of time out of the house once we were better off." I think about how different our upbringings were from one another. I was always home with my parents, even Emma and Hannah would come over to spend time with them.

"Eventually I grew up, and I didn't really have much to talk to them about..." He lowers his head and heavily sighs. "We have a better relationship now, but I was quite selfish in high school and university once things started to take off for us. I don't think my parents minded, but I think I took it for granted. I try my best now to visit them when I can." I cover my hand with his. I can see he feels uncomfortable talking to me about this. I mean, my parents are gone, and I would give anything to have them back. I spent so much time with them as a kid and teenager, and now I don't have any time with them at all.

"Hey, you can talk about them. I know that my parents not being here can impact me, and some days are worse than others. But I like hearing about your past, about who you were before you moved to this small, hick town." I give him a reassuring smile. "I have so many things to remember them by. I have spent my entire life within these four walls, and although I have updated a lot of it since they passed, they are still here. A piece of them will always be within these four walls."

"You're amazing, you know that?" He pauses, "you kept going, even though I'm sure you wanted to give up many times... you're the strongest person I've ever met. I think your parents would be so proud of who you have become." His voice suddenly became unsteady.

My eyes water slightly, "Thank you." I whisper. Auston rises from his seat and rounds the table to grab me. He holds me in his arms for a while and I just allow myself to feel this emotion.

Our conversation became heavy, but I don't feel anxious. I'm okay.

Talking about my parents used to bring a penetrating ache to my heart. Grief never goes away, no matter what anyone says. Time doesn't always heal that kind of pain; it just dulls it. The feeling of devastation, loneliness, and sadness is always here with me, but some days it's manageable, and others I feel like I may collapse and mourn their young lives.

I need to start living, if not just for myself, for them as well. I loosen my hold on Auston and look into his eyes. "Thank you. Not many people understand, but you being here, trying to understand, means a lot. Emma and Hannah were the only two who stuck by my side, no matter what. It nice to know that support has expanded."

Auston leans down and captures my lips in a soft kiss. "You aren't getting rid of me now, gorgeous. Any highs, any lows, I'm going to be here for you."

After an emotional, yet healing breakfast with Auston, I persuade him to come to a nearby city with me to buy new frames for my memory wall. After stopping to grab his car from Kline's, we head to his place for him to change. I've never been to Auston's place. When he asked me if I wanted to follow him to his place after getting his car, so he could shower and change, I couldn't say no. I'm curious to see where Auston lives. We spend a majority of our time at my place, which I don't mind because I love being home.

After driving for ten minutes, we pull into the parking lot beside the condo complex along the water in Port Dover. I park my car and get out and look at the murky water beside the condo. This condo was built beside the water a few years ago, trying to give that lakeside view that is usually obtained in the city. It fell quite short, considering it's beside the channel where boats come in and out.

"I didn't know you lived in the lakeside condos." I meet him by his car, as he lifts his body from his seat.

"I rent it. There weren't many options for luxury rentals around." I laugh because he's not wrong. Although Simcoe has started to grow, it's still not at the level of luxury many would want. It would be really out of place to throw luxury into the mixture of a small country town. Everyone has an opinion in a small town and with that usually means some very outspoken people have something to say about certain changes. I remember when this plot was sold for condos, many people were unhappy. They didn't want some big building blocking the beauty of the town, but alas, those with deeper pockets won the battle.

I don't even realize Auston is dragging me around, until we reach the door to his condo. I look down the hall and it doesn't seem like anything too crazy. The floors look like a ceramic tile and the walls are painted white, with dark brown doors. Auston unlocks the door and waves his hand for me to enter first. I walk in and the kitchen is immediately to the right, flowing into the living room. Auston isn't living in an end unit, so the only light that comes in is from the floor-to-ceiling wall opposite the door.

"It's only one bedroom, but it works for me. The rent isn't terrible, but since I was new to the area, I didn't really know what to look for." I walk towards the windows and notice it looks down into the downtown core of Port Dover. In the summer this area is usually buzzing with tourists, retirees, and teenagers. There are a lot of quick to eat spots and the beach is literally two minutes away.

"I mean, this place is perfect for the summer. The beach is minutes away, and since we have summers off, you can spend a lot of time enjoying everything Port Dover has to offer when the sun is shining." I smile back at him as he lifts his T-shirt off.

"I hope I'll be spending more time with a specific some-one, rather than at the beach...alone." He grabs my hips and before thinking, I blurt,

"Maybe by then you won't need to be renting anymore?" My eyes widen, and my body stiffens at my omission. I didn't mean to insinuate that he should move in with me. My eyes wander around his place, not wanting to make eye contact. Slight tightness is in my chest; I've never lived with a man before. I don't know why I blurted that out. We've only been seeing each other for a bit, moisture collecting in my palms.

"Hmm..." I hear him mumble across from me. He reaches out and grabs my shirt, stretching it towards him, "Is that your way of saying you want me to move in? Become roommates?" He questions, and I scoff a laugh.

"I didn't mean to blurt that, but I mean... I wouldn't..." I shake out my hands and take a deep breath.

"Relax, gorgeous." He laughs, "I would love to move in with you. Stop working yourself up over this. Are you sure though? I know you enjoy your space, and I wouldn't want to disturb you..." He cocks his head and bites his lip to keep from laughing.

"You're enjoying this, you ass." I scoff and shake my head, leaning it on his chest. The vibration of laughter radi-ates from him. "Fuck, if you're actually going to make me say it, yes. Yes, I would like it if you moved in with me." I lean my head back and look into his shimmering green eyes, excitement highlighted within them.

He's fully shaking with laughter now. He's really enjoying me being out of sorts over this.

"I mean, I rent this place month-to-month. I'm nearing the end of the month... I could let the landlord know? Unless you prefer we wait until the summer?" He tilts my head up and looks into my eyes, so much hope shining in his.

"I think…" I pause, "I think I would love that." I give him a timid smile because oh my goodness, Auston is moving in with me. I mean, we're adults. It really isn't that big of a deal, but to me… it's the next step. One I've never experienced before.

"Great," he kisses my nose. "Decision is made. Now, let me go shower before we head out to go frame shopping." He walks towards his bedroom and I glance around, noticing his place is sparse. There's almost nothing in here to give it any homey qualities, unlike his condo in Toronto. He has a small brown leather couch which looks super uncomfortable, and a TV mounted on the wall opposite the couch. Behind the couch sits a live-edge wooden desk with a black seat. I run my finger along the live-edge; I've always loved the look of it. A laptop and a few books sit atop the desk, but other than that, this place doesn't have nearly as much personality as his place in the city.

I sit at his desk and roll the chair to the window, watching people walk around. Spring is finally shifting into the air, so shops are starting to open up in the downtown core and people are finally coming out of the winter blues.

I hear the shower turn off a few minutes later, a freshly showered Auston comes out in a simple pair of jeans, and a black button down with a light grey bomber jacket. My eyes run down his body and he looks good. His hair is still wet, but he seems to have just run his fingers through it to style it.

He meets my eyes and smiles. "Let's go." He slips on his shoes and we make our way out the door to head to Ancaster, a small city about an hour-ish away.

After hours of running around to different stores to find picture frames, Auston and I are sitting on the wooden floor in the hallway with pictures scattered all around us. I took some more pictures of us today as we were out and about. We grabbed ice cream and walked around a park in Ancaster. I got a photo of us smiling into the camera and another when I pushed Auston's ice cream cone into his face, laughter evident on both our faces.

I realize we have more photos together than I thought, so I spent some time printing them out and now I'm trying to figure out where to place them. Auston has situated them all into frames, but the hardest part is deciding where they will go.

"Fifty-two, fifty-three, fifty-four... holy shit, Vic. There are fifty-four frames lining this wall." His eyes widen in shock. I glance up and look along the massive hallway wall. Along the top there are cute wooden letters that spell out "memory wall," surrounded by images. I have images from my childhood, my parents, my girls, Auston, his friends, and everything else that has impacted me in my twenty-eight years. I smile as I look at all the smiling faces along the wall. To many people this wall would look crowded, but to me... this wall is the reason for my heart beating.

"Yeah, I know. I stopped counting after picture twenty-five. I know it's a lot, but this wall is my favorite part of the house." I smile as I look at the pictures at my feet. We're both sitting cross legged on the ground, Auston looking mildly uncomfortable. His legs are bent drastically to fit his body in the hallway surrounded by pictures.

I grab the pictures from in front of him and set them beside me, motioning for him to stretch out his legs. He laughs and stretches them out. They still sit at an awkward angle due to his height, but it's more comfortable than having them crossed.

"I remember when I first saw them, I felt like I knew you.

This wall is like your memoir." He glances up at the wall and I smile. I never looked at it as a memoir, but I like that.

A memoir of memories.

Maybe I need to go buy some new wooden letters to change my memory wall namesake.

"Well, now you are part of the wall too." I smile and start to stick thumb tacks into the wall. I've never actually measured how I put my pictures up, I just hold them up and if I like the look, I stick the tack in the wall. I start to move other frames around to better suit the look of them. I spend about twenty minutes bossing Auston around to hold certain images in certain places, and getting him to hand me certain frames.

I take a step back and stare at the wall, "fifty-five, fifty-six, fifty-seven, fifty-eight, fifty-nine, and sixty." I point out all the new images that are now hanging on the wall. Five of the pictures are of Auston and I, and the last one is of me and the girls at Kline's the other night.

Auston wraps his arm around my shoulders from behind and I rest my head against his shoulder.

"Should we go make some room in your closet for me?" Auston whispers in my ear and tightens his hold on me. I bring my hand up to rest against his arm.

"Fuck… I didn't even think about that. I don't know how my clothes are going to feel sharing their home with all your fancy suits… they may get intimidated." I say playfully, and he rolls his eyes.

"I think your sexy outfits will keep my suits in great company." He laughs as he drags me to my bedroom.

CHAPTER TWENTY-TWO

The weekend came and went. The days are going by much faster now that I'm genuinely in love. I'm not complaining...okay maybe a little bit. I want to bask in the happiness.

Auston went home last night around nine o'clock, wanting to get ready for the new week ahead. He also joked about getting some packing done for his big move. I can't believe we're moving in together, I never saw this happening so soon, but it feels right to take the next step with him.

I'm sitting at my dining room nook staring out the window with a coffee in hand. The snow has melted and the flowers are starting to peek their way through the hardened ground.

I sit and stew on how my life has been an unexpected whirlwind, but I'm happy with the cyclone of chaos that has burst into my life. I felt myself getting stuck in a routine between work, spending my time with Hannah and Emma, and being alone. If I wasn't with the girls, I was in my own head worrying about some things that are out of my hands, and others that I needed to let go of. Now? I have Auston, and even his friends in my life. He has helped me gain the strength to see how worthy I'm, while also accepting the fact that my past still impacts me largely. Regardless of that though, everything that was meant to happen did. I'd like to think my parents are looking down on me with a smile on their faces. Although it took me twenty-eight years to figure myself out, I think it's okay. I don't think we're meant to figure things out right away, let alone after something traumatic happens...

I think if I had met Auston when I was younger, nothing would've come of our relationship. I would have been too in my head from my parents' death, and insecure as a young adult. I think everything was meant to happen at the right time though.

I finish my last sip of lukewarm coffee and get up to put the mug into the dishwasher. I check the time. Seven thirty already! I'm a little later than usual, so I pick up my pace, maneuvering around the island.

I speed-walk into my room and check my reflection once more. I'm wearing a black turtleneck, tight dark blue skinny jeans, and black heeled booties. This outfit portrays my hourglass figure but is pretty casual compared to my usual attire.

I grab my black bag from the ottoman near the front door and my keys and leave for work. Auston had mentioned us going out for dinner tonight after work, which sounded perfect to me. We're slowly building a routine around one another. In a few weeks that routine is going to change again... because we will be living together. A giddy shiver courses through my body and I can't help the smile that claims my face.

My drive goes by peacefully, the sun is mid-sky and there is a slight chill in the air. Some soft music is playing in the background as I turn down the road that leads to the school.

The road is straight, until it hits some jarring twists. The girls and I used to speed a little quickly down this road as teenagers and would whoosh back and forth with the bend.

My phone starts buzzing with Emma's name flashing across the screen and I decide to ignore it as I'm a few minutes from the school. The buzzing stops, only for Hannah's name to start flashing across my screen again. The constant buzzing beside me is causing the familiar pressure in my stomach, it's never a good sign.

I shift in my seat and push the turtleneck away from my neck, feeling suffocated. I'm probably making it worse in my head, but old habits are hard to break. I press my foot down harder on the gas which causes the car to lurch forward. It causes my stomach to flip and suddenly, my heart beating faster. I rest my head back and try to take deep breaths, focusing on the road in front of me.

Did something happen to someone? Hannah? Emma? Auston?

Fuck, fuck, fuck.

I finally see the school in my vision and there are two cop cars sitting out front with their lights flashing. I add a little more pressure to the gas pedal and throw my car into park as soon as I get into the parking lot. I don't even know if I'm in a spot, but I make a dash out of my car and notice a young girl, maybe late teens, in the arms of a man sobbing. Her shoulders are shaking, and her face is blotchy with mascara.

What's going on? I glance around to see Emma and Hannah holding one another's hands. I rush up to them, "What the hell is going on?" The girl behind us starts to wail as the door opens to the school.

Emma's eyes widen, and Hannah shakes her head, uncertainty flowing through her irises. We all look towards the door after we hear it being shoved open by a man in a blue uniform.

"Fuck…" I hear Emma whisper beside me, as she takes a hold of my hand. My stomach twists, my morning coffee on the rise from the sight in front of me. In a perfect grey suit, with a white button up, Auston is walking alongside the two officers, with his arms handcuffed behind him.

I glance at the girl and my breathing becomes erratic, my heart beating out of my chest.

Auston looks emotionless, like when I first met him, as officers direct him to their cruiser. His posture is tight, his eyes are narrowed, and his face is pale.

Just before he's lowered into the car, his eyes rise and meet mine. I feel paralyzed in this moment, my body is locked up, tears begin to brim my eyelids, and my chin quivers.

"I'm sorry," he mouths to me as he collapses into the seat and a loud sob leaves my throat. The girls are immediately behind me, holding my body upright. The world feels like it has just swallowed me whole. My perfect bubble from this morning has popped, I don't know what is going on, but the abandonment that fills me is scorching.

"What…" I choke on a sob. "What's happening?" I cry lightly as I stare at the cruiser pulling away, with Auston in it. I glance up at the girl who is crying and a sense of familiarity rushes through me. My emotions are all over the place, I can't wrap my head around what's happening.

"Babe, I'm so sorry… we have no idea what happened. Hannah and I were just pulling up when we saw the officers head inside. We saw the girl crying, in what I assume is her father's arms, and we started calling you because we thought she may be your student?" Emma looks just as beaten as I do. Hannah looks speechless. She's usually the one who knows exactly what to say, but right now… she has no idea what's going on. The same question flashes through all of our eyes though;

What did Auston do?

I give my head a shake, letting them know I have no idea who this girl is.

"I'm going to call my dad, he might be able to find out some information for us." We nod our heads at Hannah as she walks away with her phone already against her ear. I run my finger shakily under my eyes to remove the tears that keep falling. The air is chilly against my tear-soaked cheeks, but nothing compares to the chill in my heart. I glance around trying to find answers, anything that can provide me with some insight as to what just happened here.

The familiar anxiety begins to creep in and cause doubts.

It was too good to be true.

Nothing ever goes as you want it to, Vic.

You are destined for a world of misery.

People will always leave you.

I begin to blink rapidly to keep the tears from flooding down my face. The feeling of abandonment comes back full-force, and I don't realize I'm griping Emma's hand in a vice-like hold until she starts shaking me.

I'm brought back to reality and out of my head when Emma's face comes into view, full of concern. "Babe let's get you inside. Hannah said her dad is going to make some calls. For now, you need to get to class. It's too late to try and find a substitute." Emma guides me into the school and I'm lost. My heart is heavy, my eyes are brimmed with tears, and a sob is caught in my throat.

Was Auston involved with a student? Is that who that girl crying was? Was Emma's jokes about him with a student true? Is that why he moved to Simcoe? All these questions are floating around in my mind and there are no answers. I can't believe we never talked about his past work life. We were always so immersed in one another, or our present life, that we always veered away from talking about work, especially his work. I should have asked him more questions, there were signs when we talked about certain things, weren't there?

My hands become clammy and I'm going to vomit.

Images of Auston with a young girl flash through my mind and before I know it, my head is face first into a garbage can, as I empty my breakfast into it.

Emma rushes beside me and is holding back my hair.

"Emma... you don't think he slept with a student, do you?" I question, and Emma looks uncertain. I can see it in her face, there's a chance that that is exactly what happened.

Oh God... the rest of my coffee comes up, leaving me with nothing left in my stomach and I take a deep breath. I wipe my mouth with my hand and stand back up. I don't say anything to Emma as we make our way to my classroom. I unlock the door and realize I don't even have my bag. It's still in the car.

Fuck...

Just when I'm about to tell Emma I need to go back outside, Hannah walks in with my bag in hand, "you left your car unlocked, so I grabbed your bag and locked it from the inside." Hannah hands me my bag. What I would do without these women, I have no idea. I'm so grateful for them, as always. I set my bag on the floor beside me and sit my ass in my chair.

"My dad said he's going to head to the station and see if he can get some more information. He said he will do everything he can to find out what's going on with Auston." Hannah explains, and I just nod my head.

"Thanks, Hannah." I'm grateful, so grateful for Hannah's dad at this moment. Praying that he can find out soon what happened because I don't know how I'm going to teach in this state. I can't think about anything but Auston. As scary as the other thoughts are about his past, I just want to know he's okay. No, I need to know he's okay.

The bell is about to ring. "Let me know if you hear from your dad. I'm going to play movies today, I just... I can't teach," I say. The tears rise to my eyes again and I lean my head back, staring at the bright light above. Never have I not been able to do something. Even when my parents died, I pushed and finished my degree... only taking a week off to mourn. Everyone thought I was crazy for not taking more time off, but I needed the distraction. I feel hopeless right now because I can't find it in me to do my job. Teaching the kids won't distract me, if anything talking about tragic love stories will break me down in front of a bunch of teenagers.

"We will talk to Michelle and see if we can find anyone to come replace you at lunch." Hannah hugs me, and Emma joins in beside her.

God, if it wasn't for these girls...

"I love you two." I breathe out and they tighten their hold. They both say it back and release me. They walk out, concern etched across their faces and I take a seat again. I grab the modern adaptation of Romeo and Juliet and slide the DVD into the computer. Students start to make their way into the classroom and I take a deep, shuddering, breath.

You just have to make it through these next two classes, Vic.

CHAPTER TWENTY-THREE

The days begin to blur together. I've called in sick to work the last two days, still not knowing what's going on with Auston. It's eight o'clock at night and all I've had to eat is a piece of toast, which hasn't helped ease the feeling of nausea from my stomach. I'm curled up in bed watching meaningless TV to keep me distracted. My phone vibrates beside me and I notice the unknown caller and debate just letting it go to voicemail. I haven't spoken to anyone these last few days. Hannah has texted me saying her dad is still getting roadblocked from finding information because the Toronto police want to get involved since it apparently took place there, so I don't know what to think anymore.

I pick up my phone, something inside me urges me to pick up this call; so, I do.

"Hello?" I whisper cough. My throat is so dry from all the tears I've been shedding, and my water intake hasn't been the greatest. I grab my water bottle that hasn't been touched in two days and sip some to give my throat some liquid.

"Hi Victoria, it's Amara...Auston's mom." I hear the

sadness in her voice and I never even thought about how this could be impacting his parents. Whatever "it" could be.

"Hi Amara," I pause. "How are you doing?" I shift my body and sit up. I'm not sure how she got my number, but she's the last person I thought I would hear from. I never really thought to reach out to Auston's family, but I've only met them once, so I wouldn't really know what to say.

"I've been better, hun. I'm not sure if you've heard anything from Auston, but I thought I would reach out because we're still working with our lawyers to find out what's going on. They aren't releasing much to us." I hear tremors in her voice and I can't help but my heart pulls for her. It's been three days since Auston has been arrested and having no idea why can make someone go crazy. I thought he would have been released, but it seems they have concrete evidence.

"I'm so sorry… I'm at the same loss as you are. My friend's dad is the chief here and I'm still waiting for him to find out more information." I lick my dry lips, my voice shakes. "I…I don't know what's going on." My voice shakes, and I lean my head back and try to steady my breathing. The last thing I need to be doing is crying to Auston's mom. I've isolated myself these last few days and talking to someone who's probably feeling the same worry and fear as I am probably won't help the weighted feeling in my chest.

"Oh, Victoria… we will figure this out. I know he had some problems in the past, but those were dealt with. We will figure it out, I promise." She says in a soothing voice. It doesn't give me much reassurance, but I nod my head, as if she can see me.

"I hope so…" I sniffle. "I'm trying to stay optimistic, but my life hasn't given me the best track record with people I love." I wrap myself tighter in my blanket. My abandonment issues have been making themselves known within these last few days. It's like every time something happens though, it comes slithering out from around the corner to get me. The therapist I used to talk to said this could happen. If there was ever a chance that I got into a relationship that would potentially trigger my abandonment issues that stem from my parent's death. I always shrugged it off because I never thought I would meet someone. But now I'm feeling the weight of it because I'm scared Auston is going to abandon me. While I know whatever happens is not my fault, my brain can't help but try and pin it on me. I take a shuddered breath and try to calm my racing thoughts.

"Oh, sweetie." Amara pauses. "What you've been through already in life is something nobody should ever have to go through, especially as a child. Death carries on forever and there is no time limit on when to stop grieving; however, just remember your parents are always there. There is never a moment when your parents aren't beside you, holding your hand, and helping you through a tough time in your life." I get shivers from what Amara just said. My mind is playing games on me, thinking my parents are at my side, or maybe I just need rest. At this point, I'll never know. I'd like to believe though, that what she is saying is true.

"Thank you, Amara. I needed to hear that," I say as I wipe the snot away from my nose with a tissue. I didn't realize how many tears I was shedding during our conversation. "I feel the weight of these last few days catching up to me. I haven't been sleeping, but I probably should. It's just hard to imagine what Auston's going through and why we don't have any answers."

"I know sweetie, but we will figure it out. Auston is the strongest man I know, don't tell his father that." We both laugh lightly. "Go get some rest, I will call if I hear back from our lawyers." I bid her the same and end our call. I look down at my phone and my lock screen sits awake with a photo of Auston and I. It's the photo from our date at the Italian restaurant in Toronto, which also sits on my memoir of memories.

What's happening right now is out of my hands, I can't try to change anything, but I can continue to be hopeful. Not allowing my abandonment issues to consume me is a start; I have to fight it.

It's now Saturday morning and Hannah's dad has finally made some progress with Auston's case. He's been in custody for five days now and I think we've all been worried sick at this point. Amara said her lawyers were working on it, but I haven't heard anything else from her since Thursday. We're sitting in Hannah's car as we drive to her parent's house at eight o'clock in the morning because I didn't want to wait a second longer. These last few days have been some of the hardest, aside from my parent's death. When I fell in love, I didn't expect it to consume me, or to happen so fast. I thought I would settle down, but apparently there was a different narrative playing out. Auston made my heart beat out of my chest. From how we met, to how he's helped me; it can't be the end for us.

It just all depends on what we see today, if after everything my heart will be left broken or not.

"My dad said he found out what happened and was able to get a hand in some of the evidence for us to look at." Hannah looks over at me and I give her a small smile of reassurance. As soon as Hannah and Emma picked me up, I could see the worry that graced their faces. I showered this morning, finally, but it didn't seem to help with the blotchiness from crying or the bags that have made themselves at home under my eyes. I thought I would get some sleep last night, but my mind decided to play tricks on me. It was Auston and a student in a sexual embrace, I walked in on them and immediately woke up. That dream shook me to my very core; the one thing I don't want to believe is that Auston would have sex with a student. It would tarnish everything we've ever had together.

We arrive at Hannah's parent's house ten minutes later. Situated in a quiet suburban area, most of these houses look the exact same, but it's in the new area of Simcoe, so it's quite nice. We all get out of Hannah's car and her mom, Cheryl, is already waiting outside for us. I take it that her parents know about Auston and I because of the look of sympathy in her eyes.

We walk up towards the front door and Cheryl's arms circle around me, and I burst out crying, a sob making its way through my throat. Both Emma and Hannah's parents have been like my own, so when I feel the motherly touch, I break. I completely sob into her shoulder as she rubs my back.

"Come in girls, I'll make some tea." She pulls back and wipes under my eyes, "It's going to be okay, darling." She wraps her arm around my shoulder and guides me into the house. Hannah's dad, Eric, is sitting at the table with a few folders in front of him. He's staring at them with a look of disgust and anger.

That can't be good. My eyes drift to the folders in front of him, I feel like someone is squeezing my lower belly because those folders, those few pieces of paper, are holding what could break Auston and I.

The girls and I sit down at the table with Eric. I take a deep breath and look up into Eric's eyes. They hold anger, and I know whatever is in that folder is going to break me. If

Auston had sex with a student, I don't think I would ever be able to look at him the same. He would've taken advantage of a poor girl, which is one of my many insecurities and he knows it. He knows that it would destroy me, which is probably why he said sorry before getting in the car. I should feel anger, but instead I feel defeat. My whole life seems like a battle I can't seem to win.

"I have some photographs here," he sets his hand on the folder. "They are graphic and if you don't want to see them, I don't blame you, Victoria." He rests his hand on my shoulder and a brick has fallen in my stomach.

I look around at the girls and they're feeling just as off as I'm. I mean, I got to know Auston on an emotional level, but the girls have gotten to know him too over the last few months. This folder could change everything, I don't know if I would ever be able to trust again after this.

I slide my hand over to the folder and look up as I open the folder. I hear two gasps next to me and know those came from Emma and Hannah.

"Fuck babe, I don't think you need to see this." Without listening to her, I look down and see images of two bodies pressed together. There are no faces in the image, just bodies tangled together. I begin to flip through the pages and they just become worse and worse. Bile travels up my throat and tears begin to fall down my cheeks slowly.

How could he do this? I close the folder and put my head in my hands. My shoulders shake with the cries that are taking over my body, I have no idea what to think of this. I lean my head down towards my chest and heave in a shuttered breath.

I hiccup as I look into Eric's eyes, asking "When did this happen?"

"The young girl came to her father late Monday evening

and said that it happened over the weekend. Her father was away on a business trip this weekend and she said that Auston visited her late Saturday night. This young girl has accused Auston in the past, but she had just lost her mother, so people thought she was acting out." He pauses to look at me, "There are records from Auston in the past saying this student was very forward, but he thought it was due to trauma. However, these images have proven that maybe the girl wasn't lying." My eyebrows come together in confusion, a sudden blossom of hope shoots through my veins.

"Wait, she said that it happened this weekend?" I ask Eric and he nods. Eric's condensed idea of the statement doesn't make any sense.

I quickly throw open the folder and start to analyze the photographs before me. I stare at the man's side and notice it's empty. His tattoo isn't there. If his tattoo isn't there, then this isn't him. Maybe this is some kind of mistake? Did the police even show these photos to Auston? My heart is heavy in realization.

"Earth to Vic, what is going on through that head of yours?" Emma shakes my arm lightly and I look at all of them.

"This isn't Auston." I breathe out, relief evident in my throat, "I was with him all weekend long. From Friday night to Sunday night. I have videos and pictures as evidence. We went to Ancaster on Saturday and spent the day there, then came home and added pictures to the memory wall." I try to recall what we did that night and heat creeps up my neck. "He... he couldn't have been there, since we spent a majority of the night on the porch swing." My hands shaking, I grab the images and set a bunch of them out on the table.

"Auston has a tattoo on his torso, and none of these photos show his tattoo. His tattoo would be evident in these photographs, especially from this angle." My voice shakes from exhaustion over everything that has happened lately.

"The young girl must have lied. There would be no reason she would know about Auston's tattoos. He's a Principal, so it's not like she would've ever seen him shirtless. Is there a chance she may have lied about this?" Hope laces my voice. I continue to look through the images and folders that Eric has given to us, as he calls down to the station. I flip over the next folder and push myself away from the table as a familiar face appears.

Both Emma and Hannah raise their concerns as bile slowly moves its way up my throat. I swallow it down, but it just leaves me with a sour feeling, *everywhere*.

Holy fuck.

I recognize who the young woman in the photo is. She was the young woman at Dallas Pub causing a commotion… and the girl I met in the garbage chute in Auston's building.

"Vic, are you okay?" Hannah grabs my hand and I shake my head.

"This is her, this is the girl from Dallas Pub and the girl I ran into in Auston's building in Toronto. I was taking out the garbage before we left the city and she was in the garbage room. She was angry, when I asked her if she was okay, she had muttered a bunch of things that didn't make sense… now they do…" I whisper. "We need to go down to the station."

Eric's still on the phone but I can tell he overheard everything I just said to the girls. He motions for us to follow him as he grabs the keys to his truck. I have hope, hope that I've figured this out, but there is still worry nagging at me. What if I'm only seeing what I want to? What if I'm in such a state of disillusion that my mind is making me think it's her? I open the truck door and get in the back seat, trying to focus on my breathing. My body breaks out in a cold sweat when a hand grabs my own. I look over at Emma and she gives me a reassuring squeeze, something in her eyes tells me I'm right. We don't actually know, but feeling her hope sends a rush through me, which eases the tremors that are making me sweat.

"Eric, when you get there can you see if Auston's building has functional cameras? Maybe then you can see when we were there, and maybe her coming and going from the garbage room?" I rattle off the date and Auston's address. He proceeds to tell whoever he's on the phone with and I rest my head against the headrest.

When we arrive at the station after ten minutes, Eric walks with purpose through the doors I assume lead to the cells and offices. He disappears through the doors and all we can do is wait. The person at the front of the desk sends us small smiles here and there, but it feels like time has slowed down. Eric is still in the back, and all we can do is wait.

And wait.

And wait.

It feels like hours have passed and my stomach is in knots as I watch phone calls between Eric and the other officer through the little glass square in the door. He's been talking back and forth with others, but we don't know what's happening. The girls have only left my side to grab drinks and bathroom breaks. I haven't left once, I can't. My stomach is turning from not eating anything all day, but I don't think I can stomach anything until I find out what happened. I look down at my phone and notice six hours have passed by.

"Well, Vic, you were right. We got video surveillance of Tara in the building. We caught the end of her altercation with you when she left the garbage room. She seems to look in distress as she leaves the room." Eric states as he's walking over towards us, "I also had the guys check Auston's torso for a tattoo, and you are correct there's one there." A sob release, but one of pure relief.

"Well no shit dad, Vic is dating him. She would know." Hannah exclaims, angrily. I think we're all high on emotions, and low on food.

I just need to see Auston, I need to know he's okay after sitting in the same four walls for five and a half days.

"When," I'm cut off when everything starts to feel like it's moving in slow motion. I get the familiar tightness in my body as I wait to see if it's Auston who walks out the large metal doors. The doors are pushed open wider by an officer, as a defeated looking Auston walks out. It's unlike any other time I've seen him. His eyes are bloodshot, his hair is a complete mess from running his hands through them, and the top buttons to his shirt are undone and his pants are wrinkled. It doesn't look like he's changed in the last five days.

I stand and rush over to him, "Oh my God…" I wrap my arms around him and feel the tears brim my eyes…again. I rush towards him on impact.

"Victoria.." His voice breaks as he shoves his face into the crevice of my neck. "I didn't know if you would show up. I'm so sorry. I should've told you about Tara." He sounds completely broken, and I hate it. Seeing him as anything but strong and confident breaks my heart, this isn't him.

"Don't worry, we figured it out." I lean back, and he rests his head against mine. "Hannah's Dad has been working hard these last few days to get us some answers. At first… I felt betrayed, like you had lied to me about who you were…" I sniffle slightly and turn my head to wipe my eyes and nose with my sleeve.

"I should've told you. I stopped working at the high school in the city because of Tara. At first, I thought it was harmless. She would say good morning to me when she arrived at school, then notes began showing up in my work mailbox... and then my home mailbox. I didn't think anything of it. But then..." He looks up and his jaw tightens. "She showed up at my condo in complete distress. Her mother had passed away two weeks prior and she was a mess, I didn't know what to do. So, I let her into my condo and contacted her father. She tried to come onto me then, but I stopped it. I told her it was best we waited down in the lobby. It was my mistake letting her into my condo..." He runs his hands through his hair. He grabs my jaw, rubbing his thumb along my chin. I look into his green eyes and torment flows through them. Alongside the stress lines around his eyes, small red veins are evident in his eyes from lack of sleep.

"After that incident, I didn't feel right working there. I knew this girl was unstable, but I didn't want to cause her any further stress after her mother, so I left. I decided to move and start anew. Somehow, she still found me, and you've witnessed the rest." He grabs my hand and we walk towards Eric and the girls. So many questions are swirling in my mind... Why did this girl have random photos? Why didn't Auston want to tell me why he left? It's a jumbled mess, but honestly... I'm relieved the accusations were all a lie. As much as it pains me knowing that Auston hid this from me, I understand. He wanted to keep his past in the past.

"Thank you, sir, for helping Victoria with this. I wasn't sure what was going to happen, but I'm grateful for your work." Auston reaches out his hand and shakes it with Eric's.

"I would do anything for Victoria and Emma, they're like daughters to me." He gives a small smile to Auston, "however, this isn't over yet. The guys and I are going to have to fill out some paperwork and we're going to need both your statements about Tara."

Auston and I both agree and it's well past ten o'clock at

night by the time we've given our statements and the paper-work is done. Eric agrees to drive Auston and I back home, since I came over with the girls.

The car is extremely quiet. I think we're all trying to come to the impact of this past week's actions. Why did nobody think to question a poor girl who was ridden with grief? She may have thought she had some sort of obsession with Auston because he helped her one time, and maybe that triggered something. Everyone handles grief in different ways, some can lead to denial and ignore it, like me. Others can take a darker turn which impacts not only themselves, but those around them.

I can't help the relief that I'm feeling though. An allega-tion like this could have ruined Auston's career and the life he's built. I take a deep breath and Auston tightens his hold on my thigh and I give him a weak smile. I'm exhausted; mentally and physically.

We arrive at home and all of us exit from the vehicle. We all give our thanks to Eric for all his hard work, especially Auston. He's extremely grateful that Eric helped him and helped the police come to an understanding about the situation.

"I'm glad you're okay Auston. I was really worried there, I assumed the worst of you and I want to apologize for that…" Emma grimaces, admitting she thought Auston may have been in the wrong.

"No, I understand. Honestly, I didn't want any of this coming with me here. I should've told you from the start about my past. If I'm being honest, I didn't want your opin-ions of me to change. I know that Victoria values your opin-ions, and if there was any chance that this could've changed that, I know it could have broken us." He admits. He looks sheepishly towards me because this is the first time that he's shown me that he holds the same fear as I have about us losing each other. My heart pulls for Auston. His childhood was spent full of judgement from others and I don't think he ever got over that, always trying to please others and look perfect. It never really hit me that Auston may also deal with some of the backlash from his childhood subconsciously.

"We get it, really. There are no other secrets though, right?" Emma squints her eyes at him, and he gives her a weak smile while shaking his head no.

"Good." Emma hugs both of us and gets back into Eric's car with him in tow.

"I love you, babe." Hannah squeezes me, and I say it back. I don't know what I would've done without Emma, Hannah and Eric. They are my lifesavers. This day could've gone completely worse if I didn't have them.

Auston hugs Hannah goodbye and expresses his gratitude in everything she did today for both him and I. She smiles and heads to her dad's truck and they leave, waving as they go.

There's heaviness in the air as we try to come to terms with everything we've been through today. We make our way into the house quietly. I set my bag and jacket down on the ottoman and turn to him,

"Do you want to shower?" I twist my fingers together, my anxiety creeping back in after the long day.

"I would love nothing else in the world." He grabs my hand and we make our way towards the bathroom attached to the bedroom. We begin to undress and leave our clothing piled in a heap on the bathroom floor. Auston turns the shower on and steam slowly begins to trickle its way into the room.

We step into the shower and Auston lets out a groan at the feeling of warm water. I turn towards him and his lips meet mine. It's a chaste kiss; the love he's softly pressing on my lips is evident.

"I never thought that nightmare would continue here, gorgeous. I never wanted to put you through this, it killed me seeing you that morning. When I pulled away and you completely broke down, I thought that was it. I thought that would be the end and you would never speak to me again…" He breathes heavily and I wrap my arms around his naked torso.

"I'm not going to lie to you, I was fucking scared… I was scared you lied to me and had done the unimaginable." I whisper against his chest. He moves us around so that the warm water is cascading down my body, relieving some of the tension that has made itself at home with my body these last few days.

"I know and I'm sorry. The moment it all happened, the only thing I could think about was you." He admits. I grab the soap and begin to wash his body, knowing that he could use a little extra after today. I can't imagine the things going through his head. He's put together really well, but when he walked through those doors, I had never seen him look so broken. He looked defeated and ready to give up, knowing that there was a possibility that he would be wrongfully convicted, and his life would be over. My heart pulls in so many different directions. Knowing there are girls who have actually gone through an event like this, and others who have had their entire lives ruined to such lies. It's so hard to understand things in life sometimes. We want to believe that everyone has good in them, we want to believe that when something horrible happens, that it's true. However, I know first-hand how bad mental health can get, especially when death is involved. I feel for the young girl who latched onto Auston, and I hope that she can get the help she needs. She made a mistake and although it could've cost Auston his life, thankfully it didn't. I just hope that there's something we can do to help her.

"I love you." I kiss him and Auston lifts me up and I wrap my legs around him. I feel weightless in his arms. I wrap my arms loosely around his neck and rack my nails lightly along the back of his neck. Goosebumps begin to raise on his skin and I can't help but smirk.

"You're the other half of me that I didn't know I was missing, gorgeous." He mumbles against my lips and I stare into his eyes. I'm tongue tied by this man because I feel like he's my other half too.

He stops kissing me to slowly travel his lips down my neck.

Suddenly the air feels hot, and not from the steaming water traveling down our bodies.

"I've missed you so much." Auston groans as he latches onto one of my nipples and tingles of awareness make their way down towards my core. I bite my lip and can't help but move my hips in indication that I want more. He slowly begins to move his hips, his cock sliding through my folds, hitting my clit at the perfect tempo. My eyes look towards his and he grabs my neck with one hand and keeps one under my ass for support. He takes my mouth in a passionate kiss that doesn't end.

"Make love to me," I whisper, and Auston peels his head back.

"Always." He brings his hips back just a touch to allow himself the space to slowly slide himself into me. The fullness feels like home.

"Oh, Auston." I gasp as he fills me completely and slowly starts to move forward. His hand travels down my body, tweaking my nipples, and then slowly heading towards my clit. His pace is consistent, and our bodies move together as one. I bring his mouth to mine as the familiar build climbs towards my core. I thrust my hips awkwardly against his, which he picks up on and quickens his pace slightly. With one more flicker of his fingers on my clit, my pussy tightens and a shiver exudes from my body. He groans out my name as he thrusts a few more times and then freezes, tightening his arms around me, as he releases into me. He slowly puts my legs down and rests his head on my shoulder.

"I'll never get enough of you, Victoria Mateus." He kisses my bare shoulder, and I smile.

"I love you, Principal Scott." I bite my lip and his shoulders shake with laughter. Life really does need to have certain things happen, so it can direct us to where we're meant to be. If this young girl had never done these things, Auston wouldn't have moved to Simcoe, and we wouldn't have fallen in love. Life is uncertain, and although it tests us to points we feel like breaking, sometimes all it is really doing is showing us how strong we are.

EPILOGUE

Two Years Later...

I stare into Auston's tear-filled green eyes as we say our vows to one another. He's wearing a charcoal grey suit with a blush pink button-up underneath that really compliments his features. His smile takes up his whole face as he says the simple, but impactful words, I do. The officiant announces us as husband and wife, and Auston reaches forward and bends me backward, taking my lips in a passionate kiss I feel all the way to my toes. When he straightens us back up, I can't help but hear the excited shouts from our friends and family. Emma, Hannah, Garrett, and Axel all stand to our sides with large smiles on their faces. The girls are in long blush pink dresses, and the guys are in light grey suits with blush pink shirts to match Auston. I look down at my dress and smile. It's a full white lace a-line dress with sleeves and a one meter train that flows behind me. I had tried on hundreds of different dresses, but found this one a few months back and fell in love with it. The sleeves are a delicate lace, which allows my body to breath and not feel too hot while enjoying the beautiful day. We decided to get married in the Fall due to the temperature not being too hot, and not being too cold. It was the perfect day, two years after the crazy incident, for us to get married.

After everything happened with Tara, she got the help she needed. I had stayed in contact with her for a few months, but Auston had opened up to me and said how he wasn't a hundred percent comfortable with us talking, so I stopped. Tara understood. When everything happened, I had explained my own situation with my parents and she felt some sanity knowing that someone else understood the anguish she was feeling. We both handled it in different ways, but eventually got a handle on the new reality we had been dealt. Right before we stopped talking, she mentioned how she spoke to a therapist twice a week and was pursuing a degree in psychology. Although Auston is still guarded with students, he has opened up much more now that he has me at his side as his significant other. Once students and colleagues found out about us, it seemed to give him a sense of serenity because he didn't have to worry about anything happening with students. When we weren't teaching or doing work, we were at one another's side. I usually go to his office during my spares, and we both just sit and do work. It's become a routine that I love.

And after a long day working, we drive home—together. After everything that happened with Tara, we didn't stop our notion of moving in together, he did it the following week later because he didn't want to be away from me any longer. I didn't complain one bit.

And then one magical night, during our summer break, we were sitting on the porch swing with a glass of white wine in hand. Auston had taken my glass from me, set it down on the ground, and got down on one knee. The sun was setting behind him in the farm across the street, and I remember it like it was yesterday. I cried a lot, but was so happy. I didn't even let him ask, I just screamed yes and launched myself off the swing. I had knocked over the wine, soaking our clothes, but I didn't care. Auston had asked me to officially become Mrs. Scott.

That emotion has carried on for two years, and now he's officially mine.

My very own GQ model…

"Ready to get your party on?" Emma whispers from behind me and I laugh. The girls have stuck by our side through it all. These last two years our friendships have gotten even closer, if that was even possible. Except, we now have Axel and Garrett alongside too.

"Let's go, Mrs. Scott." I laugh at him and roll my eyes giddily. We walk down the aisle as family and friends throw rose petals on us. I look up at Auston and see happiness shining in his eyes. My own bashful smile directs back at him,

"I love you, gorgeous." He smiles down at me and the butterflies that fluttered when I met his gaze at Dallas Pub years ago, still happen today.

"I love you, Principal Scott." I smirk, and he laughs. He tightens his hold on me and presses a kiss to the top of my head. Right before we walk into the tent where the reception is going to take place, we're interrupted.

"Excuse me, Victoria?" I look up to see a man I recognize standing nearby.

"Yes?" We get closer and I notice that this is my parent's lawyer, from when they passed away. An odd feeling rises in my chest, what's he doing here? I look down and notice a simple white envelope in his hand.

"This is for you, a gift from your loved ones. Congratulations to you two." He smiles and hands me an envelope. I think both Auston and I's brows furrow because we have no idea what is inside this envelope.

My curiosity is piqued as I glance up at Auston. His concentration is divided, he hasn't been able to take his eyes off me since I walked down the aisle towards him. Auston raises an eyebrow at the white letter in my hand, which I slowly tear open. I unfold the piece of paper and recognize the handwriting instantly.

Dear Victoria,

Our amor. If you're receiving this letter, it's because one of us, or both of us, have unfortunately passed away. You know me, I always wanted to be prepared for anything. Your father however wasn't entirely on board with this, but I couldn't imagine not having anything for you on your special day, in case something unfortunate happened. We have given three different letters to our lawyer, in the case that we passed. We hope that they never make it to you, but if they do, just know we love you so much. If you are getting this one though, be sure to ask for the other two because they were both written specially for you, from one of us.

We're sorry we're unable to be here physically on your special day.

We were always here though. Whether in skin, or not, you know that we're both with you holding your hand through everything that life throws at you. You handled a lot as a teenager, and I have no doubt whatever else life throws at you, you will be able to handle it with an iron heart.

You've probably gone on to do great things in your life, which we always knew you would. However, we hope that you're doing these great things with someone who loves you at your side. Loves you for who you are, because you are worth every damn thing, amor.

We always tried to show you a loving relationship because we wanted you to have one too. We hope you've found the kind of love that blossoms through your heart and allows you to wake up every day with a smile on your face.

We are so proud of you, and know we are here with you. You never have to doubt our presence because we are here, watching you thrive because that's just who you are.

We love you so much,

Congratulations to you and your new husband, may you love each other forever and all eternity.

P.S. There should also be a little something to get you two started on your new life. Just because we aren't there doesn't mean you can't give us grandbabies... So get going.

Love, Mãe (Mom) and Pai (Dad)

Emotions swirl in my stomach, tears streaming down my face. I hiccup and clutch the letter in my hand. I look up to see Auston's eyes glimmering with tears as well. I hand the letter to Auston and open the envelope further to find a check nestled inside.

I feel so much right now. My heart is hurting knowing my parents aren't here to celebrate my special day physically, but they're here. I can feel their love today. It's really strong today, and I can feel it all the way to my heart.

"I'm sorry, gorgeous. I wish they were here today." Auston hugs me to him, and I shake my head. I can't believe they had a letter prepared, even if only one of them had passed, this damn letter would have been prepared. They were always ready for anything...

"I..." I take a shuddery breath, "I'm not sad. I know if they were here, they would've just said this to me in person. They made sure I was always taken care of, no matter what.

This is just… a lot." I rest my head on his shoulder and he kisses my forehead.

The girls walk over with the guys tailing them. They are all laughing until they see both Auston and I's tear rimmed eyes.

"What happened?" Emma's concerned gaze passes over both of us, and I can't help but laugh. This day is perfect. I hand them the letter and watch them read it, the girls start to tear up themselves. They finish the letter and Emma launches herself at us.

"I love you guys." Emma blubbers and I laugh. We all get ourselves together, even Axel and Garret are a little shaken from reading the letter and I smile at them all.

"Alright guys come on. This is supposed to be a celebration, enough of this. Let's go party." I exclaim and they all laugh and head into the tent. I shake my body out and run my hands one more time under my eyes. I look up at Auston and smile. His green eyes are glimmering back towards me, looking like the most beautiful shade of green I have ever seen. I could fall in love over and over again with this man,

"Strongest women I know, I swear." Auston bites his lip down at me. His eyes speak a thousand loving words, that he doesn't need to say out loud, because I know.

"We will see about that eight months from now, when I'm giving birth to our first child…" I wink at him and he freezes, his eyebrows rise, and his mouth opens like a fish.

"Are you…?" His voice shaky, he reaches out to palm my laced clad stomach.

"Come on daddy, this is our night to celebrate." Auston swoops me off my feet with the largest smile I think I've ever seen on his face. I hear the beginning intro to Hot for Teacher by Van Halen and know that's our moment to make an entry. This song will always have a special place in my heart, the memory of us on our way to Langford Hall while he sang it to me, while pursuing the innuendo of our story. Auston spins me around and then shouts to everyone about how he is going to be a dad. I can't stop laughing watching my husband realize he's going to become a dad. He carries me further into the tent and shouts the news to everyone over and over and over again. The girls scream and run over to us, launching themselves at us, which makes us fall onto the floor in a giant pile. Obviously, the guys are just as rowdy as they join and start to tackle Auston. I laugh and notice our photographer catching this perfect moment, another addition to the Memoir of Memories.

Looks like this party is going to be a wild one with all the excitement of the day, but I'm going to watch it sober because this mommy can't drink. I rest my head on Auston's stomach on the floor as all our friends extend their excitement over our news. His fingers run through my hair and I sigh happily.

I really did get my perfect love story; my parents are just the narrators of it.

THE END

Want to read a short story about Joe the bartender? Keep reading for a sneak peek at *Hot for the Bartender*!

a short sexy
second-chance
romance

Hot for the

BARTENDER

ALEXANDRIA GONCALVES

PROLOGUE
JOE

I tuck a piece of hair behind Rox's ear, gripping the side of her neck, my thumb caressing her cheek, as I thrust upwards into her wet cunt. No matter how many times we've done it, it always feels like the first time.

Like we were made for one another.

"I see that sappy look in your eyes, Joe." She smiles playfully as she runs her fingers through my shoulder length hair while continuing the slow movement of her hips.

"I'm always going to have this sappy look in my eyes when I'm looking at you, old lady." I wink at her and she leans down to bite my nipple, making me groan.

"You don't get to call me an old lady, until there is a ring on my finger." She throws her wild black locks over her shoulder and quickens her pace on my cock. Feeling my balls tighten, I grab a hold of her hips, aggressively pushing her down on my cock. She begins to whimper as I take control of her body. My girl never has been able to stay in control for too long, she likes being controlled more. I bite my lip as I watch her. Her face in ecstasy. She scrunches her eyes telling me she's almost there. Her pouty lips open slightly, her skin aglow.

She's breathtaking.

Feeling the familiar tightness in my balls again, I bring my thumb to her clit to get her here with me. I slam her down one last time, as she yells fuck. That's my sign and I release with her, my abs tightening and the feeling of weightlessness coming.

I shuffle our bodies so I'm now sitting up against the window of my truck with her straddling me, I grab her face, bringing it softly to mine for a kiss.

The California sunset is behind her, giving her the look of a goddess – my goddess.

"What are you thinking?" She runs her hand along my jawline.

"About how beautiful you are, more beautiful than the sunset behind you." I shrug shamelessly. She turns her body slightly to look at the sunset and gasps.

"You know what? It never gets old. I could turn around every night and seeing the sunset will always bring this warm feeling." She admits, while watching the sun slowly descend into the horizon.

"One day, I'll marry you under the sunset." I admit and she whips around and glares at me with a smile.

"Don't say things you don't mean, Joe." She goes to poke me, but I grab her finger and bring her close to my face,

"I mean every fucking word, Rox. I'll marry you under every sunset, as long as I get to see this look on your face forever." I bring our lips together in a whisper, smiling when she pushes them together for a passionate kiss. If anyone heard me talk to Rox at the club, they would say I'm pussy-whipped. I don't care though, this woman with her long dark hair, stunning green eyes, and infectious personality is my everything. I'd do anything to protect and love her and everyone knows that. I've made my intention with her very clear in front of everyone at the club. I even broke one of my brother's fingers for looking too long at Rox's ass while she was walking to her Dad's office. The perk of being in a motorcycle club is that most things are forgivable, so when someone looks at something that's mine, they should expect brutality. Luckily we're good now, but it showed everyone in the club not to look or touch what's mine.

While Rox looks like a Greek goddess, she's got fire. I'm the only one who gets to see this fire ninety percent of the time, but when something heats her up, there isn't anyone who can put that fire out. She almost stabbed a member once for making a jab at me, but her dad walked out just in time. If it's not me, it's her dad she'll listen to. He's the president of the club and he accepted me into the club without a problem after being a prospect for less than a year. I showed my loyalty to the club, I didn't really have anything else to live for. They became my family, and Rox became my everything.

It's been the best years of my life, and being in the club, I found a place I can call home. Maybe not so much a place, but a person.

I joined on a whim a few years ago, becoming a prospect for just a short period of time. It was only short because there wasn't much that I wouldn't do and our president liked that about me. Does he abuse his power sometimes? Yes – but I'm always the first one ready to take on the action without hesitation. I didn't join a brotherhood to stand around. I joined to find a family and work, my relationship with Rox was a welcoming surprise. I was only a few months into being a prospect when I saw some guys harassing her on her way to the club. I'd seen her around a few times, but hadn't spoken to her. That was my bad boy moment of shine. I pulled my bike over beside her, hopped off, and held a knife to the guy's throat. Not only did that shut him up quick, but it made Rox look at me like her knight in shining armor. I've spent five years living up to that title because she's worth it.

I grab her and smirk as I watch her pull her rose covered dress down to mid-thigh.

"Why are you covering up that sweet body?" I practically whine as I play with the hem of her dress. I brought her up to the cliffside to watch the sunset because I know how much she loves it.

"I'm covering up because you caught me in a moment of lust and I can't be caught naked in the bed of a truck." She fluffs her curls and leans back in-between my legs. I laugh and wrap my arms around her because she's not wrong. We had come into the bed of the truck to cuddle and watch the sunset, but I had her naked and moaning my name in less than five minutes.

I move her hair away from her neck and place a small kiss there as we face the sun. The sky has officially darkened, but the blue-pink hues are still prominent in the sky.

I watch the irises of her eyes get bigger as she watches the hues take up the sky. It's a breathtaking moment. I can see the reflection of colors in her eyes, and I feel this fullness in my chest that comes whenever we're alone. "Forever," I whisper as I lower my head into the crook of her neck. I don't have to watch the sunset to be mesmerized when I have this woman in my arms.

CHAPTER ONE
JOE

Thirty years later...

"What's the point of having workers, if they don't listen to a damn thing you say?" I grumble to myself as I haul cases of beer into the fridge in the back of the bar. I need to get four kegs, at least, into the bar for tonight. Running out of booze on a night where my bar is full of bikers isn't going to work. Lifting a couple more boxes, I'm feeling the strain in my arms pulling. I'm not a big guy but I throw my weight around in the gym every now and then to make sure I stay in shape and the pain is evident today. I force myself to keep putting stuff away, regardless of my arms feeling like they're going to go limp any second now. I grab the final box and stack it on the last case of Stella Artois that's leaning against the far right wall. Taking a step back, I realize my back room looks like a rainbow of booze. From the beer cases that stack along the bottom, to the shelves of various alcohol, it's a sight to see.

Walking out of the fridge, I glance around, at least the kitchen staff cleared the space. The smell of grease is pretty pungent since I decided to have a Thursday wing night for the Toronto Geese game. Victoria, Auston, Emma, and Hannah came by and it was a good night for a Thursday. They're all off for the summer due to their teaching positions and Auston has been helping his dad during the odd times. They've been around a lot more and it's made things more bearable. I swear the older I get, the more I think about the past. It's like a fucking nagging old lady that never goes away. I snicker to myself at the thought because I figured by now I would have myself an old lady – but the universe had different ideas in place for my life. I'm not mad with the way my life turned out, I'm actually grateful I got out when I did because most likely, I would've been six feet under by now.

Lifting up the last keg of beer that I need from the back room, I maneuver my way around to the front of the bar to connect it to the tap. With the summer crowd starting to kick up, I've been ordering more and more kegs of beer due to all the students coming home from college. Today is special though, because it's Friday the 13th. To the locals, it's a regular day that bikers come from all over North America to spend time in a nearby town with fellow bikers. It reminds me of my old life, the one I had before I was forced to leave.

The familiar rumble of bikes passing brings me comfort. I stopped riding as soon as I moved here. I felt like I needed to disconnect from my previous life as much as I could. Buying the bar was the closest familiarity I could get to without giving anyone any idea of who I am. I moved here thirty years ago, so the odds of someone knowing who I am would be slim. Moving from California to a small town in southern Ontario, I knew I didn't have much to worry about.

I swing through the door to the bar and come to a halt.

There's a woman sitting at the bar, but it isn't just any woman. She's got a leather jacket on, with a familiar crest for "Devils Rejects" covering the back. Her long hair peppered with gray draped in waves down her back. Suddenly, the weight of this keg feels like it's tripled as I stare at her back.

It can't be.

ACKNOWLEDGMENTS

Phew, well this has been a long two years in the making.
When I started to think about the idea for this book, I was
sitting on the Toronto subway blasting *Hot for Teacher* by
Van Halen. I was in the middle of finishing my undergrad in
English Literature and had been wanting to write a complete
book since I was fourteen. Well, almost ten years later, I can
say that I finally did it.

There are so many people I could thank for helping me get to
where I am today, as a published author. However, that would
take a few more pages and I know nobody wants to read all
that sappiness. So, I'm going to keep this quick.

Thank you to:

My fiancé, for always supporting my wild passion for
everything romance.

My amazing friends Steph, Katie, Jessi, Bri, Dana, Amber,

Willow, and Sophie for helping me bring this to life with your excitement, feedback, and love.

My amazing cover designer Emily who helped bring Principal Auston Scott to life on my cover.

Writing this has been a whirlwind of a journey. I hope you take the time to review my novel, let me know what you think (critical feedback is always welcome), and take the chance on my future work.

ABOUT THE AUTHOR

Alexandria Goncalves is from a small city in Southwestern Ontario, where she resides with her fiancé. Her passion for writing came at a young age and she found romance novels to help cope with the downsides in life. She pursued an undergrad in English Literature to help improve her writing skills and prepare for a career in writing. She writes a variety of romance that ranges from contemporary to dark and taboo—and everything in between. When she's not focused on her writing, she's nose deep into a book, spending time with her fiancé, posting on her Instagram or TikTok, or laughing with friends. Visit her website at www.authoralexandriagoncalves.com.

instagram.com/authoralexandriagoncalves

Made in the USA
Las Vegas, NV
06 March 2022

45143699R00177